I0541264

Food Court Justice

Sage Ardman

The Adjusters series #1

R.L. Ranch Press

Greenville, South Carolina

Books by Sage Ardman

The Westerley Series:

#1: *Executive Sweet*

#2: *I'll Get You My Pretty*

#3: *Seductive Synchronicity*

The Fame Series:

#1: *The Fiery Boys*

#2: *Rock Con Roll*

The Adjusters Series:

#1: *Food Court Justice*

#2: *Two For the Money* (coming)

Food Court Justice

Copyright © 2024, Sage Ardman

Print ISBN: 978-09914205-82
EBook ISBN: 978-09914205-75

Book layout by: Steve Rubin
Cover art by: Diogo Leite (bookdesigncompany.com)

Printed and bound in the United States of America. R.L. Ranch Press holds exclusive rights to this work. No part of this book may be reproduced or transmitted in any form or by an electronic or mechanical means, including photocopying, recording, or by an information storage and retrieval system, without permission from the publisher—except in the case of brief quotations embodied in reviews.

All rights reserved. For more information, please contact: R.L. Ranch Press, 711 Crescent Avenue, Suite A, Greenville, South Carolina, 29601. Or visit rlranchpress.com.

Disclaimer: This is a work of fiction. Any resemblance of characters to actual persons, living or dead, is purely coincidental.

Acknowledgments

This book was shaped significantly by Amy Lansky, my publisher, editor, collaborator, close friend, and so much more.

My other editor, Jena Roach, continues to push me to do better. She takes my unpolished ideas and makes them sparkle. Thanks also to Mark Manasse and Izaak Rubin, early readers of the book, and a special thanks to the members of my writer's group, Paul Garrett, Allan Stevenson, and Michael DiRe, who gave it a final polish.

Diogo Leite of Book Design Company did a great job on the cover art.

Table of Contents

For all the tricky women in the world
and the men who support them.

One

"I had to hack two government agencies to find these people, so you know I've been having fun." Penny tooted a quick trumpet herald as she slid a piece of paper across the food court table. Then, collapsing into the plastic chair like someone seeking relief after a hard day's work, she took a sip of her drink, a dark green concoction from her favorite food stall, the Juice Moose.

Elle eyed Penny carefully, noticing how her friend's smile kept growing and retreating as if she was struggling to keep something under control. The two of them liked to play little games, challenging each other to stay sharp, and it made Elle wonder if there was something tricky on the piece of paper that would explain the unsteady smile.

Penny could be hard to read. A few years ago, she was a trusting and friendly high-school queen whose popularity brought fun to every party. Now she was guarded and could be surprisingly abrasive when provoked. That guy who groped her last month was surely surprised later when he couldn't find his wallet.

Of course, Penny hadn't lost the ability to be a party girl —she knew how to work it. And she had the looks. Tall and thin, with long black hair and bright blue eyes, one warm smile could melt any heart. She was even more unusual looking since getting a silver nostril ring a few months back. Few could resist staring. Unfortunately, those who did sometimes got snarls from the skinny wildcat who no longer tolerated what she considered to be the wrong kind of attention.

Elle and Penny sat in a Los Angeles mall, wearing jeans and T-shirts. Penny's faded black shirt was from a local eatery. The front had the restaurant's name, curved in an elegant ribbon. The back had the address. Some stupid boy from school had taken her to that restaurant a few months ago, then bought her the shirt. Afterwards, feeling like he deserved something more for treating her, he'd tried to extract payment in the front seat of his car. Penny's disinterest made no difference to the boy as he aggressively pursued his reward, so she was forced to use some of the skills Elle had taught her. The boy stumbled from the car with a bloody nose, some of which stained the shirt, making it one of her favorite tops.

Elle would never wear a T-shirt with a story. Nor would she wear one with a restaurant name. None of her clothing had any name, word, picture, or piece of art. Con artists needed to hide and never wear anything memorable, which meant plain T-shirts in faded colors. Today's unmemorable color was russet-brown.

Elle wondered about the piece of paper on the table. Penny wasn't providing any clear signals about it. Normally, she'd flash exaggerated facial expressions to goad Elle into snatching the paper and reading it. But not today, and that made her realize this was serious—her friend had actually done it. The very information Elle had craved for years was laying right there on the table. Penny's wavering look of pleasure was simply pride for having uncovered such life-changing information, layered with anticipation over how it would be received.

"I didn't think I'd be so nervous." Elle forced a laugh. She'd been certain she wanted this, desperate for it, in fact.

But now that she had it, she needed a moment before reading what was printed there. Her hand hung inches above the paper, advancing and pausing in a dance of indecision. Finally, with a loud exhale, she snatched it from the table.

For a moment, Elle couldn't bring herself to confront the truth on the paper, even though she held it close. Instead, her eyes focused elsewhere, kids lined up for burgers, shoppers chatting on their phones, fast-food servers working their cash registers. When her heart stopped beating like a drum corps, she let out a small sigh and scanned the page, reading two names along with an address and phone number. Exactly what she wanted.

Now more calm, Elle flopped back in the flimsy chair. "How about that?" she forced a chuckle to dispel the remaining tension. "They're still together—both of my parents are at the same address." She read the page once more then tossed it onto the table, offering Penny an embarrassed smile. She was usually tougher than this, and it made her feel a little silly. "Sorry for making this into such a big deal. Don't know why I got all twisted up."

"Oh, come on!" Penny set her juice cup on the table and leaned forward. "This is intense. You're entitled to a moment here. Also . . ." She reached into her backpack and pulled out another piece of paper. "I have a birth certificate, fresh from the city recorder." She flipped it across the table like a playing card, landing it softly on top of the first piece of paper.

Elle studied it, her eyes wide as she scanned the document. "Huh. My foster mom didn't lie about my birthday. I *will* be 18 next month. And look at that! My birth parents didn't even give me a name, just wrote 'Baby girl Burnside.' How did you know it was me?"

"Easy. I followed you through the system then worked back to the birth certificate. This is you. And as for the 'Baby Girl' name, there are tons of vaguely named kids in foster care. Your parents must have known they were going to give you away."

Elle got up and raced around the table to give her friend a hug. "Thanks for this. You're the best."

"I know!" Penny beamed. "So ... Call them up. Introduce them to their missing daughter." She took another sip of her juice, a blend of kale, coconut, sea salt, and lime.

Elle squinted at the cup, wondering how Penny could drink that stuff all day. "OK then, time to call my folks."

Nothing could stop her now. Her birth parents were finally going to talk to the daughter they'd abandoned so long ago. She entered the number into her phone then aimed her finger at the call button. One insignificant touch on the glowing green dot. She stared at it like it was a life raft, her only succor in a vast, empty sea. The green circle seemed larger and brighter, as if demanding to be tapped. Could it be that her phone understood the importance of this call, accentuating the button to help her find it more easily? Or was her mind playing tricks, encouraging her with this once-in-a-lifetime opportunity? Whichever it was, the universe seemed to be conspiring to make this happen, to get her to make that call and move forward with her life.

But she couldn't do it. Something felt wrong about calling up these strangers. A phone call seemed too distant for such an important encounter, too easy for people to hide their feelings. Besides, she was completely unprepared and had no idea what she'd say. With a groan, Elle set her phone down on the table.

"I'm not ready, and I think it's wrong to do this on the phone. I have to go there." She glanced at her new parents' address. "They live near Portland, just a day or two drive from here. Want to come along?"

Elle was asking nicely, but she desperately wanted her friend along. The two girls had been inseparable for the past few years, ever since she'd saved Penny from those high-school goons. And both of them had their driver's licenses, so they really could make the trip now.

Penny nodded. "Sure, I'd love to come along. I can't wait to see what happens when you knock on their door." She took a sip of her juice and grinned more than usual, probably visualizing the scene to come. Then she started planning. "We might lose a few days of school, but who cares? My schedule is free. What about you? I know you don't care about classes, but are you working any side-jobs?"

"Nothing's happening right now, but I don't have a car. I'll ask my mom." Elle paused as she considered her new family. "It's funny. Now I've got two people I can call 'mom.' Of course, Bea hates being called that, and for once I have to agree with her. She's never been any good at being a mom."

"Oh come on! You have a totally cool foster mom, much more awesome than my real one."

"Well, she's taught me lots of tricky things," Elle admitted. "But she stinks as a mother. Feeding us has always been optional in her book, and there are no chapters at all about keeping us safe, caring for us when we're sick, or loving us. I wish I had your mom. She actually came over and brought me soup last year when I was sick. That's more than Bea did. Your mom is way nicer than mine."

"OK," Penny twisted her mouth into an exaggerated smirk. "Let's compare our mothers. My mom sells real estate, yours is a con artist. Point: your mom. While my mom was teaching me how to fold napkins, yours was teaching you how to pick locks. Point: your mom again. And while my mom made me take dance lessons at the local community center, yours sent you to cat burglar lessons at your aunt's house." She laughed. "Want to trade mothers?"

Penny had heard plenty of stories about Bea, so she surely knew the woman's darker side. And while Elle had certainly been taught to be tough, nobody was going to choose Bea as mother of the year. There were serious downsides to being raised by a ruthless con artist. Lock-picking lessons were harsh exercises that often included lightning tests before meals. If they couldn't pick the lock fast enough, they didn't get to eat. It forced Elle and her two siblings to spend hours perfecting their skills, often wishing they could be setting a table instead. Funny how each of them was envious of the other's childhood.

Elle shrugged her shoulders. "Hey, you don't need my foster mom . . . I've taught you plenty of stuff. You can pick locks, lift wallets, and do some awesome cons. Plus, the things you do with computers are crazy stellar. We're a team, Penny, so let's take this team to Oregon and have an adventure. I'll ask Bea about a car."

She read the piece of paper again. "Harry and Trish Burnside of Gresham, Oregon. Two children, Wendy and June." She winked at Penny. "Three children, actually. Looks like I get a whole family, including two sisters. I wonder if they have a dog."

"You want me to find out?" Penny bounced in her seat, always happy to go cyber-snooping "I can pull their credit card records and see if they shop at any pet stores."

"I don't know." Elle scrunched her mouth. "These aren't marks, they're my parents. It feels wrong to spy on them."

"Spy? You mean like what I did when I found them?" Penny arched an eyebrow. "You could have gotten this through normal channels if you'd waited until you were 18. But no! You couldn't even wait one more month. I had to use my Internet magic to hack the foster care agency. We're already spying—why worry about a little more?"

"Well, first of all, I know you love to hack. But secondly, Harry and Trish aren't our usual marks—I hate to swindle innocent people. I just want to meet them."

"Of course we're not going to swindle them. But if you think about it, Harry and Trish Burnside are the first people to ever swindle *you*, messing with your identity, your home, and your entire childhood." Elle blurted out a sad laugh over that, so Penny gave her a hug. "Your birth parents have done a number on your psyche for years. Maybe we *should* treat them like marks—study them and find out more. It's not going to be easy to knock on their door. The more you prepare, the better it will go. You taught me that."

Elle shook her head. "I'm feeling overloaded by the mere fact that my birth parents exist. Not sure I can handle much more information until I see them up close. I know you love to hack, but let's not do any more right now."

Two

Elle arrived home, anxious to tell Bea the news about her real parents. She knew it wouldn't be easy, but it needed to be done, and soon. Once she stepped in the back door though, she heard a familiar sound, a loud pounding that echoed repeatedly through the house. The mechanical slamming made her think of meat being butchered, each forceful slice followed by a quieter shuffling sound, as cut slabs were piled to one side and new stock was moved under the blade.

She laughed at her own reaction to the sound, because she knew it didn't come from meat. Bea was cutting paper. Elle had done this on many occasions, and it was one of her favorite things to do. She quickly went to the kitchen where her foster mother was busy at work.

Bea stood by the kitchen table, pausing to sip from a glass of wine. The table had a big guillotine-style paper cutter, with piles of paper everywhere. She was showing her age lately and relied on Elle for the tricky physical work, scaling buildings and shimmying through air ducts. Last year, she started wearing turtle-neck blouses to cover the loose skin around her neck. It made her look proper, a harmless older woman who men could trust. But "proper" was probably the least apropos word for Bea Kirkland.

Setting the glass down, she lined-up another bundle of paper then quickly swung the blade, slamming it all the way through with a massive thud. Noticing her daughter in the quiet after the cut, Bea scowled. "Get your lazy bones over here and finish this. This is *supposed* to be *your* job."

Elle silently walked to the paper cutter and took over her foster mother's work, aligning the next bundle and swinging the blade, though perhaps with less venom. The paper cutter was already marked so that the final product would be the size of a dollar bill. Or, more likely, a hundred-dollar bill.

Bea took a seat and started counting the cut pieces. When she got to 98, she wrapped the bundle in an official-looking strip of paper and stacked it for later. The next time they needed fake cash, they'd use this. Whatever the scam called for, fifties or hundreds, they would pad the top and bottom of each stack with real bills, making it into an authentic-looking bundle. Then they'd fill an attaché case with fake bundles to fool some poor mark into thinking he was getting much more cash.

They worked silently for a while, Bea counting while Elle sliced. With each bundle of fake bills, Bea's face relaxed a little more. When she actually smiled at a finished pile, Elle broke the silence.

"I have news."

Bea looked up with a curled lip that screamed, "Don't interrupt me." She had just started to count another bundle, and she refused to be disturbed. When she got to 98, they could talk. Elle kept on slicing.

Bea finished the bundle and set it aside. "OK then, I'm listening. What's your stupid news?"

Elle had a cut lined up, so she gave the blade one final swing. Then she took a deep, calming breath and confessed. "Penny found my birth parents."

A flash of grimace twitched to life then instantly disappeared from Bea's lips. "Well, whoop-de-do." She turned back to the cash, counting out another bundle of bills. She made it to about ten when she paused and dropped the paper on the table, now favoring her foster daughter with a big grin. "Wait a minute! We can take those losers to the cleaners!"

Elle felt like she'd been slapped. Swindling her birth parents had to be the most delusional idea yet, and Bea had no shortage of delusions. "Oh, no you don't! I'm not making enemies of my real parents."

Bea waved her hand dismissively. "Hey, they dumped you. They obviously don't care, so maybe you should teach them a lesson. And it'll be easy because we have the advantage—they don't know who you are."

Since Bea wouldn't let go, the best way forward would be to humor her, so Elle offered her most placating smile. "OK. Let's trick them. I'm going up there to check them out, see what they're worth. Penny's coming with me for the drive. Problem is, we don't have wheels. Do you know anyone with a car we can borrow?"

Bea stared at her daughter for a few seconds, then twisted her mouth. "Yeah, I get it. You want to 'case them out,' right?" She made air-quotes to emphasize that she didn't believe a word. "Sorry, but I need you here. Those fake bonds will be ready soon, and I've lined up a few marks who are desperate to give us their money."

"I won't be gone long. No more than a week, tops."

Bea's eyes narrowed to slits. "If you pull a Dee on me, I swear I'll find you."

Elle bristled at another of her foster mother's threats. Bea had become more desperate over the years, as her foster children disappeared, one-by-one. It had started seven years ago, when the oldest child, Jay, got killed while pulling a con. Dee, the middle child, had been with him that night and almost died too. It soured her on swindling, leaving her fearful of any encounter with a mark. But regardless of her protests, she couldn't escape her family's unsavory business. Bea wouldn't hear of it. It took four miserable years before Dee could engineer her escape, vanishing after a big con and taking all the money. Elle was proud of her big sister for finally sticking it to Bea, but she definitely wasn't happy to be left alone with their shocked, angry, and humiliated foster mother.

A few days after Dee left, she contacted Elle and told her she'd stopped grifting and had moved to New York City. Of course, she insisted that Elle keep this information secret. Bea did not need to know where her older daughter had gone. Dee also gave Elle some of the money she'd taken, a safety net against their uncaring parent. That had been a wonderfully useful gift.

The most thought-provoking aspect of Dee's vanishing act was the sacrifice she was willing to make in order to stop swindling. She'd given up her home, her relatives, and her friends. It made Elle reconsider her own life as a con artist. Sneaking around, hiding, and squeezing through narrow spaces was always fun, a game Elle did better than her brother and sister. And her first lie at age five earned her universal praise as well as a candy bar, so she quickly learned to lie about everything. Being a con artist was fun until it killed her brother and drove her sister away.

Dee's departure also made Elle think about the people they tricked. How were their lives changed by being swindled? Could they afford it? Did they deserve it? Bea always shut down such questions, insisting that the marks got what they deserved. But was that true?

Things at home were strained after Dee's escape, but it did have the benefit of changing Bea's approach to parenting. Where Elle had previously been treated like a slave, the youngest child who was forced to do whatever her foster mother demanded, her voice was now heard occasionally since she was the only child left. She still had to do the grunt work—Bea would never share completely. But they did discuss plans more often, and Elle learned many of the details. She heard about costumes, cars, props, and office spaces, along with everything else needed to pull a con.

Because of this, Elle knew her foster mother could get her a car. She just needed to convince Bea that she wouldn't run away, so she raised her hands in a sign of surrender. "I promise I won't 'pull a Dee' on you."

Bea's face darkened at this clearly insufficient promise. "You're not getting wheels from me, kid."

Elle had seen that stern authoritative look too many times to be affected by it anymore, and her options were far from exhausted. "That's OK." She gave her voice an artificial lift to show how little Bea's opinion mattered. "I'll ask Aunt Franny. I'm sure she knows someone who can spare a car for a week." Franny had taught Elle most of her physical skills, including how to drive, so this was no idle threat.

"Don't play games with *me*." Bea glared, hard and unfriendly. Another of her standard looks.

Elle refused to give up—she needed to get to Oregon, and she was certain Bea knew someone with a car they weren't using. She could have gone out and bought one if she wanted. Most of the money Dee had sent her was still there, more than enough for a nice new car. But Bea would wonder how she'd paid for it, and that would reveal Dee's secret money.

Elle wasn't supposed to have any money. None of the kids in the family ever did. Whenever they got back from a job, Bea would take everything to a mysterious storage locker where it was never seen again. This was fine when Elle first learned to swindle. She was happy to give up her take because she got those cherished candy bars. But the kids needed more food than that, and they wondered where all the money was going.

Jay and Dee started hiding some of the money they scammed before returning home. Dee would pull the center bill from a stack of hundreds. Bea noticed, of course, because she counted everything the kids brought home, but she blamed the mark, and used it as an opportunity to boast that she'd beaten the fools anyway.

When the kids bought food with their scammed money, Bea didn't notice because they ate it before returning. But when they bought new clothes or gadgets, that crossed the line. The goods were taken away, and repeat offenders were locked in a closet. Bea even patted the kids down when they returned home and searched their rooms when they went out. So they stuck to buying food, and added visits to a local pizza place where they spent heavily and tipped like crazy. It wasn't much of a surprise that a family of con artists would find ways to cheat each other.

Given that Elle wasn't supposed to be able to afford a car on her own, she was left with one way forward: get Bea to allow the road trip. She kept her eyes glued to her foster mother, a silent war of wills that she was determined to win.

After a long minute, Bea let go with a loud exhale. "Fine. If you're that determined to get a car, then run a con and get one." She folded her arms. "If you do it right, I'll even let you keep it."

Elle's eyes sprang open. Bea never let her children keep any of the things they swindled, especially not a car. This was a significant offer. Of course, *doing it right* was pretty vague and could mean anything. There were no guarantees it would help Elle get a car. For Bea, "right" usually meant big, which would mean getting more than a simple car. She might want two cars, or some money on the side.

Elle had her own idea of doing it right, and that had changed quite a bit since Dee left. At first, all she wanted was to limit their cons to more appropriate marks, the greedy who deserved to be taken down. But that was too easy—rich greedy jerks could be found anywhere. She wanted a challenge.

An idea came to her one day, and she instantly knew it was right. An extension of the Robin Hood scenario that robbed the rich to help the poor. She would start with that, swindling obnoxious rich people who'd cheated others, trying to even the score. But beyond that, she would arrange the con so that the marks would admit their misdeeds and renounce their greedy ways. The perfect con would fleece bad people then adjust their way of thinking so they wouldn't be as bad anymore.

Of course, with Bea as a partner, complex plans that delivered altruistic lessons were not at all likely. Each new swindle the two of them did went down as Bea wanted, ignoring any suggestions about adjusting the marks' attitudes. Still, as time went on Elle was encouraged that her concept might be feasible, because whenever a plan was presented, she could always find a twist that would make the mark proud to be cheated.

Last month they tricked a bar owner into spending money on fake whiskey, using the threat of illegal liquor tampering to stop him from fighting back. Elle would have preferred to involve the man's wife, who hated alcohol and, if played right, would be proud of him for failing to complete the deal. It would teach him a lesson and help him accept the lost money. Unfortunately, these sort of cons never happened. Instead, Bea continued to cheat people who couldn't afford it, and the only lesson they learned was that the world was a more dangerous place than they thought.

Given that she and her mother had very different views on the right way to run a con, Elle needed clarification. "So how do I 'do it right'?"

"Well . . ." Bea tilted her head back, squinting as she looked down her nose. Teacher-Mom was about to deliver a lesson. "First off, the car has to be in good shape. I don't want to see some junky beater parked out front—show some class. Also, you can't steal it or you'll have cops looking for it all the time. No . . ." She tapped her chin. "The real way to do it right is to get someone to *give* you a car. Have them throw in some cash, too, if you really want to impress me."

Elle nodded slowly already thinking of plans. All Bea wanted was a con that would trick someone out of a decent car and some cash. Beyond that, she could do it however she chose. That made things easy. She actually gave Bea a hug on her way out the door.

Back at the mall's food court, Elle found Penny at their usual table, tucked in a dark corner. The dim light spread to many of the tables near theirs, which they liked because it kept people away and let them talk freely. Few ventured into this poorly lit nook.

Mall food courts are rarely dark, but one day last year, the bulb over this table burned out. Elle and Penny instantly noticed the new level of privacy, and they liked it. So they took the table as their own, and they made sure that the bulb stayed off. Whenever it got replaced, it somehow managed to go out again within a day or two. The poor maintenance staff couldn't keep up.

Elle layered her fries with ketchup as she explained Bea's challenge. When she finished, Penny summed it up. "You just need to convince someone to give you a nice car and some cash. And . . ." She nodded with a knowing smile. "I'm guessing it has to be taken from someone who deserves it."

Elle ate a French fry and licked her fingers. "Yeah, no lost jobs or lost wages. Whoever gives us the car must be able to afford it easily. Like maybe a rich auto dealer. Or someone who has an obnoxious collection of cars they never use."

"Oh, oh, oh! I have an idea." Penny's eyes bugged out as she leaned across the dark table. "What if we swindle the factory that makes the cars? I was looking at some of them, and they have terrible computer security. Bet I could order an entire truckload. Let me show you one in Tijuana I was looking at last week." Penny pulled her laptop closer and started to work, her smile growing as her typing and clicking sped up.

After a minute, she stopped and spun the computer around so Elle could see. "Look at this!" The screen was filled with pictures of cars. "These are in production. I can request colors and styles, setup deliveries, you name it. Normally, dealers use this page to order cars, but I can use it to send a truckload of cars anywhere I want. Too bad I have to pay for it."

From a very early age, Elle was taught ways to make other people pay for things. So when Penny suggested that payment was a problem, Elle took that as a challenge. "Look for slush funds at the plant. There are always little pockets of money in a company that big. We might be able to use one."

Penny dove back in, her mouth tight and her nose almost touching the screen. Elle knew this look: the concentration, the immersion, the singular drive to find a way in. She ate another french fry and sipped her milkshake while her friend did her stuff.

After a few minutes, Penny brightened. "Look at this! There *is* a slush fund." She clicked and typed a bit more. "Wow! A big fat slush fund. And it gets a steady stream of deposits from random cost centers around the factory. God! It's got millions of dollars in it." She clicked some more, and her eyes grew large. "Oh snap! Someone's making periodic withdrawals from the fund, all going to the same bank account." She pushed away from the laptop and waved her hands excitedly. "I think I just found an embezzler."

Elle scooted closer to the screen, suddenly very interested. She studied it for a few seconds, then she shrugged. "What's so suspicious about the withdrawals?"

"Well, look at the international routing number on them." She pointed to the screen. "I know that country code —the money's all going to Switzerland."

"So someone at the plant is siphoning money. How convenient. And the account has plenty in it." She ate another French fry. "Can you use it to pay for the cars?"

"Let's see. I'll put the slush fund's account number in the ordering form . . . then click the 'charge' button . . ." She tapped her fingers on the table for a few seconds, then she gasped. "Oh my God, it worked! We can now get more cars than we know what to do with. Bea wants a big con? I bet she'll be impressed when a truck delivers eight cars in front of her house."

Elle laughed. "What about license plates and registration?"

"No prob. I'll hack the DMV."

"No, wait!" Elle shivered with excitement. "I have a better idea. We're going to do it exactly like Bea wants. We'll get properly registered cars, one for me and one for you. And we'll get some spending money too."

"Sounds good." Penny took a sip of juice, then cocked her head. "What's your plan?"

"Well, first of all, you need a fake driver's license."

"Why can't I use my real one?"

Elle shook her head. "We're swindling cars now, which requires that we have driver's licenses. And since we never give out our real name and address in a con, you need a fake. My license is made out to Lisa Fisher with a nonexistant address."

"OK, easy. What else?"

"Well, let's see." Elle scanned her phone. "I see a dealership in Glendale that sells these cars. The owner is a guy named Sam Brennan, and he's going to be our target. We need to get access to his phone, which is probably not possible when he's at work. Check him out and let's find a way to get that phone."

"Let's start with his expenses . . ." Penny resumed her rapid clicking and typing. It took a full minute, longer than she usually needed, then she turned her laptop so Elle could see. "Here's his latest credit card statement."

Elle read the screen. "Hmm. There's a liquor store, a few restaurants, an adult toy shop, a supermarket, a bar . . ." She sucked a rapid lungful of air. "There it is! A golf club." She pointed to the screen. "Golfers usually turn off their phones when they play, so that would be a good time to get it. Can you see if he's really a member of this club and when he's playing next?"

"I'll check the club's site . . ." Penny worked the laptop some more, muttering happily as she typed. It didn't take long. "OK, I've got the green schedule, and . . ." She scrolled through the information. "Yep. Brennan plays every Saturday at ten. He'll be there tomorrow."

"Perfect. Now comes the hard part."

Penny beamed proudly. "Nothing's hard on a computer."

"Yes, but you don't get to use your computer for this." Elle tilted back and studied her friend. "You're too skinny, Penny. You need to get out more, and eat better things than vegetable juice. When was the last time you ate a burger?"

Penny had switched to an all-juice diet a few years back, easier because of the Juice Moose shop in the food court. Elle preferred "real food" such as burgers, fries, and milkshakes. Of course, Penny had a few choice words about her friend's notion of "real."

With a look of someone cleaning the zoo's monkey house, Penny pointed to Elle's plate. "You want me to eat that? I'll pass."

"But it's so good." Elle peeled a ketchup-coated French fry from her plate and waved it in front of Penny's face. "Yum, yum. It doesn't get any better than this."

Penny waved away the greasy hunk of spud. "I'll stick to juice." She held up her dark brown glass. "Yum, yum. Beets, limes, and carrots *with carrot tops*. I've never found a place that was willing to juice the carrot tops too. I'm telling you, Juice Moose is the best. I hope they have one up in Oregon."

"We're not in Oregon yet, Penny. First, we need a car, and in order to do that, you've got to put down the juice *and* the computer. You need to get outside." She leaned closer, one hand on her friend's shoulder. "Ever worked as a caddy?"

Three

The next day, Penny sat in a golf cart, prepared to swindle some cars. She had two missions today: to plant the seeds of the con and—more importantly—to hack Sam Brennan's phone. Brennan, the owner of a local car dealership, was playing a round with some of his buddies. Sporting gray hair with a salt-and-pepper beard, his portly body barely fit in the charcoal polo shirt, and the belt holding his tan slacks struggled to stay in place.

To her dismay, Penny was not wearing her favorite color, black. All the caddies wore club uniforms, so she'd snuck into the locker room and borrowed a white shirt and—to her horror—a pink skirt. Then she asked around and found the caddy who was scheduled to be working for Brennan. A sharp-looking boy, he was delighted when Penny offered him a hundred dollars to take his place. He even gave her a few tips about the course as well as some of Brennan's quirks, and he warned her that the man was a cheap blowhard who wouldn't tip her.

Brennan was already in the cart, looking for his caddy, when Penny arrived and introduced herself. He and his golf friends gave her appraising looks and traded rude comments about Sam's cute caddy. At least they seemed willing to let her do the job.

Penny had spent the previous night watching golf videos and could now make a reasonable guess as to which club was needed. She did her job quietly while watching and listening, waiting for her moment.

As Elle predicted, Brennan silenced his phone but kept it handy, sticking far out of his back pants pocket. Penny itched to get her hands on it, and the opportunity arose at the third tee. Brennan squatted down to plant his tee, and it broke. Keeping low to the ground, he demanded another one. As Penny handed him a new tee, she could hear Elle's voice like a whisper in her mind, chanting the pickpocket's mantra: *Distract and lift, distract and lift.*

The lift would be easy with the phone sticking so far out, and the distraction wasn't too hard, either. She squatted down to hand him a tee, placing her body between the phone and the other golfers to block their view. As she got back up, she stumbled, brushing against his leg and shoulder before finally righting herself. Brennan arched an eyebrow, so she apologized sweetly for chronic clumsiness, then walked away with his phone tucked in her waistband.

Over at the golf cart, Penny pretended to sort through the clubs while the others played the hole. She used a special cable to hack the phone, then she set it on the driver's seat. He'd find it there and think it fell out while they were driving. Her main mission was done, and each step she took away from the cart made her feel lighter.

Unfortunately, before she could return to the golfers, Brennan noticed the problem. He reached back in search of his phone and stiffened when his hand fell over emptiness. Soon, he was doing a full-body pat down, looking for his phone in any pocket he could reach. He completed his search, then turned to glare at Penny.

"Where's my phone!" Penny felt her entire body go rigid. Brennan somehow knew she'd taken it, and now the con was ruined. Elle had given her this job because it was simple, something an inexperienced grifter could handle. But she had failed miserably, and feared the worst from her mentor. She stood frozen, trying to figure out how to respond.

"I'm asking you a question." Brennan's angry red face hovered inches away.

Before admitting defeat, Penny decided to try one last maneuver, something Elle would do. She would give him the same emotion he was giving her. Brennan was mad, so she would be too.

"Don't look at me!" Penny slapped a hand to her chest, both to steady herself and as part of the act. Then she leaned closer and snarled. "Why would I take your stupid old phone?"

"Because you're the only person here I don't know. Who else would take it?" He grabbed Penny's shirt at the collar and shook her.

"Jesus, mister, take a chill pill. I don't have your phone!" Penny swatted his hands away and walked off in the opposite direction from the cart. She took a few calming breaths, but a prickly heat tickled at the back of her neck. Hopefully, Brennan would find his phone before she sweated through her shirt. Elle would never lose her cool like this, even when things were truly falling to bits. Someday she hoped to be that good.

Fortunately, one of Brennan's golf buddies called out with the good news. "Hey Sam! Your phone's in the cart. Right here on your seat. Good thing your fat ass didn't crush it."

The others joined in to tease Brennan as he walked over and grabbed his phone. On the way back, he muttered unhappily then shoved it in his back pocket where it still stuck far out, waving like a rooster's tail.

Penny wiped her brow. Brennan had never really suspected her. He was merely shifting the blame to the most vulnerable person, something he probably did all the time. She had to remind herself that she'd done well. Her main mission was complete.

By the fifth hole, all the small talk had been exchanged, and the men fell into silence, punctuated by occasional bursts of bragging about money, booze, or women. Penny wanted to hack all of their phones. At the start of the seventh hole, one of the other golfers entertained everyone with a money story. Apparently, he'd gotten an extra sixty dollars from a customer who read the amount wrong on an invoice.

Brennan laughed. "That's nothing. Last year, the guys at the plant in Tijuana screwed up and sent me the wrong cars. I complained, so they offered me a discount for my trouble, a few hundred dollars off my next shipment. It gave me an idea . . ." He elbowed his buddy in the ribs. "I started making ambiguous orders, always doing something a little confusing so I could complain when the cars arrived. Worked like a charm. So far, I've gotten three more discounts from them." He bellowed out another laugh.

This was Penny's chance. She realized there could be no better time to complete her mission, so she spoke up quickly before the laughter faded out.

"Sorry for butting in, but my dad works for that plant, and he can get you a much better deal. Half price on an entire shipment of cars."

Brennan turned to her with a frown, his eyes glazed as if he couldn't remember who she was. "Look here, little girl. When I want your advice, I'll ask for it. In the meantime, hand me my driver." He turned to his golf buddies and rolled his eyes, sharing disdain for the presumptuous caddy.

Fully expecting this response, Penny continued with her task. "Hey, you don't want a golden shipment? Fine with me

—your loss." She pulled out his driver, offering it with a sweet smile. Brennan looked warily at the mysterious caddy who was holding his club, then he snapped it out of her hands.

Penny's smile never wavered because she was truly happy. She'd accomplished her second mission too and was done for the day. She could look around for the first time and appreciate this man-made nature reserve, each blade of grass mowed to perfection. At least the sun was genuine.

When Penny got to the mall, she turned her laptop to Elle, showing Brennan's chat history. They studied it for a few minutes, trying to find someone Brennan would trust.

"This guy." Elle pointed at the screen. "When he talks, Brennan pays attention. Let's be him."

Penny sent a fake message that Brennan would think was from his friend. "Hey, Sam," it read. "You really need to check this out. A guy is offering something he calls a golden shipment. Deep discount cars. Dealers in Arizona are making out like bandits."

A response came quickly across Penny's screen. "Heard about that today. What's the deal?"

Penny replied. "Insider at the plant. His daughters take care of business. Don't want to say any more about it . . . Let's keep this on the down-low. *Capiche*?"

The reply came quickly. "OK, but how do I reach them?" Brennan was hooked and hungry. Penny sent a phone number, then they sat back to wait.

Seconds later, the phone in Elle's backpack started to ring. Penny glanced at her friend. "You're on."

Elle pulled out the phone and let it ring a few more times before answering. She held it between herself and

Penny so both of them could hear. "Yeah?" Her voice indicated boredom and irritation.

Unfazed, Brennan spoke with authority. "Tell me about the golden shipment."

"And who are you?" Elle's condescending reply oozed disinterest.

"Sam Brennan. I got a dealership in Glendale."

"Hmm, OK. Let's see." She paused, tapping her fingernails on the table to make it sound like she was typing. Then she resumed the conversation. "I think we can help you out, Mr. Brennan."

"Did I talk to your sister today? Skinny girl with black hair."

"Sounds like her. Do you play golf? She caddies at the club."

"Yeah, that's her. So how do two teenage girls get me cheap cars?"

"Not us, Mr. Brennan. Our dad runs things. My sister and I just make arrangements. Meet me at the mall near your dealership and I'll explain."

"I can be there after work, say at six thirty. Where do we meet?"

"I'll be sitting on the edge of the fountain in the center of the mall, facing the watch store. And don't be late, because I have homework tonight." She added extra pressure to make sure he really cared about the deal. If it was going to happen, he needed to be the one who wanted it more.

"Homework? Jeez, what a lame operation! Maybe I should talk to your dad. Who is he, anyway?"

"Forget him. You deal with us. Besides, he won't talk to you—safer that way. And for your information, I'm only *slightly* interested in talking to you, so be prompt. If you're not there by six forty, I'm gone." She ended the call, then she and Penny fist-bumped on their way to get a celebratory juice.

At six thirty promptly, Sam Brennan sat down next to her by the fountain. "So, the caddy and her sister sell cars. What's the deal?"

"The deal is that I can get you an entire truckload of cars for only ten grand each, less than half price. There are only two catches. First, we keep two of the cars." She held up a hand to stop Brennan's expected protest. "Don't worry, you only pay for the cars you get. But you will handle the registration of those two cars to me and my sister."

Brennan smirked. "Are you even old enough to drive?"

"Certainly. We'll show you licenses, insurance, and everything else you need."

Brennan shrugged. "OK. What's the second catch?"

"You pay in cash."

Brennan threw his head back and howled with amusement. Then he launched forward to get in Elle's face. "What kind of a fool do you take me for? You want me to hand you cash for a very dubious shipment of cars? Not a chance."

Elle didn't flinch, even with Brennan's anger rising red and his bulk hovering close. She let him finish, then smiled. "You pay when the truck arrives, not before. We front the bill up to that point. When you've seen the cars for yourself, you pay. Don't like them? I'll have the truck take them somewhere else. You're not the only dealer around here."

Apparently pacified, Brennan squinted and thought for a few seconds. "What's wrong with the cars?"

"Nothing. Fresh from the plant, full paperwork, regular driver. Only difference is, you pay me."

"I don't know. This sounds all kinds of fishy."

"It may sound fishy, but it works exactly as I'm saying. Look at this." She handed him her phone. Penny had set it up so Brennan could order the cars.

He looked down, then arched an eyebrow. "This looks like the same ordering form I use."

"It is. Exactly the same. If you want a golden shipment, pick one from this phone. I'll have it delivered right to you at only ten grand per car."

Brennan worked his mouth as he examined the shipments. She let him explore for a bit, then she cleared her throat. "Look, I've got a big test tomorrow, and I've got to study. You in or out?" She grabbed the phone and stood up.

"Wait, I'm in. What do we do next?"

Elle sat back down and pointed at the phone. "Pick any batch that hasn't been assigned to a dealer yet. That batch of nine cars near the top, for example. It can be at your place next Thursday." She pointed to another order at the bottom of the screen. "This batch can be at your dealership the following week." She handed him the phone to let him choose.

Brennan studied it briefly and nodded. "That first shipment looks good. If I ordered it, which ones would you keep?"

"Let's see . . ." She examined the phone. "We'll take the two tan cars, the sedan and the hatchback. Modest vehicles, not very flashy." Elle had learned the importance of hiding, of not standing out in any way. Con artists needed to disappear easily, and a tan car was perfect for that. Few people noticed the little brown cars on the road.

Brennan nodded. "You have a deal."

"OK. There are nine cars in this shipment, so you get seven of them. That means you'll pay us seventy thousand dollars in cash." She stood again, staring at her watch as she tapped her foot. "Can you get that much money ready by Thursday?"

"Of course!" Brennan curled his lips, as if it was the stupidest question he'd heard all day. "Thursday, then." He got up and walked out of the mall without looking back.

Once he was gone, Penny came out of hiding. "Did you get me a hatchback?" She hopped excitedly.

"Indeed I did." The two of them hugged and went to dinner.

"To us!" Elle called out when they returned to their table. They tapped their glasses, one with juice, the other a milkshake. Remembering something, Elle grabbed her phone. "I've got to take care of one little detail. Hang on." She smiled when the call went through. "Vance, old buddy. I need you for a job next Thursday. You available?"

Vance was part of Elle's extended con-artist family, the son of her Aunt Franny and Uncle Carl. All of the kids worked cons, including Vance, but he really didn't have the chops. Growing up, she'd heard story after story about Vance's inability to do a job right. The consensus was that you couldn't expect him to do anything critical, but he had a great scowl, so he could be useful when a show of force was necessary.

Elle listened quietly to Vance's reply, her foot tapping while she grunted, "Uh huh" a few times. She finally got him to agree to the job. "OK. I'll meet you Thursday morning. Thanks, Vance. Bye."

Penny wrinkled her nose. "Seriously? You're asking your dumb cousin Vance to help with this scam?" Even Penny had heard stories of his many epic fails.

Elle shrugged. "All I need is his scowl. With any luck, I won't even need that."

On Thursday the truck pulled up to Brennan's dealership. Elle and Penny had been waiting, and by the time he came out, the cars were being unloaded. He looked at the two girls and winked at Penny. "I remember you. The skinny caddy chick."

"Not any more," she folded her arms. "I quit."

Brennan's scanned the paperwork, muttering approval. Then he pulled out a pen and started signing various pages. Other men came out of the building to help unload the truck.

At one point, Brennan was standing next to Elle. "I'm impressed! That whole shipment for half price. How did you do that?"

"I didn't do a thing. My dad takes care of shipments."

Brennan propped his hands on his hips. "So why should I pay you anything? The paperwork has my name all over it. Perhaps I should keep my cash and kick you two out of here."

"Perhaps you should." Elle stood tall and stepped right up to the big man, unafraid. "And perhaps my dad's goons should come out of hiding and kick your ass into the Pacific Ocean." She indiscreetly looked off into the distance where a few people were gathered across the street.

Brennan looked around, then folded his arms. "You're bluffing."

"I am?" She pulled out her phone and made a call. "Hey, Vance. Put down your gun and wave to the nice car salesman." She pointed to a building across the street from the dealership. Up on the roof, Vance stood tall and waved. Elle had made sure he looked particularly scruffy today. "Still think I'm bluffing? Maybe you'll believe me when you see a targeting laser dot on your chest. Want me to ask him to get you in his sights?"

Brennan's bluster evaporated instantly. "I believe you!" He quickly moved behind the truck to hide from Vance. Safe behind the massive delivery vehicle, he scooted into the building, keeping his head low. Elle and Penny did their best not to laugh.

Back inside the dealership, he pointed to the two tan cars. "So, you want those two ugly hunks of metal?"

Elle agreed, so he pulled out the necessary documents and handed them to an assistant. He ushered the two girls into his office and gave them a briefcase full of cash. Elle quickly counted it, then snapped the case shut. Brennan directed them to a sales associate, who handled the paperwork. Elle got the sedan, and Penny got the hatchback.

A few hours later, two happy grifters drove off in brand new cars, along with seventy thousand dollars in spending money. Bea would be proud, but since she always took any cash Elle brought home, they stopped at a few banks in town to make generous but limited cash deposits. Elle's half of the take was now down to only three thousand dollars. She could face Bea with that much.

Then the girls went to the mall where they tapped drink cups to toast their success. Across town, Sam Brennan was probably celebrating as well, eager to tell his buddies about the golden shipment.

But down in Tijuana, an accountant was staring at his computer screen, eyes growing wider with every click.

Four

The house was a simple, small box surrounded by dozens of identical neighbors. Except this one looked worse. Weeds grew up through gaps in the walkway, a big crack zigzagged across the living-room window, and one of the rusty gutters had taken an unfortunate leap away from the building, making it dangerous and no use at all in a storm. The place had known better days, and Elle wondered about the people living there, her parents.

As she stood on the sidewalk, her heart beat so heavily that she could feel it in her throat. Would her parents be happy to meet her, or would they be angry that she'd barged back into their lives? And more important, what would they think when they found that their long lost daughter was a con artist? They might wish they'd never met her.

In the fading dusk of evening, she could see dim lights inside, along with the blue flicker of a television. She walked slowly to the front door, Penny by her side. Above the chipped and yellowed doorbell button, someone had scrawled "Broken." She tried the button anyway, but the graffiti was right. Elle knocked and stepped back.

A man opened the door wearing jeans and a torn T-shirt from a local basketball team. This could be her father, and she swallowed hard as she searched his eyes. Having been raised by a foster mother, Elle had no sense of what to expect from a father. Given what she'd seen of her friends' fathers, many of them were disappointments, and some were even tyrants. She'd never missed having one when she was younger, figuring that the reality could be much worse.

But Harry Burnside seemed like a nice man, smiling and relaxed. Average height with a slender build, he had an open face and straight blond hair. Behind him, the television commanded the attention of two younger blonde girls, who looked up briefly, then resumed watching their show.

Her sisters were blondes? Elle was brunette, but her father and sisters weren't. She looked at the door again to be sure she was at the right address.

The man's gaze hopped between Elle and Penny. "Hello."

"Um, hello." Elle faltered for a second, then recovered. "Are you Harry Burnside?"

"Yes, I am. Who are you?" So this was the right address, but all the blond hair made her wonder if Penny's information was wrong. She needed to meet Trish Burnside to be sure, but even with the wrong hair, she felt an affinity to this man, a sense that he really *was* her dad.

"My name's Elle, and this is Penny." She wrapped an arm around her friend to pull her close, holding on to something familiar as she dove into the lives of this unknown family. "We're . . . wow, this is so weird. Is your wife, Trish, around? I have something for both of you."

"Yeah, she's here." Harry paused and held up a finger. "You know we don't need Girl Scout cookies or anything else you're selling."

Elle smiled at him. "I promise we're not selling anything. We really don't want your money, just a moment of your time."

"Oh, I get it. You're Jehovah's Witnesses, right?"

"Nope. This isn't about religion. I'll explain everything if you let us introduce ourselves to you and your wife."

Harry shrugged. "OK, come on in."

As Elle walked slowly across the living room, tears welled in her eyes, and she had to force herself not to scream out, "Dad!" She was here! In her parents' home for the first time. This was the moment she'd anticipated for over a decade. It should have felt like a homecoming, a place of love where she could be at peace. Too bad everything looked so broken.

The inside of the house looked even worse than the outside. The furniture was threadbare, and the faded rug was chewed up in one corner. A computer sat over to the side, dating back to the time of the dinosaurs, with a big clunky box for a screen. Even the television was an old console model, the color flickering in and out of true. The only piece of recent technology was a small drone, sitting on a shelf and looking rather beat-up.

Her father led the way through the living room, past the girls who still watched television while glancing once or twice at their new guests. Wendy and June, according to Penny's information. Harry continued into the kitchen where four mismatched chairs surrounded a small card table. "Trish, we have visitors."

Trish Burnside was standing by the sink, wearing torn jeans and an amber tunic with three-quarter sleeves. Elle let out a huge breath when she saw her mother. Finally, someone with brunette hair! And more than that, Trish definitely looked familiar, slim and short, with a similar mouth. Now Elle knew for sure that she'd come to the right place.

"Well, hello! Would you like some soda?" Trish's enthusiasm made Elle wonder if her mother knew who she was. But after watching carefully, she rejected the idea. Trish was simply being friendly, something Bea would never be caught doing unless she was running a con. The contrast was almost laughable.

Elle accepted the offer of soda, but Penny opted for a glass of water. The three of them took seats while Elle's mom busied herself with the drinks. Sitting next to Elle, Penny pointed at Trish and whispered, "I can see the resemblance. This is definitely the right place."

"Shh! Give me a chance." Elle looked around to see if anyone had heard, but they hadn't. Harry and Trish still didn't have a clue.

Soon, Trish joined them at the table, setting down their drinks. "So who are you two?"

"Well ..." Elle began, then paused, her body unexpectedly tense. Once she made this announcement, there would be no going back. And although she wasn't going to talk about her life of crime, they'd find out at some point. How much damage would that do? These people worked hard and no doubt took only what they earned. She didn't want to burden their already-difficult lives with a strange and troublesome daughter. Part of Elle felt like running away and leaving these poor people alone.

But she'd come this far so there was no stopping now. She'd wanted to see them, now here they were, sitting at a table together. So she faced her parents and let it out.

"I hope you'll forgive me for being blunt . . . I'm your daughter."

The silence that followed this was so sharp that the television in the living room suddenly seemed loud. Harry and Trish stared at Elle, then turned to each other. Finally, Harry spoke up.

"Really?" He frowned. "How old are you?"

"I'll be turning eighteen in a few weeks, on the fourth of March. I even have a birth certificate, which lists you as my parents." She pulled a page from her backpack.

Harry grumbled as he glanced at the paper, but Trish didn't need any further assurance. She bolted from her chair and ran around the table toward the girls. This startled Elle, but when she noticed her mother's huge smile, she stood up in time to get a big hug. "Oh my God! You've come back! I've been worried about you for years." She pulled away, holding Elle at arm's length and studying her first child. "You've grown up beautifully! It's wonderful to finally meet you." She hugged her daughter again, tears streaming down her face.

Harry stood up but didn't approach. Trish looked up at him waved an arm. "Come on, Harry. It really is our daughter. Get over here!"

He nodded bashfully then joined the hug. "Welcome home, Elle. I'm really sorry we had to abandon you. It . . . it wasn't a good time for us."

Elle turned to survey the tired kitchen. "If you don't mind me saying, it doesn't seem like a very good time now, either."

Trish sighed. "You have no idea. This is luxury for us. When you were born, we were living in a car, scrimping to get enough to eat each day. Neither of us could find work, and we had no idea what we were going to do with a baby."

"What about your parents?"

Harry shook his head. "My parents died long ago, leaving me in foster care. Trish's parents hated her for taking up with a lowlife like me, and when she got pregnant they actually cut her off. We were stuck, so we gave you up for adoption. I did OK in foster care, so we hoped you would too."

Trish scowled at her husband. "That didn't make it right. You always used your own foster care experience to justify giving her away, but you know I never saw it like that." She turned to Elle. "I was miserable when we had to leave you. But there wasn't anything we could do. If we hadn't let you go, Child Protective Services would have taken you anyway." She dabbed at a tear. "I'll never forgive myself for that, Elle. I know we did a terrible thing. I'm so sorry."

Elle hugged her mother tightly, all of her worries swept away. "It's all right. I'm here now, Mom." She stopped suddenly, aware of the strangeness of her words. "I hope you don't mind that I call you 'Mom.'"

Trish laughed. "I don't mind at all. In fact, it's a huge relief. I've wondered for years what it would be like to meet you, and my worst fears were that you'd be so angry that you'd never want to be a part of our family again. Having you ask if you can call me 'Mom' is the best thing you could possibly say."

Harry smiled at his wife then turned to Elle. "She's right, we're delighted to meet you again, and we want to do what we can. Are you in trouble? Do you need a place to stay?"

"No, certainly not. I live in Los Angeles with my foster mother, Bea Kirkland. She adopted me when I was only two years old, so I've had a relatively stable life. I finally found your names recently, which is why Penny and I took a little road trip to visit you. But we won't be staying."

"So your name is Elle Kirkland?" Harry let his smile fade. "We never got around to giving you a name. 'Elle' is nice."

"Bea named me. She likes names that sound like single letters, so she's Bea, I'm Elle, and the other two foster kids in our family are Dee and Jay. I'm the youngest."

She didn't dare tell them why they'd been given these names, how they were intended specifically for con artists. Fortunately, she didn't have to because Harry had more questions. "So do you have a good home in California?"

"It's OK." The nature of her home life would have to wait, so she dissembled by switching to her brother and sister. "Dee lives in New York now, but Jay died years ago. It's just me and Bea these days. We're—how can I put it— unusual." She looked at her father. "What about you? What was foster care like when you were a kid?"

Harry's eyes twinkled. "Good. I was lucky to grow up in a home with loving parents. Sounds like you did too."

Elle flattened her lips. "I got plenty of love from my brother and sister and even from an aunt and uncle who were very close. But my foster mother . . ." She shook her head. "Not so much." Elle didn't mention Bea's I-saved-you-from-starvation-and-gave-you-a-home righteousness that let her treat her children like slaves and take everything they scammed. Nor did she explain how her foster mother's idea of love was a chocolate bar, given to any child who came home with cash.

Elle needed to get back to the present moment, and try to understand a family that's capable of love. So she turned toward the living room. "Looks like I have two sisters."

"Oh my God, of course!" Trish got up and called out, "Wendy, June! Come here, please." She turned back to give Elle more details. "Wendy is twelve and June is eight."

The girls must have been listening at the door because they entered the kitchen quickly and stood by the sink. "Girls," Harry began, his voice wavering with uncertainty.

"Mom and I have told you we had some rough times before you were born. Well, one of the things that happened back then was that Mom got pregnant and had a baby. A girl."

"Wait!" Wendy held up her hand, a surly narrowing in her eyes. "You're saying there's a third sister in this family that you never told us about? Is it one of these two?" She squinted at the visitors, then pointed to Elle. "You look like Mom. Are you my sister?"

Elle swallowed. "I am. I'm Elle and I'm seventeen. You must be Wendy." She turned to the younger girl. "And you must be June."

Wendy's brow wrinkled as she turned to her parents. "How come you kept her a secret?" Harry and Trish dropped their heads, unsure how to proceed. Wendy glowered as she stood waiting for an answer.

June picked this moment to run up to Elle and give her a hug. "I'm your sister, too."

Elle hugged her back, tentatively at first, then with as much enthusiasm as June was giving. Her little sister! She had a sister less than half her age! "It's nice to meet you, June." She gave one final squeeze, then stepped back.

Wendy didn't seem at all mollified by June's acceptance of their mystery sister. While the other two hugged, she tapped her foot for a few seconds, making a big show of her displeasure. When her younger and older sisters finished hugging, she started for the door.

Harry stopped her and wrapped her in a hug. "Look. We never told you about Elle because it's hard to explain to a young child. You're old enough to understand, but we would have liked June to be older first. Now it doesn't matter. We'll be telling both of you." He paused for a moment, anticipation filling the air, then went on. "When Elle was born, we couldn't raise her. We had no home, no money, and barely any food. So we had to give her up for adoption. Some other family raised her, and we never saw her again until tonight. We're not proud that we lost our first daughter, but she seems to have done well, and we're really happy to finally meet her again."

Wendy wasn't ready to stop being testy. "Are there any others?"

"No, I promise. We have three daughters, and that's all." Harry gave Wendy another squeeze, then he hugged Elle with his free arm, bringing his two oldest daughters together for the first time. Wendy wasn't squirming away, but she wouldn't yield completely, so Elle looked her in the eye.

"You're right to be suspicious, Wendy. I certainly would be if someone told me I had a new sister. If it's too much to handle, you and I could start by being friends. Get to the sisters part later. What do you say?" She held out a hand.

Wendy's sullen look melted slightly as she pulled away from her father, but she folded her arms and refused to shake. "Maybe." She glanced at Penny. "Is she your friend, too?"

"Penny's my *best* friend. But she's not my sister." She gave Wendy a deep smile then opened her arms for a hug, and the two sisters finally connected. Elle could feel the tension still in her sister, but she said nothing more.

Trish ushered everyone into the living room where they chatted for an hour until the girls had to go to bed. Wendy and June shared the second bedroom upstairs. Elle promised she'd stick around and would see her sisters soon, then she and Penny sat back down with the grownups.

Elle got right to the point. "How bad is it?"

Her father sat up straight, his chin raised. "What do you mean?"

"Well, let's just say I see trouble here. You might not be living in a car like you were when I was born, but you look like you might be back in that car soon. What's going on?"

Trish's shoulders sagged as she turned to her husband. "Go ahead. Tell her."

Harry sighed and slumped down next to his wife. "You're right, we're close to losing the house. The bank sent an eviction notice if we don't pay in the next month. The girls don't know it yet, so please don't tell them. I haven't had a job in over a year—bad times, you know. And we're stretched to the limit on Trish's salary. We never should have refinanced the house."

Trish huffed. "We never should have bought lots of stuff. That barbecue, the drone."

"Hey, Wendy loves the drone. She's got a real knack for flying it."

"Yeah, but we still can't afford it."

Elle could see that they were talking about small expenses while avoiding the bigger issue. "So what was wrong with the refinance you did?"

"Well . . ." Harry groaned. "It seemed like a good deal when that man from the bank knocked on our door last year and offered a much better rate. He demanded that we sign quickly to get the offer, but he gave us a pretty suspicious loan. I think he cheated us."

Trish snorted. "He *definitely* cheated us. We had to initial it all over, but some of the things we signed had nasty fine print. Now we're ruined. They nailed some of our neighbors, too. From what I've heard, this whole street is likely to get repossessed. People here think they purposely targeted our neighborhood so they can build overpriced mansions. I swear those bankers are all a bunch of con artists."

Elle and Penny looked at each other for a few seconds, suppressing knowing smiles. Finally, Elle turned back to her parents. "Tell me more."

Five

Elle's parents insisted that she and Penny stay the night, but the house didn't really have enough space. When they started rearranging furniture in the living room, Elle put a stop to it. "This is too much for you. We'll get a motel room."

"Oh, come on," Harry resisted. "That's too much money."

Elle threw her arms around her father and gave him a hug. "This is a special trip, so it's totally worth it. Tell me when I should come back and I'll be here."

"Well, we're going to church in the morning. They're having a picnic after services, and . . ."

"No," Trish cut him off. "Forgive me, Elle, but you need to know that you are a huge secret. We got this house only five years ago, after struggling for over a decade, and nobody around here knows we have a third child."

Harry seemed confused. "Our friends won't think less of us."

"It's not that. I don't care what people say or think. But we need more time first, to get to know our daughter. And Elle probably wants to get to know us before being stormed by our friends. This is church, Harry!" She spun her head in a circle of feigned dizziness. "If she goes with us tomorrow, we'll be bombarded with questions that even we can't answer. No. We need much more than a half a day together before we can deal with any of our friends, especially the ones at church."

Elle gave her mother a nod. "Hey, I get it, folks. Besides, I'm here for you two, not the whole community. And Penny and I may have some things to do tomorrow, so why don't we come back Monday?"

Trish let out a long breath, clearly relieved. "That sounds great. Come at noon and we'll have lunch. Harry will be home, and I always come here to eat." With hugs all around, they parted for the night.

Penny drove the car while Elle fumed in the passenger seat. "Oh my God, Penny! Those bankers are driving my parents out of their home. We've *got* to do something."

"We scored seventy grand from the car scam. I'll donate my share, if you like. Let's pay down their mortgage."

"But what about all their neighbors who are being cheated too? Those bankers need to be taught a lesson, and I think we're the ones to do it."

"Yes!" Penny pounded the steering wheel as a big smile grew across her face. "Now you're talking. I knew you wouldn't be able to resist a con."

"And you know what else?" Elle laid her hands on the sides of her face as if that could contain her excitement. "This is the first time Bea isn't around to meddle. We can run the con however we want."

Penny laughed. "We? *You're* the mastermind when we do cons. It's all up to *you*. So sure, run it however you like."

"Well, if we're tricking greedy bankers, we don't have to worry about taking from people who can't afford it. That's good news. So why not take it to the next level. Let's find a way to make them admit their guilt and change their ways." Adding this challenge made her even more excited.

"You've been dreaming about that for a long time. What was the word you used?" She wagged a finger as she tried to remember. "Right! Adjustment. Adjusting the marks' thinking so they gladly pay back the people they cheated. Sounds convoluted. Are you sure you want to make things even trickier by throwing that in? These are bankers, Elle, and they're not going down without a fight."

"Hey, I can dream, can't I? But you're right, it might not be possible. It's too soon to tell—we've got work to do first." Elle chuckled quietly. "I knew we'd be busy tomorrow."

They got a room at a nearby motel, using fake IDs to pretend they were old enough. As expected, the two of them spent all night online, learning about the mortgage scam.

The next day, they went into Portland in search of a mall with a food court, a place where they could sit and talk for hours without anyone caring. As they stepped into the first mall's dining area, Penny started to scream. "A Juice Moose! They have my favorite juice shop!" She ran off to score sustenance.

Elle easily found her favorite food: a burger and fries with a strawberry milkshake. She knew she should eat properly, more like Penny did, but Bea had trained her foster children well, giving them candy bars as prizes when they pulled successful cons. It cemented a lifelong association between grifting and junk food. And since they were planning a con, she had to have some junk.

Food in hand, she scanned for a place to sit. This food court didn't have the luxury of dark spaces where they could hide, but she did find a less crowded area that offered a good view.

Penny came soon after, dancing and twirling as she cradled a cup of juice. "You're not going to believe this, but they found my juicing plan down in Los Angeles and they made the perfect juice: kale, carrot, ginger, and lime." She took a sip and let her eyes drift closed for a few seconds of concentrated delight.

Elle squinted at the cup. "Looks kind of brown and scary to me."

"Hah!" Penny lounged back in her chair. "I declare this mall's food court to be our official Portland hangout." She flipped open her computer while Elle worked on her burger and fries.

By the time the burger was gone, Penny was muttering unhappily. A few minutes later, she shook her head like a dog shedding water, then emerged from the grasp of her computer. "There are two guys at the bank who are real pieces of work. Damien Artemis is CEO, and he came up with the idea of targeting your parents' neighborhood, as well as a few other streets in the city. I found a story of one woman who went to see him and ask about all the unfair fees in her mortgage. The guy was not only unsympathetic, he was aggressively rude. He yelled at her and called her an idiot for not reading the paperwork before signing. Then he told her that as punishment for wasting his time, her home was now higher on the eviction list. The woman started getting rude visits from collection agencies, and when she and her husband couldn't pay, they were roughed up by hired thugs, then thrown out of their house."

Elle curled her lip. "Wow."

Penny pointed at her screen. "And here's another banker who's in this up to his neck: Galt Baxter, the Bank president. He drafted the mortgage with a special low interest rate to get people to agree. Then, in a boring stretch of wording, he buried a tiny footnote that demands a massive balloon payment as well as an assortment of hidden fees. They seem innocent, but they add up quickly, and some of them are surprisingly large. The mortgage charges for administration, application, documentation, origination, processing, recording, and underwriting. Oh, and also a fee to lock-in the low interest rate. It adds up to over twenty-five thousand dollars, and the surprise balloon payment means people need a new mortgage at a higher rate. That's why they're losing their homes."

Elle frowned. "What's an underwriting fee, anyway? Is it under-handed?"

"It's all underhanded. Baxter sent people to sell this mortgage in certain neighborhoods, for example where your folks live." Penny turned her laptop toward Elle. "See? Their home is near a more upscale area of the city with trendy shops and boutique hotels. Your mom had it right: they want to redevelop the street and turn it into luxury housing. And when I looked at the addresses of the two dozen families with similar stories, they all fall near places with more wealth."

Elle considered the map. "So it's settled. We're going to swindle some bankers." She took a sip of her milkshake.

Penny sighed. "You know we're going to need help. The two of us can't do everything. We don't know the Portland area, and it would be nice to have a grown-up for some things. Back in L.A., we have your foster mom, your Aunt Franny, Uncle Carl, even Vance when you need someone intimidating. You and I don't look very tough."

"I know." Elle shrugged her shoulders. "But I can't involve Harry and Trish. It's too soon." She flopped back and cradled the milkshake to her chest, taking another sip. Penny said no more about it, but their thoughts continued to churn.

In the relative silence, a voice carried over from one of the food shops. "Oops! Sorry about that. I'm only trying to get rid of all these singles, and I know how shopkeepers like them. I meant to give you ten singles for that ten dollar bill. Here's the extra one—now there's ten. But how about this ... I'll give you another ten, then you can give me twenty."

Elle and Penny sat up at the same time; their eyes wide. The boy over at the counter was running a classic change-raising scam on an unsuspecting cashier. They recognized the patter, the fast-talking blur of numbers that only loosely resembled the amount of cash each person had. The first ten-dollar bill was the cashier's, and the boy had taken his ten singles back. But the presence of the bill on the table, along with the second ten dollar bill the boy had placed down, made it seem as if he could rightfully trade them for a twenty. Elle and Penny leaned closer to watch the game wrap.

The boy grabbed the two tens and held them out to the cashier, not giving the poor clerk time to consider that he was being scammed. Numb from his boring job, the clerk reached into the till and handed over the twenty. The boy thanked him and left with his profit. He'd successfully exchanged a ten dollar bill for a twenty.

As the boy walked away from the counter, he nodded discretely at another young man, bigger and looking slightly older, who got up too.

"You know," Elle grinned, "I think we found some locals who can help with the con."

"You trust them? They don't seem too sharp to me, running petty little scams."

"No, I don't trust them. Yet. Let's follow them and learn more."

Elle and Penny followed the two young con artists through the mall. They ended up in a game shop, with fast-moving graphics on every wall, and thunderous weapon fire overwhelming every conversation.

Elle pulled Penny aside. "Stay up front in case they try to get away. I'm going in." She flipped up her hoodie and slunk down as she moved through the shop.

Elle followed the boys to a private room where customers weren't allowed, sneaking in after they went back there. The two of them were showing off their hauls, and the bigger boy had a huge smirk on his face. "You only got ten bucks? I got sixteen. You lose, Neil."

The smaller boy snorted. "Yeah, but you didn't get all sixteen from the change-raising trick, Andy. I saw you dip into the tip jar."

Andy sneered. "Have I taught you nothing? We do what it takes."

Andy was clearly the leader, and he dressed more properly with a button-down shirt, a denim jacket, and a tie. He had a thin beard shadow and stylishly messy brown hair. Stocky and muscular, he exuded confidence as he lectured his friend.

Neil, the smaller boy, had piercing blue eyes and messy black hair, similar to Andy's. Probably younger than his friend, he was thin and cute, with jeans and a blue T-shirt.

Andy turned to look at a pile of boxes in a corner. "So did you rig that carnival game for the open house this weekend? Kevin's counting on us . . . if this brings in the dough, we'll score some free games."

"Yeah, this'll bring in plenty for the shop. It's a ring-toss game, and I bet you can't beat it." He pulled a few boxes away to reveal nine milk bottles in an orderly square, a set of rings draped over the middle bottle.

Elle slid closer, low and slow. This was her special skill. Her brother had been the expert safe cracker in the family, and her sister was an incredible forger. But Elle was a sneak, able to get into or out of any place without being seen. Of course, given the noise in the store and the way the boys were so focused on their scams, approaching them was easy.

Neil grabbed the rings, stepped away, and tossed one which landed on the neck of a bottle. The second one missed, but the third one also landed on a bottle. "Now you try."

He handed the other rings to Andy, who carefully tossed them at the milk bottles. They missed completely. One of them even looked like a perfect throw, but as it approached the bottle, it fell off course and hit the floor.

Andy rubbed his chin for a few seconds, then he brightened. "You have two kinds of rings, right? The ones you threw are good, but the ones you gave me are rigged. Watch!" He retrieved the rings Neil had thrown and gave them a toss. None of them finished on a milk bottle, either.

Neil laughed. "Hah! Fooled you. This game's going to take in lots of money." He retrieved the rings and tossed them, looping more than half over a bottle.

Andy studied the milk bottles for a while. "Aha!" He gave Neil a big smirk. "Hand it over."

"Hand *what* over?" Neil seemed flustered. Elle could tell that Andy had discovered the secret.

"The controls for the electromagnet. I see that thing sitting under the bottles. You turn it on, and the magnet deflects the rings."

Neil hung his head. "Can't fool you, after all." He pulled a tiny remote from his pocket and showed it to his friend.

Elle had seen enough. Standing directly behind them, she stood up straight. "Well, I think it's clever."

Both boys jumped and spun around to face her. She gave them a small smile. "Hi, guys. I saw you two at the food court, pulling a change-raising con. You'll never make any money that way, you know. The people who end up paying are the poor cashiers, especially when you steal their tips. And as far as these crooked carny games go . . ." She glanced at the ring toss game. "Don't get me started."

Neil looked at her closely. "Who are you, anyway? Ninja mall cop?"

"Nah. I'm a fellow grifter. But seriously, you need to up your game if you expect to get anywhere."

Andy folded his arms. "A grifter, eh? What's your angle? Why should we trust you?" He turned to his friend. "Let's get out of here, Neil."

"Oh come on! Give me a minute. This could be worth a lot more money than the games you're playing."

Andy squinted. "Look, I know this stuff is chump change. But we're doing just fine, thank you, and we do plenty of serious cons. Three Card Monte, Fiddle Game, you name it. Neil and I were bored, so we figured we'd score a free lunch. Think you can do any better?"

"I can do *way* better. Come on back to the food court and I'll tell you about it." She led them out of the shop, glancing discretely at Penny as they passed by. When they got to the court, Elle started to sit at a table, but Andy stopped her and pointed to a different table in a dark corner that she hadn't noticed.

Elle almost broke out laughing as she looked up at the missing light. These boys had pulled the same trick to get some privacy—she liked them already. The best seat was farthest in back, with a clear view of the rest of the food court. Elle sat there, with the boys on either side of her.

After the three of them were seated, Penny arrived and took the seat across from Elle, with her back to the food court. The boys stared at her with typical interest, so Elle did the introductions. She noticed that Neil hesitated to make eye contact, especially with Penny. This boy might be a con artist, but he definitely needed to work on his confidence.

Once the introductions were done, Penny looked the boys over, then turned to Elle with a frown. "You really think these amateurs can help us? They seem like two-bit players to me, and we need solid grifters."

Andy took up the challenge. "Hey, sweetheart, we're as good as you need us to be. We've done long cons, too, not just short grifts. There's nothing we can't do." He winked at Penny, who ignored his cocky attitude and continued to scowl.

Elle returned to the interview. "Can you work with a larger crew? Can you handle serious money?"

Neil shrugged. "All money is serious to the people who lose it. And we've worked with others before. Last year we worked in a boiler room, doing phone swindles with a dozen other people. So what's your story? How big a con are you putting together?"

Following a planned script, Penny held up her hand to stop Elle from answering. "Hang on here, the two of us need to talk this over." She reached out to pat the boys on their shoulders. "Tell you what, let's meet back here in two days. Tuesday at noon, OK?"

Andy frowned. "Cute chicks who think they're con artists. Geez!" He shook his head slowly, eyes rolling upward. "I'll be here Tuesday, but will you?" He got up and walked off, Neil following him into the mall crowd.

Elle turned to Penny. "Did you tag them?"

"Sure. You want Andy or Neil?"

"I'll take Andy."

Penny took Elle's phone and tapped on it briefly. When she handed it back, the phone showed a map with a blinking red dot moving slowly across the screen. "That's Andy. I've got Neil on my phone." They held their phones next to each other so they could compare the boys' paths. "Yep, they're still together. Let's go." They got up to find out more about their potential new coworkers.

Neil set off on bicycle from the mall, but Andy got in a car. Elle followed in her car, continuing past when he stopped at a fancy apartment building. She parked around the corner then came back to investigate.

Scanning the names by the building's door, she found an Andy Burr on the second floor. She quickly crossed the street and watched until some lights went on. Then she crossed back to climb a trellis and a drain pipe, finally arriving at his balcony where she hid in a corner.

Inside his apartment, Andy pulled a beer from the refrigerator, then he wandered down the hall. The balcony door was easy to unlock, so Elle slipped inside. Andy's place loudly announced that a single man lived there. The living room furniture was modest, with every piece facing an oversized television. The art on the walls was all posters for bands, especially ones with attractive women. In the kitchen, the cabinets were filled with bags of pretzels, potato chips, and beef jerky. The refrigerator had exactly one thing in it: beer. No ketchup, no butter, nothing perishable. This kid never ate at home—there weren't even any empty take-out boxes to be found.

Elle crept down the hall and saw Andy sitting at a computer in his bedroom. She hid outside his room, observing discretely, but all he did was watch videos. She retreated to the balcony but kept the door cracked so she could continue to listen.

At one point, he went to the bathroom, and Elle could hear a shower running. She took the opportunity to go back inside and explore his bedroom, including his wallet, his computer screen, his dresser, and his closet. The closet surprised her the most. Instead of clothes, Andy had an impressive collection of forging tools in there: inks and paper and even an ID card printer.

When the shower stopped, Elle returned to the balcony. Satisfied with her investigation, she was about to climb down when she heard his doorbell ring. This could be interesting, so she tucked herself into a corner and waited.

Andy went to open the door. "Hey, Neil. Want a beer?"

"No thanks. I came to make another driver's license. Business is hopping." He headed toward the forging gear in the bedroom closet.

Andy followed lazily. "So what do you think about the girls?"

"I like them."

Andy leaned closer. "You mean you like *Penny*. Total babe material. But Elle . . ." He blew out his breath. "What a bitch."

Neil groaned. "Interesting how when you boss me around and tell me how to trick people, you're my mentor, but when a girl does it, she's a bitch."

"I . . ." Andy waved his hands in the air, clearly trying to find a reason to continue bashing Elle. "Well, she's much younger than us, so what can she possibly know?" He turned away to get another beer from the kitchen.

"Honestly, Andy," Neil called out after him. "You're a total dick-for-brains."

Beer in hand, Andy wandered back to his bedroom and stood outside the closet. "Dick-for-brains, eh? Maybe. But you're all brains and no dick! Come on, I bet you like Penny, too. But are you going to make a move on her? No!"

"Oh, and you are?"

Andy bobbed his eyebrows. "I might, if you don't."

"Uh huh. Or you might not." Neil stepped out of the closet, holding a driver's license. He turned it over a few times, then he handed it to Andy, who gave it a single grunt of approval before handing it back.

Elle had seen enough. Andy was more experienced, but he was a jerk and he thought he knew everything. Neil was still learning, but he was reasonable and had forging skills. She wondered if she could get Neil to help with the con but leave Andy behind.

She climbed down from the balcony just as a car pulled up in front. Hiding along the side of the building, she watched as Penny stepped out. Of course—Elle had taken their car, so Penny was following Neil using ride-shares.

Elle ran up to her. "Hey, girl. Looks like the boys are together again."

Penny surveyed the building. "They're pretty thick, those two."

"I've already scouted out Andy's place." Elle pointed to the lit window on the second floor. "He's 19, lives alone, and according to some pay stubs I found, he works as an electrician's assistant. Oh, and he thinks you're hot."

Penny held a hand to her chest. "Little old me?" She grinned. "I already knew he was a total lech. And I doubt he's willing to treat you fairly, either."

"Yeah, according to him, I'm a bitch." The girls rolled their eyes in a sign of shared exasperation with boys everywhere. "But get this: Neil stood up to him and defended me. Now that's unusual."

Penny pursed her lips. "So is Andy any good?"

"Probably. If the cash I found in a suitcase under his bed is any indication, he pulls in much more money playing con games than he does by going to work. Oh, and get this: Neil has a nice little forging setup that he keeps in Andy's closet."

"I know." Penny smiled. "I hacked Neil's social networks. He's selling fake licenses to other kids at school."

"He's still in school?"

"Yeah, Neil's our age, 17, and he lives with his parents. But I don't think he spends much time at school or at home. Andy's place is his real home. Those two have known each other for five years now, and from what I can tell, they've been pulling cons the whole time."

"So, we have two young con artists who know the local scene and might be willing to help us out. This is good news . . . if you can deal with Andy's leering."

"I get leering all the time—Andy's nothing new. But what about you?" Penny tilted her head. "Can you handle being his bitch?"

Six

On Monday, Elle went back to her parents' house for lunch. Penny offered to back out so the three of them could have some private time, but Elle refused. She had too many secrets she needed to keep from her new family, so she wasn't ready for any serious sharing. With Penny there, the conversation would stay lighter, avoiding questions about her nontraditional upbringing.

Harry and Trish welcomed the girls with open arms, and the four of them settled in the kitchen. With both of Elle's sisters in school, it made her father wonder. "Shouldn't you be in school?"

"Yeah, I should be, Penny too. Let's just say we're on vacation."

"And your foster mother doesn't mind?"

"Well, she has her concerns. What parent wouldn't? But this is important." A perfect lie that would make Harry think Bea was concerned for Elle's health, safety, and education. But Elle knew her foster mother's issues laid solely on missed opportunities to swindle someone.

"Is she rich?"

Before Elle could stop herself, she blurted out a laugh. Harry's question should have been a reasonable one, but questions of money were awkward issues, especially with Bea. Her house was no bigger than Harry and Trish's, and they never spent money on themselves for cars, clothes, or even food. Given how plainly they lived, Bea seemed anything but wealthy. But she and her foster children were con artists who pulled plenty of successful tricks, so there should have been lots of money somewhere.

Harry wanted to know if Bea was rich, and he seemed perplexed at Elle for laughing at the question. Bea would say she wasn't, but her children knew that was a lie. Still, without evidence to the contrary, Elle repeated the lie. It was easier than explaining mysterious fortunes that nobody had seen.

"Sorry, but I doubt my foster mother's rich. Comfortable, at best."

Harry looked outside the front window. "She sure bought a nice new car for her seventeen-year-old daughter. Or is that a rental?"

"No, Dad. It's . . ." She didn't want to start a thread of lies about the car, so she decided to be as truthful as possible. "It's mine."

"Wow! I never had a new car. Your foster mom can't be doing that badly."

With a loud exhale, Elle turned to her father. "OK, listen, Dad. Forget about the car. My foster mother didn't buy it, and neither did I. It was a gift. For . . ." She was stretching the truth here and paused to find the best way forward. "For helping someone with their finances." She smiled at her ability to find words that were almost true.

Harry's eyes narrowed. "You're just seventeen and still in school. How can you be that good with finances?"

"I know it seems strange, but I've been doing it for years. It started as a hobby, but it's gotten serious lately. I've even helped my foster mother get money, which she really appreciates."

Now that she'd broached the subject of her so-called financial skills, Elle decided to push forward with her plans. "Money problems are kind of a specialty for me and Penny.

We help people in difficult situations, and we think we can help you and Mom with your bank troubles."

Harry frowned. "I don't see how that's possible. We're just another broken family, living on the edge of the American dream. We got tricked, Elle. The bank is demanding twenty-five thousand dollars in fees, plus a balloon payment of about seventy-five thousand dollars. We might be able to get a new mortgage in time to pay off the balloon, but I don't know where we're going to get the money to pay those fees. How can you fix that?"

"I don't know yet—it's too soon to say. We need to do more exploration, first. But I'd like to try. Are you interested?"

Harry said nothing, his arms folded in obvious doubt, but Trish jumped right in. "Yes!" She turned to her husband. "Come on, Harry. This could be the opportunity we've been waiting for. If we ignore her, I have no idea how we'll make it. We promised ourselves that we'd do what we could to survive, and she's offering us that chance. What have we got to lose? Let her try."

Harry blew out a weary breath. "You're right. But it sounds too good to be true, which worries me."

Elle smiled at her father. "You're right to be skeptical. You don't really know anything about me and Penny. But I promise we won't ask you for any money. All we ask is that you give us some time, OK?"

Harry sighed. "Sure. Why not?"

"Good." Elle hugged him. "Let's start by looking at your mortgage papers."

When lunch was over, Trish went back to work. Elle and Penny spent the afternoon with Harry, examining finances. The mortgage papers had the same deceptive wording that they had read about online. A tiny footnote demanding outrageous fees and repayment of most of the loan. Harry's initials were next to it, but he told them he was rushed by the shameless banker who claimed the offer would soon expire.

Later, they went with Harry to pick up Wendy and June from school. Wendy was now willing to accept her new sister, and she was much more friendly. The five of them came home, where the girls talked for hours about their favorite music, favorite videos, and in Wendy's case, favorite boys. Elle remembered her early enthusiasm about boys, especially her only boyfriend and the single kiss they'd shared. Too bad their relationship had ended badly when he found out his girlfriend was a con artist. It taught Elle that boys were a luxury she couldn't afford.

When dinner was over, Wendy and June went off to do their homework. Elle decided it was a good time to return to the subject of money. "You said that some of your neighbors are also being threatened by the bank. Can we meet them?"

"Sure." Harry nodded. "Chip and Quincy live two doors over. Come on, I'll introduce you. Unfortunately, I can't stay long—I promised June I'd help her with a school project."

He, Elle, and Penny walked a short distance to another house and knocked on the door. This house seemed to be in better condition than her parents' place, but she noticed a few loose shingles on the roof and an old rusted car in the driveway. These people were struggling, too.

The man who opened it was not at all what Elle expected. With names like Chip and Quincy, she imagined stuffy old British men with pasty white complexions. Instead, she looked up at a tall black man in his mid thirties with close-cropped hair. His blue silk shirt and shiny black pants showcased a reasonably muscular build, and his gold necklace glimmered in the light. She didn't think it was possible to wear more than ten rings, but this man managed to overload his hands with so much bling that it nearly blinded her.

At first, he seemed confused by his visitors, but when he spotted Harry, his face brightened. "Hey, neighbor. What's up? Come on in!"

The three of them entered a dog-themed living room and sat on a sofa piled with dog-themed pillows. In addition to a leather dog bed, an indoor doghouse, and dog-silhouette wallpaper, they even had a dog, an Airedale who jumped into Quincy's lap as soon as he settled in his overstuffed chair. He wagged his finger. "Down, Prada." The dog obediently climbed off and curled up on its bed.

Harry apologized for being in a hurry. He introduced his new daughter and briefly explained how Elle and Penny were trying to help people with their mortgages. Then he left to attend to June's homework.

As Harry was leaving, Chip came home. Like Quincy, Chip didn't match his name very well. Instead of a younger-looking man with a diminutive nickname, Chip was more like the stuffy old British man Elle had expected: stocky, bald, bearded, and white. He looked to be a little older than Quincy and was neatly dressed in an immaculate gray three-piece suit with a red striped tie. Dark horn-rimmed glasses made him the picture of proper.

Chip and Quincy kissed each other, then Prada laid down by Quincy's feet for some loving attention. While this went on, Quincy introduced Elle and Penny who explained that they were trying fix the problem of bad mortgages. The men told the same story as Elle's parents: twenty five thousand dollars due now in suspicious fees and a balloon payment that could cost them their home. Not surprisingly, they took much less time to get interested in Elle's offer of help than Harry and Trish had.

"You're not saying this out loud," Chip observed. "But from the sounds of things, I'd say you were planning on stealing some money from the bank."

"No." Elle shook her head vigorously. The last thing she wanted to do was rob a bank. "Our plan is to get one of the bank officers to make good on the bad loans they've written. We like to find creative solutions, so we do *unusual* things, but I promise I won't ask you to do anything illegal." She'd save the illegal activities for herself.

Chip and Quincy looked at each other with arched eyebrows, silently communicating. After a nod from each of them, Chip turned to look at Elle. "We're in."

Quincy sat up straight and smiled. "Tell us more."

Elle smiled sheepishly. "We may want to use you in our plans, but we haven't made any plans yet. For now, we're just glad we met you . . . we want nothing more tonight."

Elle and Penny now had all the people they needed including two local grifters and two older men. Together, they hoped to make a lot of people very happy, and even score some money for themselves.

Seven

As Elle and Penny approached the darkened corner of the mall's food court, Neil was having an enthusiastic conversation with Andy. He slapped two driver's licenses onto the table. "See? You can't tell which one is fake."

Elle looked over Andy's shoulders and nodded. "Nice work. They look pretty good."

Andy spent a bit more time, then he tossed one of them to Neil. "This one's fake; it's got a little smiley-face in the corner."

Neil snorted. "That's my signature, so I can tell which is which."

Andy blurted out a laugh. "Neil, you doofus! Never put your name on a forgery."

Neil glanced heavenward. "Jeez, Andy, I know that! If I hadn't put it there, you wouldn't be able to tell them apart."

"Well, I might . . ." Andy studied them a bit more, then tossed them back. "Take your stupid name off that fake and show me again."

Neil let out a long groan and turned away from his mentor. Then he looked up at Elle and Penny with a tentative smile. "So, uh, what's new?"

Elle unwrapped her burger and fries, then started squirting ketchup packets on everything. Penny set up her laptop and was sipping a very brown-looking beet, apple, and kale juice. When enough of Elle's food had ketchup on it, she turned to Neil. "We'd like to do a job with you two. We plan to go after some seriously fat cats, and we're going to take one of them down. Interested?" She picked up her burger and took a bite.

Neil chuckled. "Well, when you put it that way, sure!"

"Wait a minute." Andy grumbled. "You're the boss now? Don't I get a say in this? I'm the oldest here, and I have the most experience. You should probably let me run the job."

Elle expected something like this. "Oh yeah? How long have you been grifting, Andy?"

"Five years. I've seen it all and done it all."

Elle leaned back and faked a yawn, patting her open mouth while her eyes drifted away. "I've been swindling since I was a toddler, twelve years by my count."

"Yeah?" Andy sneered. "Were you planning cons back then?"

"I was tricking, and I was learning. What's your story, Andy? Do you have a problem working for two girls?"

"I have a problem working for anyone."

"OK, if you don't want to join us, that's your choice." She took another bite of her burger.

"Ya know, Andy," Neil waved his index finger in the air to get everyone's attention. "We used to play a game to test who's the better con artist. Why don't you do it with her."

"Yeah, let's do that." Andy snagged a French fry from Elle's plate and held it up. "See if you can handle a little competition."

"See if you can handle losing." Elle snapped the fry out of Andy's hand and ate it. "What's the game?"

Andy grabbed Elle's napkin and wiped his fingers clean. When he finished, he crumpled the napkin and tossed it on the table.

"Here's how it works. The two of us leave all our stuff here at the table. No money, no phone, no lock picks, nothing. Just the clothes on our backs and into the mall. The first one to return with $50 wins."

Elle handed her phone and backpack to Penny. "I'm ready."

Andy handed his backpack to Neil, then he pulled out his wallet and phone and slipped them into a side pouch. "Ready, set, go!" He jumped to his feet and left, wandering through the mall.

Elle sat casually and watched Andy disappear into the crowd. Then turned to Neil with a sudden interest. "I notice you have the only dark corner in the food court. Who pulls out the light bulb above this table?"

Neil smiled proudly. "That used to be my job. We'd sneak in at night when the cleaning crews were around, and I'd borrow a ladder."

Elle looked up at the ceiling, far above the floor. "Used to be your job? What changed? Does Andy do it now?"

"No, but he went up there last time and cut the wires in the ceiling. Now we don't have to pull bulbs anymore."

"Good idea. Penny and I do the same thing down in L.A., keeping our table dark too. But it's easy in our mall because there's a heat vent next to the bulb. I climb through the ducts and come out next to the bulb. No ladders—much easier."

Neil regarded the ceiling. "Cutting the wires is the easiest."

"I guess so." Elle glanced out into the mall, but couldn't see Andy anywhere. "You're a good guy, Neil." She wrapped her arm around his shoulder, distracting him from her other hand which slipped into Andy's backpack and removed the wallet he'd left behind. "Who usually wins when you two play this game?"

Neil blew out his breath. "Andy, of course. This game is one of his lessons. And unless you get going, you're gonna lose. He'll be back soon. In fact, I see him heading this way. You really need to find some cash."

Elle flopped back and tossed a wad of cash on the table. "I'm done."

Penny laughed, but Neil furrowed his brow. "How did you do that?"

Before she could answer, Andy returned to the table, his eyes focused on the cash in front of Elle. "You did it already?"

Elle grinned. "I robbed someone. What about you?"

"Same. Found an old lady with a big purse. She had exactly fifty-five dollars in her wallet."

"Too bad, Andy. I hate stealing from innocent people. Instead, I found someone who could afford to lose their cash." She picked up the money in front of her and counted it. "Looks like I got over two hundred dollars."

Andy darkened. "Who did you rob?"

"You."

With a look of alarm, he grabbed his backpack and looked for his wallet. When his search came up empty, he raised his eyes in time to see Elle holding it out to him. He angrily snapped the wallet out of her hands and tried to find his cash. "Give me back my money."

"Sure. Right after you give back what you took from that old lady."

"I can't—she was leaving the mall when I robbed her." With a loud hiss, he collapsed in his chair. "How about another round?"

Elle gave her potential new colleague an impassive gaze so he wouldn't think she was gloating. "Look, Andy. Penny and I are running this con, with or without you. *We're* making the plans, and *we're* paying the expenses, so as far as I can see, that makes us the leaders. If you choose to work with us, you'll find that we welcome discussion and questions about our plans, but we expect you to follow those plans *exactly*. Now . . ." She pulled away, staring hard at the boys. "Would you like to join us?"

"OK, fine." Andy nodded his head slowly. "Sign me up for the Elle and Penny crew. Who's the mark?"

"We don't know yet. All that matters is that we take down a top executive at Tera Bank. They deserve to get swindled because they've been tricking people into expensive home refinances, using some very shady deceptions. We want to help the customers they cheated."

"Sounds good. Are we going to rob their houses? Raid their bank accounts? I'm down with anything, so long as we make some money."

Elle was relieved to see that Andy's pride didn't get in the way of his greed. "We're just getting started here. We don't know who we're targeting or how to take them down. That's our first job—figure it out. So there's plenty of opportunity for you to run things, too, depending on what we discover."

She turned to Penny who took over the discussion, suddenly energized. "I've been researching the bank to figure out who should be our mark. From what I can tell, four executives are up to their necks in this financial mess, but we need more information. Since there's four of us, we can each focus on one, study the guy, and figure out how he can be tricked. Then we'll decide who to go after."

Penny turned her laptop around so everyone could see pictures of the bank officers. "Unless anyone objects, I'm going to give each of you a bank officer. Andy, you get the president, Galt Baxter." She turned to Neil. "You get the chief mortgage officer, Marshall Crew. I'll take Orson Dearborn, the head of the upstate bank branches. That leaves Elle with Damien Artemis, the chief executive officer."

Elle smiled. "Artemis is highest in the tree, so he's likely to be the target. But I want to know more about his colleagues, so let's dig deep. Somewhere along the line, we'll figure out who to trick and how."

Andy considered this, his mouth tight. "Which of us gets to do the swindle? Who gets to face the guy and take his money? Can I do it?"

Elle made her most generous offer. "How about this: if we decide to trick any of these four men, then whoever did the investigation gets to be the person doing it. If we choose Baxter, you get to play him, but if we choose Artemis, I'm the one taking him down. Does that sound fair?"

Andy sighed. "Yeah, OK."

"Good. Now we need to do one more thing before we start working together. We need a way to communicate securely. Phones are all being monitored these days, as well as text messages. But my awesome hacker girl has a solution."

Penny showed them her phone. "I wrote an app that gives us secure communication."

Neil held up his phone. "There are lots of those. Andy and I have one already."

"Sure, your app encrypts messages and phone calls, but it doesn't hide your location. Use mine, and you're impossible to locate because it scrambles GPS and cell tower data. Each call you make seems to come from a different place around the world." She held out her hand to them. "Give me your phones." She quickly set them up. Then she and Elle left the mall, promising to meet again in a few days after everyone had a chance to investigate their banker.

Elle and Penny were in good moods as they drove back to the motel. But the mood was soured by the special ringtone on Elle's phone that warned of a call from her foster mother. She groaned and took the call.

Bea started to yell before Elle could even say hello. "Damn you! Didn't I teach you anything? I swear, Elle, you better fix this or I'm coming up there and slapping you so hard your head will face backward."

"Whoa, calm down Bea. What's wrong?"

"What's wrong? Everything! I had a visit from a private dick today. This dirtball's been looking all over for you, and he actually knocked on my door. *On my door!* Thanks to you and your stupid friend, I've got heat checking me out. Did Penny give out our address? I told you not to make friends with that girl."

"Hey! Penny knows not to tell anyone, and I certainly wouldn't. How'd this guy find you?"

"I told you, it was Penny. She's not as smart as you think. Apparently, she hacked some computer, and they traced it back to her home. Then—get this—her *mother* knows where we live and told the guy. I might actually have to move thanks to your carelessness."

"Oh," Elle barely whispered. Bea was not going to like this. "Penny's mom came over to take care of me last year when I was sick. You were gone on that cruise ship swindle, but I was wiped out and needed help. She got me through it, so of course she knows where I live."

As expected, this news didn't help at all. Bea grew even angrier. "So this *is* your fault!" Her voice trailed off into a series of mutters about the abject stupidity and total waste of time it is to be a foster parent.

Elle interrupted the rant. "Did you get the name of this guy?"

"Calls himself Larry Smith, but that sounds like a fake to me. He already knows you two are up in Oregon, thanks to Penny's blabbermouth mother. I didn't tell him anything, of course, but this is still a royal pain. Fix it! And watch your back because that guy is heading your way. No matter what else happens, make sure I never have to see him again."

"OK, OK! I'll talk to Penny."

"Maybe you should get back here before he finds you."

"I told you, Bea, I'll handle it. Thanks for the heads-up, but I'm working a job here, I can't leave yet. I'll keep my eye out for trouble."

"Working a job, eh?" Bea gave a frustrated grunt. "You *are* trouble." She ended the call.

Penny had been observing this interchange. "Did I do something wrong?"

Elle shrugged. "Maybe. There's a detective looking for us because you hacked somebody's computer. The guy managed to figure out where you live, so he visited your mom. Then, of course, she sent him to Bea, which was exactly the wrong thing to do." Elle shook her head, imagining the sparks that must have flown during that visit. "You've been caught, Penny. Whose computers did you hack?"

"Are you kidding?" Penny stared with a look of disbelief. "Whose computer *didn't* I hack? It's what I do." She took a long breath. "OK, let's see. I hacked the adoption agency and the city birth records to find your parents. Then I hacked Sam Brennan's personal finances, the golf club, and the car factory so we could drive up here. And that was just in the last week or so. Before that, I hacked our high school, a dress shop, and a shoelace factory."

"A shoelace factory?" That one sounded like a joke.

"Hey, I bought shoelaces, and I wanted to know more. Turns out they're made by the millions in Hong Kong. Anyway, I didn't steal anything or break anything, but I did hack them. You know me—I can't resist."

"Well, here's the deal. Your high school isn't going to hire a detective to get back at you for hacking. Neither will the dress shop, the adoption agency, the golf club, or the city recorder. But banks and factories might, as would Sam Brennan. Did you leave a trail when you did any of those jobs?"

"Well, I can check the doors that I opened at those places. If they're still open, then it's likely they don't know I was there. But if I can't get in anymore, that might mean they're on to me. Let's see . . ." Penny worked her computer for a few minutes. "Hmm. I can still get into the Brennan's finances and the shoelace factory. I can even order cars from the plant in Tijuana." She worked for a little longer. "Uh oh. The slush fund that paid for the cars is gone. Maybe they're the ones who are on to us."

"Alright Penny, we'll simply have to deal with this guy when he shows up. Call your mom and see if she can tell you anything. Then look online for someone named Larry Smith."

"Excuse me, but 'Larry Smith'?" Penny's withering glare was familiar. In unsuspecting victims it could cause fear, dizziness, and loss of bodily control.

Elle just sighed. "I know. There have to be a million guys with that name. But one of them may be a private detective on his way to Oregon now. See what you can do."

"OK," Penny exhaled slowly. "Sorry. This is all my fault. I don't know why you put up with me."

Elle patted her friend's back. "Don't be silly, Penny. We can handle this. We've seen worse." She decided not to point out that they'd also seen better.

Eight

Two days later, the young grifters returned to the dark corner of the food court. Each had been studying a different bank officer, and it was time to share.

Elle started off with findings about the CEO. "Damien Artemis has pretty solid security at his home, which caught me by surprise. I don't mind dealing with electric fences and dogs, but I wasn't prepared for cameras and razor wire at his house. So I decided to raid his office at the bank, which was much easier to get in. I didn't think I'd learn as much about him at the bank, but get this!" She flashed her eyes. "He keeps *all* his personal finances at work: checkbook, credit card statements, receipts, you name it."

Penny's brow furrowed. "Why would he keep all his personal stuff at work?"

"Because he's got a mistress, with a condo downtown and plenty of suspicious expenses. His personal finances are quite revealing, so he probably moved all the paperwork out of his house to keep it away from his wife."

Neil and Andy chuckled, but Penny and Elle could only trade looks of disappointment.

"I'll tell you this about Artemis: he loves jewelry. Buys it by the bucket and often buys two of the same thing, one for each woman. He even bought a million-dollar bracelet for his wife last year. There are plenty of pictures around the office of him and his wife, and a few hidden photos on his computer of him and his mistress. In every shot, the woman is *bathed* in jewels. I'm telling you, jewelry is our hook for this guy."

"Interesting." Andy tilted forward in his chair. "The guy I checked out, Galt Baxter, also likes jewelry. I saw where his office is and spotted his administrator, then I chatted with her when she went to lunch. I'm real good with the ladies, you know." He winked at Elle and Penny, who managed to ignore his sloppy male ego.

After his boasting failed to get a response, Andy continued his report. "There are dozens of stories about Baxter, and his admin knows them all. People think he's the strangest bank president, ever." Andy ticked off the points on his fingers. "He's a really loud dresser, favoring suits and jewelry that would make Versace jealous." Another finger got raised. "He's been having some suspicious visitors lately, especially one last week who arrived with five ugly bodyguards, all looking for trouble." A third finger joined the others. "He's got a safe in his office that's the subject of a lot of discussion and jokes. Most people think it's just got bank papers in it. But my informant knows better because she wandered past his office after those suspicious people left, and Baxter's safe was open. She says it's packed with trays of glittering jewelry, and he was adding more to it that she swears the thugs brought. And finally," Andy brought up his fourth finger. "She claims he has another safe at home which—and these are her words—has even more *stolen* jewelry."

Andy puffed out his chest. "So how about that? Not only does my guy like jewelry, but he likes it hot. Seems like the perfect mark. It'll be easy to take this one down." He grabbed his soda and took a long pull.

Neil cleared his throat. "OK, this is strange. I checked out Marshall Crew. I was in the bank's reception area when his fiancée came to see him. I'm not as smooth with the ladies as Andy, but since we were both sitting there, I had an excuse to strike up a conversation." Neil offered a shy smile. "I'll tell you this, she was certainly chatty. And all she could talk about was the jewelry he gives her. She was wearing a ton of it, too. Right now, they're looking for the perfect necklace for her to wear at their wedding."

Neil leaned back casually. "You'll like this. She was bringing him flowers to decorate his office, so I had a listening bug, and I slipped it in there. Check this out."

He tapped his phone and Marshall Crew's voice spoke. "Yeah, hi. Did you find anything? . . . Screw that! Try harder. I need something dazzling, buddy. Something nobody else in the world has. And don't tell me about the law. When I want to know about the law, I'll get a lawyer, not some cheap little thief." There was a beep as the conversation ended, but Crew wasn't done. He strung out a long collection of colorful words aimed at the man who couldn't get him the world's finest jewelry for his upcoming wedding.

"Wait!" Neil stopped the playback. "This is even better." He tapped again and there was a sound of knocking on a door.

"Yes, come in." Crew's voice rang out. After some shuffling, the visitor began to speak.

"Hey, Marshall. Got a minute?"

"Sure, Galt. What's up?"

Andy interjected, "Galt? That's my guy: Galt Baxter." Everyone shushed him so they could listen to the conversation.

More papers got shuffled, then Crew went on. "Got those mortgage reports you wanted. Seven more of the target people have signed up."

"Excellent!" Baxter chuckled. "We'll have that entire neighborhood under our thumb in no time." There was a brief pause, then Baxter went on more quietly. "Found anything good for your little lady yet?"

Crew grumbled. "Little lady, huh? God, she makes me crazy with this wedding crap."

"So why are you marrying her?"

Crew let out a loud breath. "God only knows."

Neil stopped the recording and flashed a satisfied smile. "So my guy likes stolen jewelry, too. And he's a colossal pig. If you ask me, we need to take him down."

Penny waved her juice cup in the air to get everyone's attention. "I have to say, you three went about it the hard way, breaking into offices and talking to people on the sly. When you want information, the Internet is your friend. I hacked into the senior vice president's accounts and found out everything I needed to know about Orson Dearborn. And some things that you three *ought* to know."

Elle leaned closer. "Such as?"

"Such as the fact that all four of these bankers, plus two other executives, are in some kind of a jewelry club where they compete with each other to see who can buy the most expensive baubles." She pointed to Elle. "Your man, Artemis is currently the top dog after his million-dollar bracelet purchase, so the others are scrambling to outdo him. My guy, Dearborn, has been talking to a diamond dealer to see if he can get his hands on some big uncut rock they recently unearthed. Probably hopes it will put him on top for a while." She leaned back to take a sip of juice, then launched forward with renewed enthusiasm.

"Here's what you really need to know . . . The jewelry club meets once a month to get drunk and brag about their latest acquisitions, like little boys competing to see who can pee the farthest. The next meeting is in two weeks, so if we're going to trick one of them with a jewelry scam, we need to do it soon or else we'll have to wait another month."

"Good." Elle's head bobbed as she considered this information. "We have an angle. And since all of them like jewelry, we don't have to choose a mark. Instead, we'll make it known that we have something they want, and let the mark call us."

Andy gave her a withering look. "That's not how it's done. You have to choose your mark carefully and rope him in."

"Normally. But it's a big job to choose the right mark, win his confidence, and convince him we have something he wants. It takes time, and we only have two weeks. Since there are plenty of possible marks, what if we started with the jewelry instead? If we get the right piece, all six of them will want it. The first one who calls will be the hungriest, the one most desperate to con himself. We won't have to win his confidence, and the game will go faster."

Andy didn't seem completely satisfied. "Sounds simple. Except for the part about getting the right piece of jewelry. What do you mean by that? Are we suddenly jewel thieves? Or are we going to fake it and pretend we've stolen something?"

Neil jumped in to develop Andy's idea. "We could spread a rumor that some jewelry's been stolen."

Like a tag-team wrestler, Andy continued the pitch. "Yeah, we could drop an anonymous tip to the police and the press."

Elle blew out an exasperated breath. "Are you two kidding? You can't pretend to have stolen jewelry, then use that lie to con someone. The owner of the piece will point out that it hasn't been stolen, and the banker we target will have it checked by an expert. If we really wanted to trick someone without actually having the jewelry, it would take an elaborate con where we build the mark's confidence so much that he no longer trusts anyone else. An awful lot of work that would take a long time to set up. Easier to investigate local jewelry exchanges and see what's hot, then steal it. We don't need to keep what we take, just borrow it for the con then return it."

Andy squinted at her. "You make it sound so easy, little girl. But can you break into a heavily guarded jewelry store? Can you rob a museum?"

"Sure, why not, *big boy*? It wouldn't be my first." She gave him a proud smile.

He tilted his head with a tighter squint. "Really? Then you should have no trouble robbing the French jewelry exhibit that's visiting the museum in Portland. All sorts of royal goodies from way back. Crowns and tiaras and tons of diamond-encrusted bling. Think you can steal some of that?"

"Now you're talking." Elle pulled out her phone to explore the museum.

Neil blanched. "Are you kidding? You can't really be thinking of stealing priceless jewels from a museum. Isn't that, like, impossible?"

Elle grinned at him. "Nothing's impossible. I've been stealing all my life, so this is no big deal."

Penny giggled. "You should hear some of the stories she's told. One time, she stole a painting from a mob boss's home. And that guy had tons more security than any museum. So if she says she can steal some jewels, you should believe her."

"But ... this is wrong." Neil's lips twitched. "We're grifters, not jewel thieves."

Penny propped her hands on her hips. "What part are you objecting to, 'thief' or 'jewel thief'? Because you two are certainly thieves—you steal from the tip jar at the food court, from shoppers in the mall, and even from your fellow students who pay exorbitant prices for fake IDs. Face it, if you're a grifter, then it means you're a liar, a cheat, *and* a thief."

"But can't we find a way to trick a banker without having to rob a museum? It seems like you're making this con way too serious."

Penny sighed. "Sorry, Neil, but this con is already serious. Taking millions of dollars from a smart and savvy banker is a little harder than taking change from a fast-food cashier. It's a whole new level of serious, and sometimes you have to do extreme things to make it work. Elle's right— robbing a museum is not too much to do, especially if it makes the rest of the game simpler."

Neil still had issues. "I thought you and Elle liked to cheat people who deserve it. If we rob the museum for one of those bankers, we're punishing the museum and doing the banker a favor."

"Excellent point." Elle nodded. "We need the jewelry for the con, and that's important to me so I can help my parents and lots of others. But we'll return it when we're done."

Andy frowned. "Why not keep it? Millions more for us."

"Yeah, but then we're on the run for some serious theft. And I agree with Neil . . . we want to punish the bankers, not the museum. Also, if we return the necklace, then yes— we still stole it—but the pressure on us will be much less. We'll make plenty of money by simply borrowing it."

"Well, OK. So what are we stealing?"

Elle looked down at her phone. "I think we should go for one of the key items in the main exhibit room, where they have all of the crowns."

Andy's eyes grew large. "We're stealing a crown? Cool!"

Elle shook her head. "We don't want a crown."

"Why not? That's mostly what they have there: crowns and orbs and scepters and stuff."

"Sure," she explained. "But nobody is going to give his wife a crown. Women want jewelry that looks good on them, even if it's stolen and can only be worn in private. That's why we're going for a necklace. This one." She turned her phone so the others could see. "Thirty-two huge emeralds and over a thousand diamonds. Napoleon had it made for his wife, Marie Louise of Austria. Check it out." She pushed her chair back and let the others gather around the phone.

Penny gasped. "It's gorgeous. And wow! Says here it's worth 8.39 million dollars."

"And yet it's not as valuable as the crowns." She took back her phone and flipped to a different image. "Look at this picture of the main room. Three display cases in a row, the middle one has the crowns. They're the big draw, the main focus of the French exhibit. The case on the right has scepters and orbs and the case on the left has the necklace. It's an incredible piece, but in the crown room, it's merely a side display, overlooked and easier to steal.

"Now look at the flow through the room. There's two doors, one coming into the center of the room to take you right up to the crowns, and the other on the right by the scepters and orbs. But there's no doors on the left, leaving the necklace tucked into a corner. Exactly where I like it."

Andy arched an eyebrow. "OK, mastermind. How do we steal it?"

Elle shrugged. "It's too soon to tell. Let's go visit the museum, then I'll know how." She got up and walked off, Penny by her side.

The boys followed behind them, muttering quietly. "Are we really going to rob a museum, Andy?"

"Seems like it." He spoke up so the girls could hear him. "You're not kidding, are you Elle?"

"Not kidding." Elle turned to face them, arms folded.

Andy considered for a second, then his mouth twitched with a hint of amusement. "I'll say this much for you— you're hardcore."

Nine

Following the museum's recommended flow, the four con artists started at the top floor and worked their way down, arriving at last on the main floor with the French jewels. One room had sculptures, festooned with rare gems. The second room had clothing, all gilt and shiny. The third room had more mundane items, hair brushes, letter openers, time pieces, and silverware, all elaborately adorned with jewels. But the fourth room was the busiest, the place most visitors came to see. It had the important items used in royal business: crowns, scepters, and orbs, as well as their target, Napoleon's necklace.

Elle walked around the display cabinet with the necklace, a solid box with treasures on top, covered by glass. In addition to Napoleon's necklace, the cabinet showcased five other items, each on a white velvet panel. The jewelry on these panels appeared to be floating in the air, thanks to dozens of tiny wires rising up and holding the piece in place. This let the light filter through the gems for a dazzling effect.

At first, it seemed that the panels were sitting on top of the cabinet's display surface. But on closer inspection, the light told a different story. The velvet panels were actually sunk into the surface, as if there were holes, exactly the size of each panel.

It made sense. The necklace was probably attached to its panel all the time, held by those tiny wires. It lived there in France, and it traveled to America still on its panel. This was certainly safer for the gems, because it avoided any handling. Here in Oregon, the museum merely had to build custom display cases with holes for each panel. Then, when the exhibit arrived, the panels could be dropped into place. When the tour ended, they'd ship the panels back, and nobody would ever touch the stones. Nobody but Elle, that is. She couldn't wait to get her hands on that necklace.

After a few minutes, they left the room and drove back to the mall. Neil angled forward from the back seat. "You really think you can rob that place?"

Elle wasn't completely sure yet, but she'd been stealing things for years, so she knew she'd find a way. "Probably. What do you think, Penny?"

Her friend took a bit longer to answer. "Looks difficult. The room has cameras and guards, which is typical. But I also saw laser emitters all over the place and sensors on the glass. Each case has a rope barrier to keep people a few feet away. It wouldn't surprise me if there were pressure sensors on the floor inside those barriers."

"OK, so it's going to be hard to take them from outside the case, but what about from below? The display cabinets go all the way to the floor, and the space under them is accessible—I saw a locked door on the back. I also noticed that the necklace is on a panel that seems to be sunk into the cabinet surface. If that's so, and if I can get into the cabinet—two big 'ifs', I admit—we take it from underneath. Then I won't have to worry about glass sensors or laser emitters or any of that."

Penny blinked a few times, her look wavering between amusement and disbelief. "You always make it seem so easy."

"Easy? No. But possible."

Soon they were back at their table in the food court, reviewing details. Penny had hacked the museum to get a security plan, and was pointing out items of interest. "As I suspected, the glass on each case is wired for tampering, the floors around them have pressure sensors, guards make regular visits all night long, and the room has lasers sensors which can spot a mouse if it dares to crawl out." Andy and Neil groaned at the thoroughness of the system.

Elle slapped the table. "Then I was right about attacking from underneath."

Penny shook her head. "You're forgetting the pressure sensors around each display. How are you going to get underneath it if you can't even get close?"

"By finding a weakness. You've told me the strengths of the room's security. Now tell me the flaws."

"Well, there are only two cameras in the room to cover the three display cabinets. Both cameras see the crowns in the center, but only one of them sees the necklace cabinet on the side. So that's good news."

Penny turned her laptop around so everyone could see the videos. In each one, visitors milled around the display cases.

Andy looked at her screen with wide eyes. "You hacked the museum's security video."

Penny rolled her eyes. "That's the easy part. Stealing the necklace is going to be harder."

Elle pointed to the back side of the display cabinet, closer to the wall. People could walk there, but few did because it was narrow and also because the labels inside the display faced the other way. "So you're saying that someone crouched down behind the display won't be seen on any camera."

"True, but take one step closer to the case, even from the back, and the alarms will start to ring. I even noticed rolling doors that drop down over the two entrances to the room, sealing it. Set off that alarm, and you won't be leaving until the guards are finished with you."

Elle shivered as a wave of excitement ran through her. This museum job would be a real challenge, and she lived for such thrills. The more she thought about taking the necklace from underneath, the more she liked the idea. All she needed were a few more details. "Can you find out what the alarm sounds like?"

"What it *sounds* like?" Penny furrowed her brow. "Why do you care? By the time you hear that alarm, it's game over."

"I like to know what to expect."

"I thought the whole idea of stealing something is to *not* set off the alarms."

"Hey, sometimes you need to make some noise. Just find out, OK?"

"Sure. I did notice a brand name on the laser sensors when we were there today, and I happen to know that this company changed their alarm sound when they started using computerized systems five years ago. From the look of the sensors I saw in the room, this system is much older. So the alarm probably makes the older sound, which is really annoying."

Elle cocked her head. "How annoying?"

Penny clicked her computer, and a honking wail started to play, fortunately at low volume. After a second, she stopped it. "That annoying. And way louder."

Elle still needed more information to be sure she could do this. But if all else worked, she might have to get used to that noise. "Send that sound file to me."

Penny seemed confused, but before she could protest further, Andy squinted at Elle. "Already have a plan?"

"I'm close. But I need to know what the computerized systems have that the older ones don't." She laid her arm across Penny's shoulder. "So?"

As Elle suspected, Penny already knew the answer. "The newer systems log every alarm event with a location and a time code, but the older systems don't keep track of anything. They just make noise."

"Ahhh." Elle relaxed back in her chair. "And that's the plan."

Andy stared at her. "That simple, huh?"

"Nothing's simple. And we've got lots to do."

Neil pushed for details. "Such as?"

"Well, let's see . . ." Elle regarded him and Penny for a second before giving them a broad smile. "For starters, I need you two to fall in love. Neil, you romance Penny with some seriously sweet texts. Tell her how much you love her. Win her heart." She turned to her friend. "Penny, you fall for him instantly. The two of you need to be convincingly in love. And don't use your security app . . . send these texts openly."

Andy grumbled. "What about me? I could go for Penny." He wagged his eyebrows.

"Because you get to be at the museum to help with the heist while lover boy here has to sit at the mall and keep out of sight. Besides, I think he needs the practice." She winked at Neil. "Of course, if you'd rather switch places, that's fine with me."

Andy flattened his mouth, silent for a moment before answering. "I hope you've got this all worked out, because I already spent time in juvie, and that was bad enough. I'm older now, and my next offense will send me to prison."

"You're not stealing anything, Andy. I am."

"Yeah, but I'm still an accomplice to your crime."

"Well then, do you want to stay out of sight at the mall, or do you want to help me rob the museum?"

Andy considered for a few seconds, then acquiesced. "OK, I'll take the heist. Nobody calls me a chicken."

Neil chuckled lightly. "Guess I'll take Penny." He gave her a tentative smile.

Elle tried not to laugh. "I hate to disappoint you, but you don't get Penny. You're putting on a show for the cops, in case they go looking at your phones after the theft. Make the romance convincing, you two. Any hint that this is fake, by *any* of us . . ." She glanced at Andy to make sure he knew it meant him too. "Will spoil it all, so don't drop out of character."

Neil swallowed as he turned back to Penny. "OK. So, uh, what do you think, sweetie pie?"

Penny grimaced. "She said convincing, not nauseating."

Neil smiled. "Got it. I'll do better in my texts."

"Now you're talking. Bring it on."

As Neil and Penny plotted their fake romance, Elle considered the big picture beyond the theft. Having Napoleon's necklace would enable them to swindle a banker, but how, exactly, would they do that? Various plans floated through her mind as she gazed unfocused into the distance. But how could she trick them into repenting their ways and being glad they got taken? That was the challenge.

Suddenly, she knew she could do it, the perfect con that leaves the mark reformed. She leaned in to talk to her three partners. "You know, we can do something really special with this job. I think we can actually use the necklace to teach our banker a lesson."

"Of course," Andy cackled demonically. "We're going to teach him not to mess with us."

"No, we're going to teach him not to mess with his customers. If we can do this, we'll get the money, help the bank's customers, and make that banker proud to have helped them. This also solves the problem of how to cool-out the mark so he doesn't come for us after we've taken his money. By making him feel good about being swindled, we're much safer."

Andy's eyes narrowed to slits. "Sounds crazy. But I'm beginning to expect that from you. What's the plan?"

Elle shrugged. "Well for starts, when I steal the necklace, I have to replace it with a fake, so we need a jewel forger. I know people down in L.A. but not up here. Any suggestions?"

As usual, Andy knew someone. "I met a kid in juvie who'd been busted for jewel theft. He liked to brag about how he'd swap real pieces for fakes so it wouldn't be immediately obvious. Said he had a source for perfect fakes. I bet he'd be willing to connect me with his jewel forger."

Elle nodded. "Give it a try."

Andy grabbed his phone and wandered off to make the call. When he came back, he sat down grandly like a conquering hero assuming the throne. "We're on. My friend's going to meet us in an hour and take us to the forger." Elle and Penny gave each other hopeful looks, tinged with the ever-present concern that this could be a trick.

They drove to a downtown address that was occupied by a trendy candy store. Next to the store, an unmarked door led to stairs. They rang the bell, got buzzed-in, and went up to meet a young man wearing a fedora and a dress shirt. He regarded the four kids with a look of confusion that cleared when he finally noticed Andy.

"Hey Bud! Been a while. Who are your friends?" Andy introduced Neil, Elle, and Penny.

They got comfortable in his room. Aside from smelling like sugar from the store below, the place was fairly nice, furnished tastefully and decorated with a few silver statues, including a large Buddha. Elle considered each of the pieces. "You have quite a collection here."

"Thanks. So, you want to get a forgery made?"

"Here's the deal," Elle fixed hard eyes on the boy so he'd know she was serious. "If you take us to meet your guy, we'll give you a $200 finder's fee. But if you connect us without insisting on coming along, we'll give you $500. In other words, we'll pay you more to stay out of our game, and the less you know, the safer you are. What do you think?"

"I'm OK with that, but my buddy won't be happy to see four strangers show up in his shop. I'll try, but I can't promise anything."

The boy went off to make a call that grew heated for a while. Finally, he returned with a piece of paper. "As I thought, he's not happy about seeing four strangers. So only one of the girls gets to go. Here's the address." He tilted his head. "Don't make me sorry I did this."

Andy clapped him on the back. "You won't be sorry." Any thoughts of sorrow seemed to disappear when Elle handed him $500.

The address of the forger was actually a jewelry store. Elle went in to ask for the man, and soon found herself in a brightly lit back room that sparkled with trays of gems, small, shiny, and rare. Tools covered the walls and crept across the tables, each with glinting steel surfaces, curved and complex.

The jeweler stood proudly by his table, wearing jeans and a sweatshirt, a well-used work apron covering it all. His long blond hair and unkempt beard gave him a scraggly look—the look of an artist, not a crook. Elle liked him already.

"I understand you need some costume jewelry made."

Elle laughed. "Yeah, costume. We're going to a party, and we want to look the part."

The man scowled. "Don't insult my intelligence, kid. I'm not in the mood, and I don't know you from jump." He waved a shiny and sharp-looking tool in Elle's face. "Sit down or get out!"

Elle sat down obediently. "Sorry. I—"

The man cut her off with a quick wave of his hand. "What are you stealing and why should I help you?"

She showed him her phone. "It's an emerald and diamond necklace, currently on display at the museum. I'm using it to scam a banker at Tera. They've been tricking people with deceptive mortgages and I want to teach them a lesson."

Now it was the jeweler's turn to laugh. "A lesson, eh? Yeah, I know about those guys. My uncle got an eviction notice last week. Really pissed him off." He glanced at the tool in his hand, then set it down. "OK, I can do this, but I'll need better pictures. Might have to visit the museum to be sure." He worked Elle's phone to study the necklace more closely. "I'll tell you this: the setting's not hard because nobody looks too closely at it. It's the fake jewels that get all the attention, and they're much harder to get right. Every piece of glass has certain imperfections that can be spotted with the naked eye. And sometimes they scratch or chip, so to be safe, you need extras. I'd recommend making enough fake jewels for two necklaces. Then I can hand sort through them and pick out the best ones. It'll cost more, but you'll get a quality fake."

"Actually, I need multiple necklaces, anyway. One to leave at the museum in place of the real one. Another to give the banker when he buys it. And a few more in case of trouble with underworld people or police. I need to be prepared for all the people—yourself included—who think they can take advantage of an innocent-looking girl."

"So, how many do you want? Three? Four?"

Elle scrunched her mouth. "At least four . . ." She paused and thought for a few seconds. "Oh, what the heck, make five of them. You never know. And I might need a bad fake. So when you sort through the gems, put the best in one necklace, and the worst in another. What's that going to cost?"

"Well," The jeweler thought for a minute. "If you wanted only one, it would cost ten grand. But since you want five and you're willing to take bad rocks, I'll charge you half price. That's twenty five grand for five necklaces, and I want half now. You got that kind of cash?"

Elle picked up the tool that he'd used to threaten her. "I might be able to get my hands on that much money. But now it's your turn to come clean. How do I know you won't take my money and cheat me?"

"You don't, of course, but I swear on any stack of Bibles you can find that I'll make five of those necklaces, and I'll have them for you in a week. Besides, I know you have three others in your team, and I don't want the four of you coming back to trash my shop, so I won't cheat you."

Elle nodded and pulled a big pile of hundred-dollar bills from her backpack, counting it out and stopping twice to reach in for more. This job was starting to cost her, but the results promised to be spectacular.

On her way back from the forger's place, she called her uncle Carl. He and his wife, Franny, were her two favorite relatives in the whole world. They'd taught her and encouraged her and protected her in ways that Bea never bothered to do. Down at their music shop in Los Angeles, Carl worked in the back room, repairing guitars and other instruments, while Franny was up front at the register. At least, that's what musicians thought.

In truth, the music shop was a front for a crew of con artists, including Carl and Franny, Bea, and a few other regulars. Carl's guitar repairing skills were only the start of what he could do. In his spare time, he liked to build fake and supposedly rare musical instruments, then sell them for outrageous amounts. Franny was an expert on the human body who'd taught Bea's children important physical skills such as running, self-defense, and the ability to read people by observing their body language. Franny also taught them the light touch of a pickpocket, and made Elle climb every building in the neighborhood so she'd be able to escape from trouble.

Penny was right to be jealous of Franny's cat burglar classes. They were some of Elle's fondest memories, learning to hide and to sneak around quietly. Every skill she had came from her aunt, and the two of them had always been close. So although Carl and Franny weren't really related to her, they were the best aunt and uncle a young girl could have.

And now she needed her uncle's woodworking skills for something else: fine jewelry cases to showcase Napoleon's necklace. Carl was happy to help, and he agreed to make five of them, one for each of the fake necklaces. They probably didn't need that many, but Elle liked to plan for the unexpected.

Carl said he'd make the display boxes in five days, and the forger wouldn't be done for a week, so Elle and Penny decided to drive back to Los Angeles to pick up the boxes. Before leaving, they spent time with Elle's new family and with their new friends at the mall. Neil's ring-toss booth at the gaming store was a great money maker, and he came home with a bag full of free games as a reward.

The drive to Los Angeles was peaceful, and they were soon back with Carl's boxes. Then Elle went shopping. She bought a half-dozen leather pouches that could hold Napoleon's necklace, and she filled them with a half-dozen cheap necklaces made out of red plastic pop beads. She also bought an assortment of backpacks, some of which she ripped apart and stapled together again in novel ways. Then she spent a few hours at a hardware store, buying all of the necessary tools for the job. A wig shop was also on her list, as well as a discount clothing retailer where she bought the frumpiest and baggiest old-lady dress she could find.

The next day, the necklaces were ready. The jeweler had kept his word, and he let all four of them come this time. Penny was familiar with Elle's excitement over upcoming cons, so she insisted on driving to the shop. She was right to get behind the wheel—Elle bounced all the way downtown.

They gathered in the jewelry forger's back room while he carefully unwrapped his work. "This one's the best." He laid it out on the desk. The piece dazzled—it looked exactly like the pictures of the real one. Elle was impressed. She would sell this to their target banker.

The forger unwrapped two more necklaces, which also looked good. Of course, he was quick to point out the wavy patterns in some of the stones. The next necklace had scratches on some of the fake diamonds, not noticeable at first, but even an amateur would spot it if they paid attention.

The last necklace looked like it had been banged around by a hyperactive child. Scratches were evident on most of the diamonds and some of the emeralds, including the large centerpiece stone. A few of the fake diamonds even had chips missing from them. This necklace had clearly been assembled last, using the remaining parts that had been passed over four times already. But like the other necklaces, it was perfect in its own way.

Now they had everything they needed. Except, of course, Napoleon's priceless necklace. Elle could feel the excitement of the heist, building like a countdown on New Year's Eve.

Ten

Andy picked up Elle at her motel, and they drove to the museum. Since it was still two hours before closing on a Saturday afternoon, they expected the place to be busier than when they'd first visited. Bigger crowds were good, because all those people helped them hide from the security cameras. But crowds could also be bad if they got so out of hand that the museum increased security or restricted full access. What if there were extra guards in the room? What if they setup ropes to guide people past the jewels? If she couldn't get to the back of the case, she'd have to abort the heist.

Elle couldn't worry about these things right now—she'd deal with them as they came. Besides, she was so excited over the theft that she couldn't think about anything else. Sitting here in front of the museum, all of her senses felt sharper, her mind alert.

Andy leaped from the car as soon as it stopped, tipping his hat and wishing her luck. Then he set off for the museum entrance, wearing jeans, a T-shirt, and a baseball cap—the same as any other kid.

They didn't want to be seen together, so Elle remained in the car. After a few minutes, the passenger door opened and a very different looking person emerged. She wore a navy dress with a floral pattern, full-length and five sizes too big to cover her heavily-padded body. A short gray wig and white gloves completed her disguise—nobody this slow and large could possibly rob the museum.

The padding around Elle's body was actually an elaborate backpack that held important supplies. She let the museum guards examine her purse when she entered, but she knew there were no metal detectors, so she could sneak anything she liked under the dress.

The museum definitely had more visitors today. Elle felt the crush, even in the main entrance area. She took slow steps toward the star exhibit, wondering how many people would be there.

The answer came sooner than expected. Turning a corner, she found herself at the end of a long line leading to the French jewels. Velvet ropes channeled people toward the entrance, and extra security guards made sure people got in line. The worst possible situation.

Elle needed to learn more, so rather than get in line, she walked down the length of it, observing the ropes, the guards, and even the people waiting to get in. The good news was that there were no ropes guiding people once they got into the room. Guards were controlling access, but once inside, she'd be free to move about. The bad news was that they were admitting people in groups, so she needed to join one in order to hide from the security cameras. She scanned the line, looking for people who would let her join them without asking questions.

She saw couples, single visitors, even a family of five near the front, but she couldn't blend with any of them. Then, closer to the back of the line, she found her dream group. A dozen older women, with hair as gray as the wig she wore. Elle squatted down as much as her padding would allow, certainly farther than someone her size would normally be able to do, and ducked under the rope into the middle of them. A few started to speak, but she muttered an apology and continued across the line to the other side, focusing on a piece of nearby art to hopefully defuse the feeling that she had cut in line. The ladies said no more, and when the line advanced, she let them walk past, joining the group after the last of them had gone by, knowing that the folks behind her would assume she was part of the group and let her be.

Standing with these women, Elle advanced slowly, keeping to the left so she'd be in the camera's blind spot when she entered the room. As she expected, the older ladies were allowed to enter together. After the last of them entered, Elle squeezed in with two others. Once inside, she kept low and hid behind people, always facing away from the camera. She wouldn't be safe until she was behind the cabinet with the necklace.

She moved through the room at a glacial pace, a few steps with a nearby person, then stopping when they did to pretend interest in a brochure while scanning for the next person she could use as cover on her journey to the necklace.

After a few minutes, she made it to the back of the case and sat down on the floor, safe from the camera. As she expected, few visitors went back there, but people moved all about, so some might notice. To look less suspicious sitting on the floor, she untied her shoelace and removed her shoe, ejecting a fictitious pebble.

Next, Elle fiddled with her dress, adjusting her bra strap. If anyone was watching, they'd see an older woman fixing her clothes. What she was really doing was unhooking the straps that held her body-sculpting backpack, letting the supplies fall over her hips and, with some squirming, down her legs to her feet, all under the protection of the billowing dress. She could now get to her supplies without anyone noticing. The first things she needed were together in one pouch: a portable drill, an air pump with a hose, wide black tape, and of course, a set of lock picks.

She took a deep breath, then looked to the other side of the room where Andy was waiting by the orbs and scepters. He was easy to see in that ball cap, and he had already spotted her. As soon as their eyes met, he gave a hint of a nod, then he quickly looked away. There was no going back now, the countdown had started. In one minute, the alarms would go off.

With her heart beating a pounding rhythm, she sat on the floor playing with her shoelaces, tying and untying them to keep busy. Across the room, Andy was counting the time. Sixty seconds after he and Elle made eye contact, he would reach into his pocket and pull out his phone. As he did this, a small rubber ball would come out and roll across the floor, under the protective rope and up against one of the other display cases.

Elle could track Andy's actions by the sounds they made, starting with his panicked yell when the ball rolled away. She imagined him diving under the rope to grab his ball, a maneuver he'd rehearsed a few times back at the food court. She visualized the heroic save he was about to make as he snatched the ball off the floor. The solid thud that followed told her he had slammed himself into the display case and would soon be laying in a crumpled mess under the protective rope, one arm defiantly holding the ball in the air. Of course, the final sound, his victory yell, was mostly drowned out by the screech and wail of the alarm.

The siren was the official starting bell, charging Elle into action. The thrill of the steal surged through her body as she scooted under the rope to lean against the display case with the necklace. This also set off an alarm but, as expected, no additional noise was made by a second breach of security.

Picks in hand, she went to work on the locked door under the cabinet. The cheap lock should have been easy to pick, but the howling of the alarms made it difficult to concentrate. To prepare for this moment, she'd practiced picking locks while this sound played in her ear buds at an annoying volume. Good thing opening this lock didn't require sound, just feel.

In the background, she heard museum patrons scurrying to the doors, trying to get out before the descending metal gates blocked their way. Since the necklace exhibit was farthest from the doors, nobody came back here to see what Elle was doing. Instead, they were gathered by the exits, hoping to get out soon. It gave Elle the privacy she needed.

The lock opened easily enough and she swung open the door, ready to dive under. But when she saw what was inside, a jolt of panic swept through her. Access was blocked.

The space under the necklace display was presumed to be empty, a large open cabinet where she could hide. Instead, she found a shelf, dividing the space in half and preventing her from getting in. The shelf wasn't being used for much, a few stacks of museum brochures on one side. But the shelf had to go. If she couldn't get it out of the way, she'd simply have to stand up and leave the museum along with everyone else in the room.

As if to highlight this setback, the metal gates completed their descent with a final thunk, sealing off the gallery and possibly her fate.

Over the continuing blare of the alarm, she could hear Andy start to explain himself, shouting his excuses to the guards. He knew to stretch things out as much as possible, delaying the moment when they'd turn off the alarm. To do this, he spoke broadly, with side stories and overwrought embellishments. From the looks of things, Elle was going to need that time.

She reached out to examine the shelf. With any luck, it would be adjustable, a loose board sitting on side pegs. If the board didn't wiggle, then it might be nailed in place, which would be much harder to remove. She'd brought a small crowbar with her, in case of things like this, but she didn't have time to do any extensive remodeling. Fingers mentally crossed, she grabbed the shelf and pushed.

Much to her delight, the shelf was loose and slid back, so it could be dropped to the floor of the cabinet, out of her way. While the alarm continued to howl, she put her arms under one side of the shelf, lifting it off its side supports. The shelf went up at an angle, then it fell off the supports on the other side. Now free in her hands, she guided it to the bottom and pushed it as far back as it would go, leaving a few inches free by the door. She'd need that space soon.

With the shelf out of the way, Elle quickly climbed in. She grabbed her backpack, her shoe, and the supplies, then she pulled the door closed, leaving it unlocked but secured with a piece of black tape.

Although hidden under the necklace display, Elle couldn't celebrate yet. She still had to get air to breathe, since she intended to spend the night here. Her plan was to drill a hole down through the bottom of the cabinet. It had an indented base that gave it the sense of floating above the floor, so a hole close to the edge would emerge outside of the indentation and give her air. And fortunately, the shelf she'd dropped to the bottom was short enough that she had access to that edge. Before the alarms stopped ringing, she needed to cut a hole.

She started up her drill and aimed it down. It had a round saw blade so it could cut a hole exactly the size of her air hose. The drill made a loud grinding sound as it churned through the wood, but the sound was masked by the alarm's shrill cacophony. Pushing harder on the drill, she urged it to cut through.

From inside the muffled cabinet, she could hear Andy and the guards shouting indistinctly over the blaring of the alarm. He was doing a great job of stretching things out, which gave her a perfect opportunity to make some noise.

Soon, Andy's conversation became more calm, signaling that he was close to establishing his innocence. They'd turn off the alarm any moment now, and she needed to have this hole drilled. The saw advanced a little, then a little more. At one point, she stopped the drill and pulled it out to blow away the accumulating sawdust. Then she quickly resumed drilling.

The drill sank deeper and deeper as it ground through the cabinet floor. She prayed that the alarm bells would keep on ringing to cover the sound. She also prayed that this hole would provide her with a decent supply of air.

Unfortunately, her first prayer wasn't answered. The siren stopped suddenly, its ringing now a slowly fading echo in the room. But a second later, the drill made it through the bottom of the cabinet, pushing into freedom with a thud. Elle turned it off and let relief wash over her. With the drill stopped and the alarm off, there was a sudden silence. She paused for a second to quietly enjoy the incredible excitement of having gotten this far. She was here, under the necklace, secure and undetected.

The sound of retracting metal gates signaled the return of normal activity. She heard people applaud their freedom and file out of the room. Andy might be questioned further, but he knew to play the dumb kid, and he'd soon exit the museum, leaving Elle on her own.

The mechanical ratcheting of the rising doors helped cover the remaining sounds she needed to make. She pulled the saw out of the hole, then shoved in the hose to the air pump, taping the pump to the wall. In order to turn on a light without it being noticed outside the cabinet, she had to cover the slivers of light coming from ill-fitting seams in the construction. Elle quickly covered the cracks with more black tape and also covered the edges of the cabinet door. Now everything was dropped into total darkness, and she could relax.

She was safe under Napoleon's emerald necklace. With only minor hitches, everything had gone as planned. Placing two fingers on her neck, she felt her pulse slowly return to normal, calmed by the quiet whisper of the fan. Of course, when she thought about holding that necklace and considered the steps that would be required to do that, her pulse edged back up. Thrills like this were rare and wondrous moments.

When she'd first visited this room, she noticed that each item sat on its own velvet panel, indented into the display surface. The question that remained was how deep these panels went. Did they go all the way through to the cabinet below? How did they attach? Would she really be able to get to the necklace from underneath, or would she need to use the crowbar and do some serious demolition? She was about to find out.

Elle turned on her flashlight and looked up at the underside of the display case. What she saw caused her to give out a silent cheer. The panels *did* go all the way through, each one sitting in a hole that had been carved for it. From underneath, they were held in place with metal brackets, each attached with a handful of screws that would be easy to remove. Having studied this cabinet from above, she knew exactly which panel held the necklace and gave it a see-you-later wink.

For now, there wasn't much to do. The swap would happen at night, when no one was around, so Elle made herself at home. She packed the drill and brought out some food and water. Her wig and giant dress had made a nice disguise, but she was done with them now, so set them aside. Even with the fan blowing air on her, the cramped display case was warm. She was much more comfortable in her T-shirt and cutoff jeans. The gloves stayed on, of course, to keep her from leaving any fingerprints. She even peeled the museum sticker from the dress and affixed it to her T-shirt.

Finally, she laid down and turned off the light. She'd done everything she needed to do, so she could stop moving. Of course, her mind raced like a cheetah, with plans and back-up arrangements. Not surprisingly, the faster her mind churned, the slower time advanced. Squeezed underneath Napoleon's necklace, time barely moved at all.

A few hours later, the museum closed for the night. Even from under the display case, Elle could sense the increased silence. She loved being alone with rare treasures, and her excitement managed to overcome the discomfort of sitting in this tight space. Unfortunately, the next step was still hours away. She ate some food, then she settled back and tried to get comfortable while waiting for the middle of the night.

Eleven

Hours felt like days, curled in the dark little display cabinet. Elle could sit up straight and even stretch her legs out, but she couldn't lay down flat. Sleep was out of the question because of the discomfort of this space, the excitement of the job, and the fear that she might make noise when she awoke. Also, she had to listen for guard activity. They had schedules, and would be visiting this room from time to time. If she could establish a pattern, she'd know how much time she had to switch the necklace. She sat and listened.

While waiting, Elle thought about her new parents and how easily they'd accepted her. What would they think when they found out what she was doing now? And what if she got caught? They might not be so accepting then. Thoughts like these were her only companions, late into the night.

By midnight, she understood the pattern of guard visits. They came to the room every hour, at roughly ten minutes past. That meant she would have one hour to remove the necklace, switch it, then get the fake back in place before the guard passed by again. A bit tight, but she'd simply have to work fast.

Finally, after the guard's footsteps faded at 2:10 am, it was time to act. Light on, she leaned back and unscrewed the brackets that held the necklace's panel in place. Then, with her light off, she released the panel and brought it down to her lap.

There was no time to examine the panel, no time to even check that she had it right. She had to get the security camera fooled, so she taped a piece of paper over the hole where the panel had been. Printed on that paper was a picture of the necklace that, according to Penny's calculation, would present the correct view to the security camera.

Before she could turn the light back on, however, she had to ensure it wouldn't leak through the picture covering the hole, so she added another layer of black plastic under the paper. Now it was safe to look around.

Elle took a deep breath then turned on her light. The sheer thrill of this moment made her want to shout for joy. Napoleon's stunningly gorgeous necklace sat in her lap, attached to its velvet panel. Even in the dim light the gems gleamed royally. She stared for a few seconds, transfixed by the stunning brilliance of this incredible piece.

Without any more delay, Elle began the task at hand. As she already knew, the necklace was securely attached to this panel. There seemed to be at least fifty tiny wires wrapping themselves around the piece, holding it perfectly still. This was going to take some time to swap, and she needed to hurry.

She started by taking pictures of the necklace so she'd know how it was attached. Then she went to work on the wire loops. They unbent easily enough, and after fifteen minutes, the necklace was free. She wrapped it carefully and hid it in a leather pouch.

One of the less impressive fakes would take its place. The best fake would be sold to a banker and would get extra scrutiny, but this one needed to fail such an examination. If it didn't have obvious flaws that could be seen from outside of the security ropes, the museum might not believe it had been stolen. But if she used the worst fake, with scratched emeralds and chipped diamonds, it would be noticed too quickly. So the museum got the second worst fake, with a few scratched diamonds.

Elle started to attach the counterfeit necklace to the velvet panel. This process took even longer because each loop of wire had to be neatly wrapped back in place, and it had to grab on to the proper part of the necklace. She consulted her phone a few times to be sure she was getting it right, but after the first few loops had been connected, the rest went more quickly.

Unfortunately, working these tiny wires was difficult while wearing gloves. The stiff, thin metal was hard to grab and harder still to bend, even with the right tools. With only fifteen minutes before the guard came back, she was barely halfway through the task. Wiping sweat from her brow, she started skipping wires, attaching only every other one. She'd fill in the rest later, if she had the time.

The tedium became automatic as she attached wire after wire, a simple job that her fingers could now do without thinking. Then, only ten minutes before the guard showed up, she accidentally pricked her finger with one of the wires, drawing blood. Muttering a curse, she quickly set the necklace panel aside so it wouldn't get stained. A little red dot on that neat white panel would be noticed by the first visitor in the morning, and all her efforts to keep from leaving DNA or fingerprint identity would be for nothing.

Elle quickly pulled off the cloth glove, now stained with blood. She nearly laughed at the wound, the most minor of cuts. Her finger didn't hurt at all, but the bleeding had to be contained. Fortunately, she'd brought extra gloves in case she needed to do unusual work, so she switched to a pair of nitrile gloves which, although less dexterous, would prevent any blood spills. Then she returned to the tedium of the necklace, working her fingers even faster to make the deadline.

She had most of the necklace in place when she heard footsteps approach the room. The guard was a few minutes early, but this didn't surprise her because they hadn't been very precise on any of the visits. She wondered if she had time to add one more loop in the middle of a section that hadn't been secured, but instead, she decided against any hasty work. Besides, no guard would notice such a minor irregularity. Would they?

She turned off her light, quickly peeled the fake necklace picture from the hole, and slid the panel up into place. With no time to attach the brackets, she had to hold it up there until the guard passed by. Sweat beaded on her forehead as she forced herself to stay still, holding the panel above her head. The slightest wiggle could be noticed by a guard. And even if she did hold it steady, the briefest glance could expose the theft, since one of the segments was now laying flat on the velvet surface instead of being held in the air. Her rational mind knew that the guard wouldn't look too carefully at the necklace, especially at three in the morning. But anything could happen in a heist—that's why she loved it so much.

The footsteps grew louder as the guard approached. They usually walked through the room with a steady gait, one foot in front of the other, never stopping. She was counting on that happening once again, and she mentally encouraged him to keep on walking, through the room and out.

The footsteps grew to their loudest as he walked by her display case, then they started to fade. With each softer footstep, her heart was able to calm a bit.

Then, without warning, the slow fade of the guard's footsteps made a terrifying sound, a sound that sent chills up Elle's spine and caused her breath to catch in her throat. The sound she heard was silence.

Where a second ago, there had been the gentle shuffle of footsteps, fading toward the room's exit, now there was no sound. The guard had stopped walking. And if she was not mistaken, he was fairly close by—only seconds had passed since the walking sound peaked.

Elle's heart shuddered as she tried to imagine what was going on. She wanted to scream at him. Keep going! Don't look around! Don't look at the necklace! Her arms trembled as they held the panel in place, and a drop of sweat fell from her nose.

The guard grumbled, then muttered, "What now?"

Oh God! He must have noticed the necklace. The theft had been discovered, and she might soon be caught. Elle tried not to think about the door to the cabinet being ripped open by armed security forces.

Terrified, Elle held the necklace panel above her head with life-or-death determination. As usual in a situation like this, all the advice she'd been given as a child was worthless. Breathe slowly? Ignore discomfort? Prepare to run like a the wind? None of these would help.

Then the guard spoke again. "Of course I ordered the pizza, almost an hour ago. Call them back, dammit."

Elle wanted to laugh, and although she couldn't make a sound, she could at least relax. The guard hadn't noticed the necklace swap. He was merely answering his phone and discussing late-night snacks with his fellow security buddy. A flood of relief renewed her enthusiasm, and she held the panel steadily in place until the man's footsteps resumed and faded into the distance.

When all was silent, she once again brought the panel down and reattached the decoy picture. With her light back on, she returned to the task of securing the fake necklace, and twenty minutes later, she'd completed the job.

Elle took a minute to relax and wipe away drying sweat. As much as she loved the thrill of a theft, the close call with the guard had shaken her. She took another drink and tried to relax.

Finally, she turned off her light, peeled the necklace picture from the hole, and raised the panel back into place. With the light back on, she reattached the supporting brackets. The swap was done, and Elle now had the priceless necklace.

She got as comfortable as she could and settled down for the night, still unwilling to sleep. Her thoughts now centered on the fake necklace and what the museum people would think when they realized what she'd done. She also found herself replaying the swap, tiny loops detaching and reattaching in her mind.

By morning, Elle needed to stretch. Spending all night in this cabinet was thrilling, but minor discomforts were now competing with her sense of excitement, turning her attention to thoughts of getting out. Her back hurt, her food supply was gone, and the wide-mouth water jugs she'd brought with her were filled with a different liquid. It wasn't easy relieving herself during the night, but she simply couldn't hold it until morning. The big granny dress, which she wouldn't be wearing again, got repurposed as a cleanup rag.

Everything was packed for her escape this morning. She'd leave the dress, the wig, the body-sculpting backpack and most of her tools, including the drill and air pump. They'd figure everything out soon enough, and she'd been careful not to leave fingerprints on any of it. She had a smaller purse for her escape, with just a few dollars and, of course, the necklace.

Elle didn't want to arouse suspicion when the alarms went off again, so today, Penny would trip them with a completely different story. She would wander into the French jewelry exhibit blindly, not looking up from her phone. She and Neil were still having their fake romance, and they would be sending little love messages all the while.

Penny would stop first at the necklace display and signal that she was ready, so Elle listened carefully, itching to get out of the stuffy cabinet. Suddenly, she heard Penny's sigh, "Oh, Neil, I love you too." That meant that the one-minute countdown had begun. Elle turned off the air fan, grabbed her purse, and put on her shoes.

Outside the case, Penny would wander to the other side of the room and continue texting. At the thirty-second mark, she would tell Neil that she wanted him to meet her parents. Neil would know that she was in place, and he'd wait another thirty seconds. Then he would send his final text.

After days of happiness, Neil's last text had a different tone. This message was a hesitation about their love, an admission of disinterest, a knife to her heart. Their brief relationship was over.

Penny howled in despair and flung her phone. It hit the display case with the crowns and slid to the floor, causing now-familiar alarms to start their noise.

In the ensuing chaos, Elle listened to the activity outside her hiding place, not easy to do with the alarm's loud wail. When the shuffle of footsteps faded, she quickly slipped out of the cabinet and sat on the floor. Just like the day before, nobody was there to watch her exit. They were all gathered by the steel doors that once again blocked the exits to the room. She pulled off her gloves and stuffed them in her purse, then she waited with her hands on her shoelaces, pretending to be tying them. When some people scampered past the back of the necklace display, she stood and followed them, staying low and using them for cover as she worked her way out. She stayed hidden until she'd made it to the main doorway, now blocked by a closed security gate. The cameras were high above this exit and faced the room, so she was no longer visible when standing underneath them.

Having experienced alarms yesterday, the guards knew the proper procedures to take. They examined Penny's cell phone and understood her anguish over lost love. There was no need for her to drag it out, as Andy had done yesterday, and her nonstop sobbing softened them enough that they simply disengaged the alarms and let her go.

Elle waited with a group of anxious visitors as the security barriers started to rise. One woman mentioned a similar false alarm that had gone off yesterday, and Elle acted appropriately interested. When the barriers were open, she filed out of the room carrying Napoleon's emerald necklace in her purse.

Her first stop was a bathroom, where she cleaned up a little, toweling sweat from her face and hair. Then she walked slowly through the museum, just another casual art-lover. But as she strolled down a hallway far from the French jewels, a most unexpected thing happened.

A guard pulled her over.

"Excuse me, miss, there seems to be a problem." He stood in her way, arms out to prevent her from walking past.

A moment of panic seized Elle as she tried to figure out what had gone wrong. How could this guard have caught her so easily? Was he part of a larger security operation? Had they been watching her all along? She took a step back from the man, but he grabbed her by the arm. Not good at all.

She looked around to see if any other guards were part of her capture, but nobody seemed to notice what was going on. Whatever this was, the guard was handling it quietly—he clearly didn't want to alert anyone. She didn't think museum security was that good.

Elle forced herself to calm down as she considered her options. She was a con artist, trained in self-defense, and a good runner, so there were many ways to escape. All she needed was one.

Twelve

Stopped by a museum guard after stealing Napoleon's necklace, Elle struggled to keep panic at bay, especially since his hold on her upper arm brought back unpleasant memories. Two years ago, when she saw those boys attack Penny, they'd held her that way, one on each arm. Penny didn't have any self-defense skills back then, so she couldn't break their grip. Elle could have gotten away easily then, and she could right now—her Aunt Franny had taught her many ways to escape such a hold. But in the middle of a busy museum, she doubted she'd be able to make a clean getaway. The alarm bells had alerted everyone, from security guards to curious visitors, and all of them would notice if she started to run. Her best approach was to wait, let things unfold, and stay ready.

Penny couldn't wait back then, as the boys dragged her away from the school building. Most of the students had gone home, but Elle hadn't because Bea would just send her back out to swindle someone. So she stayed and did homework, secluded in a small patch of trees where few people went. Naturally, she noticed the three kids who came through, Penny in the middle surrounded by two boys. Elle's first impression was that the class hottie was cavorting again. She was well-known for being at every party and in every boy's fantasy, so she seemed to be living up to her carefree reputation, today with *two* boys.

The boys, by contrast, were anything but popular, and it made Elle take notice. Most kids steered clear of those two, and Elle had seen them in places Penny would never be found. The school cutie was admired, respected, and loved, but these boys elicited the opposite reaction. Troublemakers, bullies, jerks. And the way they were holding her was definitely not friendly. Elle tried not to think about the sinister thoughts buzzing through their Neanderthal brains.

Penny struggled and pleaded, but the bigger boy gave her arm a twist, warning her to keep quiet as they led her deeper into the trees. Elle packed up her things and followed discretely, listening as the boys discussed Penny as an object of their shared desire. In the middle of the grove, they stopped and pushed her to the ground, straddling her with grunts and laughs. Elle grabbed the biggest rock she could find and scanned the trees, quickly climbing one that would let her move through the branches to get above the scene.

Fishing through her backpack, she pulled out a metal water bottle that she'd topped-off after school. She tossed a few coins off to the side as a distraction, then when the boys looked away, she poured out a few drops and watched where they fell. This let her correct the bottle's position so when she let it go, it hit the bigger boy's head with a satisfying thud, laying him out. Elle pulled back to hide in the foliage as the other boy looked up, then he turned to his friend and tried to rouse him. That's when the rock came down, knocking him out, too.

Penny had been on her back, watching everything. After the second boy collapsed, she got up to call Elle down, hugged her tearfully, and proclaimed that they were now best friends.

Penny had been hacking on the side for a few years by that point, initially to help her older sister take down some offensive social media comments. So she was fascinated by Elle's tricky ways and was eager to learn more. Elle taught her self-defense, but it didn't take long before Penny wanted to know how to fight back in non-physical ways too. That's when Elle showed her how to swindle.

Penny never told anyone what happened that day, not even her parents, so no one understood her transformation. Gone was the sunny, cheerful girl who made friends all around. In her place was a sullen, goth kid who dressed in black, pierced her nose, and scowled at boys who stared too much. The party crowd was abandoned, and many of the certainties she'd had about life were gone, replaced by new truths. One of those truths was that nobody would ever grab her arm that way again.

Of course, nobody got away with grabbing Elle's arm that way, either. Until today.

She pushed her anger down and told herself that this was a very different situation than the one Penny had faced. This was something she could handle, so she gave the guard an innocent smile.

"What's wrong?"

"Hey, I'm just doing my job. Let's go."

He tried to pull her away, but she resisted. Once he'd sequestered her in a holding cell, escape would be much harder, and if they found the necklace, it would be nearly impossible. She swallowed the lump in her throat and twisted in the guard's grip to face him. "Where are you taking me?"

"To the ticket booth."

That was a surprise. The ticket booth sat in the middle of the grand entrance to the museum, certainly far from the security office and any windowless interrogation rooms. She couldn't see how this made any sense. "What's at the ticket booth?"

The guard pointed to the sticker on her T-shirt. "To get you a ticket. You have to buy a new one every day, you know. Not sure how you got in the door with yesterday's sticker."

Suddenly, Elle understood. She looked around the museum and saw purple dots on everyone's clothes. Her yellow sticker loudly proclaimed that she didn't have a valid ticket for the museum today. Yellow was yesterday's color.

All her tension evaporated, leaving only elation. She hadn't been caught stealing a priceless necklace, she'd merely been caught stealing the price of admission. The necklace was hers!

Elle pushed away the thrill of the steal so she'd appear appropriately contrite. "Oh, God, how embarrassing." She peeled the outdated sticker from her shirt and rolled it up into a sticky little ball. "I'm such a slob that I even wore yesterday's shirt, and I stupidly assumed the sticker was still good today." Con artists often put themselves down to make others feel superior, and Elle knew it would work to call herself a slob. Besides, she *was* a slob right then. After spending the night under a display case, her hair was matted, her clothes rumpled, and she smelled bad.

The guard merely shrugged. "I don't care about your shirt. But you have to buy another ticket."

At the ticket booth, Elle paid for admission again, then she thanked the guard for his diligence. During the span of two minutes, her emotions had cycled from the stark fear of capture to the immense thrill of success. She *had* gotten away with it, and was about to walk out of the museum with millions of dollars in jewelry.

As Elle left the building, she got a message from Penny, directing her to the car. Deliriously happy and thoroughly exhausted, she went straight there and hid in the back seat, awaiting her friend. Penny took her time, purposely walking the long way around the museum before finally arriving at the car and driving off. Once they'd gone a few blocks away, Elle came up to the front seat, and the two of them were finally able to connect with howls, hugs, and laughs.

When their celebration was over, Penny winced and lowered the windows. "Girl, you need a shower."

Elle sniffed her armpit and wrinkled her nose. "A shower, some sleep, and . . ." She pulled out the pouch with the necklace. "Dazzling jewels!"

Penny sighed. "You are too much. Someday I want to be able to steal things as easily as you do. I saw when the guard pulled you over . . . you didn't even break a sweat."

"I couldn't understand how he'd caught me. I was worried, but mostly confused." She peeled the purple sticker from her T-shirt. "Of all the silly mistakes to make." Suddenly fatigued, she slanted her head against the window, watching lazily as the city rolled by.

Back at their motel, Elle bathed. Clean, but still exhausted, she flopped down on the bed and napped for a few hours. It wasn't until late Sunday afternoon that she and Penny returned to the mall, where Neil and Andy were waiting in the food court. Strutting like a queen, Elle plopped down at the table to light applause from the boys.

Penny sat down next, giving Neil a pat on the back. "Sorry it didn't work out between us."

Neil blushed. "I told you I wasn't very good with girls."

"Actually, it was perfect. I showed the guard my phone, and he seethed at that last nasty message. Pretty harsh, Neil." She glowered at him, then relaxed into a smile. "Anyway, he felt sorry for me, so he let me off easy."

Andy stared at Elle. "I can't believe you did it. You're really something."

"Thanks. Looks like we can do the job now."

"Yeah, about that . . . Who are 'we'? When we talk to a banker, who do we say we are? The food-court kids? Elle's gang?" He grinned. "Maybe we should be Andy's gang."

Neil joined in. "Oh, come on . . . We should be Neil's gang." Penny rolled her eyes, so he offered another suggestion. "OK, we'll be Penny's gang."

Elle already knew the name she wanted to use. "Since our goal is to fix these bankers, I want to call us, 'The Adjusters.' How's that sound?"

"Adjusters?" Andy squinted. "As in, we adjust the amount of money you have?"

"No. As in, we adjust your attitude so you admit to cheating and start doing the right thing. Doing cons that teach lessons also saves us from retribution when people find out they've been cheated."

"Yeah, you mentioned that. But where's the profit in getting them to do the right thing?"

"Don't worry, we'll take our cut. Much more than you'll ever get rigging carnival games or picking old lady's pockets, I'll tell you that."

Elle switched to more important issues. "What we need right now is to tell the bankers what we have. We need an important underworld figure, someone who can connect us with buyers. A bartender at the right bar, a concierge at the right hotel. Are there any local fences who will buy high-ticket stolen goods? I bet these bankers use someone like that to keep them informed of the latest in hot jewels. Who would that be?"

Andy perked up. "There's exactly one person who buys high-end stuff in Portland. I've never met the man—never stolen anything that fancy. But I've heard stories, he's definitely the guy to see. Frank Tucker, known as Frank the Fence."

"Cute name."

"Think so?" Andy frowned and shook his head. "Like I said, I've heard lots of stories about him. Nobody thinks he's cute."

Elle nodded. "OK, how do we contact him?"

"He runs a bail bond service, Tucker Bail, on the east side. But I've got to warn you, whatever game you're playing better be good, because Frank the Fence may not be cute, but *you* are. He's going to wonder what you're doing in his place, flashing a stolen necklace. Could get dangerous—the guy's got lots of muscle."

"What if I hire my own muscle? Would he take me more seriously?"

"Problem is, you never know if the bodyguard you hire is connected to Frank in some way. He has contacts all over the place. I heard about a guy who hired two guards before going there, but when they arrived, Frank knew the guards and got them to walk off the job. Bad scene."

"So I need independent bodyguards." Elle thought for a second, then realized that her parents' friends would fit the bill. She smiled at Penny. "We know the perfect people to call."

Penny chuckled. "Chip and Quincy? They're not bodyguards, but they do look the part. Bet they've never even heard of Frank the Fence."

Andy groaned. "Even with your own people, you're going to make Frank suspicious. He can get pretty unpleasant when people aren't straight with him. And since you don't intend to sell the necklace, that could set him off. He might even try to take it from you."

"OK, I get it. Frank the Fence is *not* cute. Let's give him a call." She turned to Penny. "We need some fresh phones."

Penny had managed to inch closer to Neil during the past few minutes. At this point, the two of them were leaning comfortably against each other. But work needed to be done, so Penny sat up and pulled two new phones from her backpack. She wrote "Frank" on the back of one of them in big letters, then she handed it to Elle, who called up Tucker Bail.

The line picked up quickly. "Yeah?"

Elle kept it simple. "Need to talk to Frank about some hot goods."

"Wait." Soon a different voice came on. "This is Frank. What you got?"

"There's a fabulous exhibit of French jewels at the museum. Lots of emeralds and diamonds, worth a fortune. One of the pieces may have fallen off a truck, if you know what I mean. Interested?"

Frank blurted out a laugh. "Excuse me lady, but you're full of crap. I haven't heard a word about a museum heist."

"That's because the museum hasn't noticed yet. But when they do, it'll be big news. Tell you what—let's pretend you're right. I don't have anything, and you never got this call. But when you hear about it later, call me if you're interested in managing a spectacular item." She hung up and put the phone away.

"And now, the museum." Elle picked up the other new phone and made a call. "Oh, hello. My name's Lorrie McNee, and I'm a reporter for the Gresham Journal. Who can I speak to about the theft of the French jewels?" The person on the phone insisted that the gems were safe. "Seriously? You don't know about this? Let me talk to the museum's director." She winked at the other three while she waited. After a minute, she pulled the phone closer and turned away from the noise of the food court. "Good afternoon. We just got an anonymous tip from a caller who claims to have stolen Napoleon's necklace from the visiting French exhibit. He says that the one in your display case is a fake." She paused. "No, this is not a prank. Go check the jewels for yourself if you don't believe me. This could be a huge story! I'll call back later." She hung up, then she pulled out the phone's SIM card, bent it in half and tossed it in the trash. They'd never find that phone again.

With a long exhale, Elle relaxed into her chair. "And now, we wait." She glanced at Penny and Neil, who were back to cuddling. "You two seem OK with that."

Penny gave Elle a crooked smile as she pulled Neil closer. "You know what? I think you need a boyfriend."

Thirteen

Roland Watson stood near the head of the line outside his favorite nightclub. No suit this evening, he'd left his work clothes behind. Tonight he wore a leather jacket with a blue and white dress shirt, skinny jeans, and his favorite dark glasses. Roland had a drawer full of dark glasses, for clubbing, driving, hiking, and even for work. FBI Special Agent Roland Watson was a dark-glasses kind of guy.

He stepped up to the bouncer and showed his ID while an avalanche of music pulsed from the door and flashes of light punctuated the scented smoke. The bouncer examined Roland's ID and waved him into the club, but he never made it through the door, because his work phone started to ring. With a frustrated sigh, he moved to the side.

"Watson," he barked, mixing crisp seriousness with a light layer of annoyance.

"Trouble," came the reply. His supervisor never wasted words. One was all it took, and Roland knew he wasn't going inside.

He stepped away from the door to continue the terse conversation. "What?"

The answer required a few more words. "Theft. Portland Museum of Art."

Roland furrowed his brow. He'd only been with the bureau for two months, but he knew the regulations. "I thought we didn't do art theft. Let the police handle it."

"They robbed an exhibit from France, which makes it international, and therefore on us. The French boys are *not* happy."

Roland started back to his car. "You want me at the museum?"

"No. H.Q. Yale's on his way too." He disconnected.

Great! Yale Fulton, Roland's partner, had the sensitivity of a Sherman tank. He'd burst into a room, wave his gun, then haul everyone down to holding cells, barely listening to what they had to say before assigning guilt. A former Navy SEAL, now a family man, Yale lived for beer, barbecues, and bazookas. He also took endless pleasure in teasing Roland, the new kid who—according to Yale—wasted too much time thinking and not enough time kicking ass.

Roland had a different view of his job. Catching crooks was much more nuanced than bashing through doors and rounding up suspects. He'd been educated by the best, studying Criminal Justice at the University of Southern California, then working at his father's detective agency for a year. Both places taught him to use his head for something more than a battering ram. Too bad Yale didn't agree.

As Roland drove to the office, he listened to the local news station, curious to know if the theft was public yet. All he heard was standard drivel with no mention of French jewels.

When he arrived at the FBI building, Yale was waiting in jeans and a "Don't Kill my Vibe" T-shirt, stretched tightly over his gut and definitely not his style. It took great will for Roland to avoid a comment about Yale's vibe, which was certainly long dead.

The big man squinted at his junior partner and shook his head. Roland's short brown hair was done up in a faux hawk tonight, and his thin beard gave him a stylishly unshaved look. Of course, Yale pretended ignorance about beard styles so he could tease his partner for being too young to grow one.

"Aw, look at the kid. Been clubbing? Sorry if we ruined your night."

"Are you kidding, Yale? This *made* my night. There aren't any international jewel thieves at Portland's clubs." He regarded his colleague with a smirk. "What about you? Did this ruin your paper-clip-sorting night?"

Their supervisor, a senior FBI man with close-cropped salt-and-pepper hair, called to them from his office. "Can it, you two. Get in here." They gave each other one last scowl, then headed to the office where their supervisor showed them a picture of the necklace. "Museum got a call from a local reporter, asking about the theft of this piece. They checked—it's true. Someone replaced it with a fake."

Yale blurted out, "The caller is the thief. Find him!"

Roland chuckled. "I bet you won't be able to trace that call, and the newspaper never heard of the reporter."

The supervisor nodded. "Right on both accounts. There's no Laurie McNee working at the Journal. And even stranger, the call looks like it was made from Fiji."

Roland's eyes grew wide. "They can do that? I'm impressed. Did the call get recorded?"

The supervisor touched a button to play the message. *"Hello Ms. McNee, this is the museum director. What can I do for you?"*

"Good afternoon. We just got an anonymous tip from a caller who claims to have stolen Napoleon's necklace from the visiting French exhibit. He says that the one in your display case is a fake."

"Is this some kind of a prank?"

"No, this is not a prank. Go check the jewels for yourself if you don't believe me. This could be a huge story! I'll call back later."

When the playback ended, Roland tilted his head and considered. The caller sounded like a young woman with a slight valley-girl lilt, like so many women he'd met at school. Could she be from Southern California? And she was unusually excited about the theft, almost bragging about it. Yale was wrong that the thief was a man, but he was right that the caller was the thief.

Their boss had more. "You'll like this. The museum's alarm went off in that room both yesterday *and* today, both times for supposedly innocent reasons."

Yale slammed his fist against the table and laid out his plan of attack. "Innocent, my ass. Find the people who set off the alarms and beat the truth out of them." He leaned back with a smug look.

The supervisor arched an eyebrow. "Too easy, Yale? Maybe you want to stick with the diplomat assassin case and let Roland handle this?"

Yale looked down at his fingernails, swiveling his hand from side to side. "Yeah, too easy. Give it to the kid." He looked up with a grin for Roland. "Try not to get killed by Lorrie McNee. She sounds dangerous." He cackled and flashed a fake look of horror, then he hoisted himself up and started for the door.

Roland gave his fist an enthusiastic shake and muttered a quiet, "yes." He'd been following Yale all over Portland since he started work, and the man was tiresome. He wanted his own case, and now he had one. This would be his chance to show them what kind of agent he was, how he could solve a crime all by himself.

"I'll start at the museum." He shot up from his chair and raced for the elevator before anyone could change their minds. Of course, he had to suffer his annoying partner's antics all the way to the lobby.

The Museum of Art was anything but quiet. Roland counted four police cars flashing red lights, three unmarked cars parked haphazardly, and a handful of news vans. He found the local police officer handling the case and got introduced to the museum's head of security, who explained the obvious.

"This could be related to those false alarms. We rarely have alarms go off, so having it happen two days in a row is unusual, even though the causes were innocent."

Roland nodded. "Have you done a fingerprint sweep?"

"Police are doing that now. We also checked the security footage to see what happened when the alarms went off, but nobody touched the necklace."

"When was the necklace last checked?"

"Well . . ." The security man paused to clear his throat, a light flush rising in his face. "The exhibit has only been here for a month, but nobody's bothered to authenticate any of the pieces since they arrived. I suppose it's possible that the necklace has been fake all along."

Roland smiled. "If that's true, then it's not your problem or mine. But somehow, I doubt it. If the swap was made over a month ago, why would the criminals wait until now to tip you off? No, I'd say this happened recently—your suspicion about the alarms is probably right. Let's look at the room."

The security man led Roland to the exhibit room. No visitors were in the museum now, but the room was still full of people. Officers were picking over the space, dusting for fingerprints, running chemical tests, and taking pictures.

Roland looked at the necklace now in the display case. It was a pretty good fake, but when he leaned closer, he saw irregularities in some of the stones, clearly hunks of glass. "This necklace is pretty nicely displayed. Look at all the little wires holding it in place. If someone switched it, they had plenty of time on their hands. Almost makes me think it *was* switched before you got it."

"Ugh!" The security chief dropped his head in his hands. "The Parisians insist that they delivered the real thing. I really don't want to get into an argument with them. They'll blacklist our museum and we'll never get a special exhibit like this again. It would almost be better if it was stolen."

"Almost?"

"Well, only if you get it back."

Fourteen

Elle knocked on Chip and Quincy's door, nervous about bringing these men into the swindle. Her parents' neighbors would be ideal for the show of strength she needed when visiting to Frank the Fence. Given their problem with the bad mortgages and their interest in fixing things, only one question remained: could they handle this somewhat-shady activity?

Elle still hadn't told her parents about any of this. They might be able to help, but she simply couldn't approach them. Harry and Trish Burnside were important people in her life, so she didn't want to ruin things by revealing her particular skills. She'd have to explain everything at some point, but not until her trickery was over. For now, their neighbors would be the first to know the truth.

Chip answered the door with a big smile on his face. "Hi, again Elle. Come in." He led her to the living room where Quincy turned off the television so the three of them could gather around the coffee table.

Elle perched forward, hands on her knees. "Let me start by saying that I'm shocked that the bank cheated so many people in this neighborhood."

Quincy grunted an unamused chuckle. "It's way more than our neighborhood. I posted our troubles on the web and it grew into a huge conversation. It let me collect the names and addresses of everyone who has this problem. We're talking almost two hundred families."

Elle sat up straight. "Really? Can you send me that list?"

"Well sure, but . . ." Quincy tilted his head. "What are you going to do with it?"

"We're going to fix things for these people including you and my parents."

"Fix things?" His eyes rolled heavenward. "How? The only way to fix our problem is to give us enough money to pay the bank. And if you wanted to help everyone who got cheated, it would take millions." He shook his head slowly. "I doubt you can fix this problem."

"Well, actually, I think I can. Penny and I have found a way to get the money. But to do this, we need your help."

Quincy frowned. "To do what? Rob a bank?"

Elle chuckled. Why did everyone assume that bank robbery was the easiest way to get money when actually, it was one of the hardest? She'd been involved in bank heists that were much more involved than her recent fun at the museum. "We're not going to rob a bank. Instead, we're going to convince one of the bankers to do right by his customers. If this works, he'll give you the money you need to pay for your sketchy mortgage."

Quincy's frown held fast. "That sounds suspicious. Is it legal?"

Elle hesitated. "Before I answer that, I've got to tell you that my parents don't know any of this, and I want to keep it that way. I promise I'll tell them at some point. But for now, this is a secret. Can you handle that?"

Quincy leaned back on the sofa. "So this *isn't* legal, and you want us to get mixed up in it. I don't know . . ."

Elle propped her hands on her hips. "First off, I'll never ask you to do anything illegal. But secondly, you two are about to lose your home. Wouldn't you like to have enough money to save it? I get that you don't know anything about me, and I admit I can be a troublemaker, but I promise you'll never have to do anything that will land you in jail. Now, do you want to know more, and can you keep it secret?"

Chip's eyes grew wide as he scooted closer to her. "Honey, you walked into your parents' life a few days ago without any hint about where you've been. Quincy and I have wondered ever since. So yes, we can keep a secret. Are you an international thief, on Interpol's top-ten most wanted list?"

"No, no," Quincy interrupted. "She's a commodities trader who swings billion-dollar deals using insider information." He faced Elle, grinning like a school kid who'd aced the test. "Right?"

Elle slumped down in her chair. "You're both wrong, but Chip is closer. I've never left the country, which means I'm not an international anything. And no, Interpol doesn't know about me, as near as I can tell. But I have stolen things, so yes, I'm a thief."

Both men stared with even wider eyes that seemed to beg for more, so Elle took a deep breath and resumed. "OK, the truth is, stealing is only part of what I do. I'm really a con artist, and so is Penny. Right now, we're hoping to trick an officer of the bank into helping you out."

"Whoa there." Quincy darkened. "If you're a con artist, then shouldn't we be doubtful of everything you say? Are you even Harry and Trish's daughter, or is that a trick, too?"

Elle shook her head rapidly. "I know you don't have any reason to believe me, but I swear they're my parents. I recently found out who they are, and I came to meet them. I honestly didn't expect to swindle anyone. But when I found out what Mom and Dad are going through, I knew I had to help." She sighed. "You've got to understand, Quincy. This is what I've been doing since I was a baby. My foster mother is a con artist and she raised three con-artist kids. Now I want to do the right thing with my skills."

One corner of Quincy's mouth curled in a hint of a smirk. "Well, I think tricking a banker is cool. But if we help you, aren't we accomplices to your crime?"

"I just need you to come with me when I visit someone. It's not a nice neighborhood, so I could use company. We'll be there less than an hour."

Quincy leaned forward. "And what's happening during this visit?"

"It turns out that some of the bank officers love expensive jewels, so I'm luring one of them with a rare piece that's been on display at the Portland Art Museum. A necklace full of emeralds and diamonds. Really quite pretty."

Chip folded his arms. "Napoleon's necklace? I heard it got stolen from the museum yesterday. Don't tell me that you're the one who stole it."

"OK, I *won't* tell you that I'm the one who stole it." She gave him a sly smile.

Quincy's mouth fell open. "Oh my God! You weren't kidding when you said that you were a thief. You actually robbed the museum! I heard that they didn't even know they'd been robbed until someone phoned it in. They're still looking for you."

Chip laughed. "Well we found her, right in our living room. And by the way, those jewels are from France, so I was right. You *are* an international thief."

Quincy pulled Chip aside. "This is much more serious than I expected. Are we sure we want to get involved in a museum theft?"

Chip sighed then shrugged his shoulders. "She's got one thing right. We're being forced out of here. Maybe we have to take a chance. And she did say we won't do anything illegal."

Quincy paused, then blew out a long, calming breath. "OK, but please don't tell us anything about the theft . . . We don't want to know."

"Good. And remember, my parents don't want to know either. This is our little secret."

"*Little* secret?" Quincy choked out a laugh. "This secret's so big that we can't tell *anybody*. And by the way, it's not very nice to make the French pay for the bank's bad loans."

Elle held up a hand. "Contrary to what you and the French may think, I didn't steal that necklace. I just borrowed it. My plan is to get you the money, then return the necklace to the museum."

"So why did you take it? No, wait!" Chip held out a hand to stop Elle. "I don't want to know that, either. Who are we visiting?"

"We're visiting a guy who calls himself Frank the Fence. He's a tough guy who appreciates tough visitors. I want you to be my bodyguards."

Chip snapped his head. "Bodyguards? What makes you think we know anything about that? I'm a department store floor manager, and Quincy teaches English at a community college. The last time I shot a gun was in summer camp, at least twenty years ago. And I definitely don't want anyone pointing a gun at me."

"All that matters is the image, not the reality. And you guys do look like bodyguards—you're big and strong. Dressed in black suits and sunglasses, you'll be perfect. I'll even give you toy guns so you can have that threatening bulge in your pockets."

"Wouldn't it be better to have real guns, in case of trouble?"

"Definitely not!" Elle waved her hands. "You only need to *seem* like bodyguards. Trust me—if there's any trouble, it's best if you don't have guns."

"Then what *do* we do if there's trouble?"

"Show them that you're harmless, tell them anything they want to know, then go. As my foster mom would say, 'Don't do anything stupid.' Understand?"

"But what about you?" Chip protested.

"No! You are *not* there to protect me—I can defend myself just fine. And if I know you're not worrying about me, then I won't have to worry about you. If there's trouble, everyone saves themselves. Got it?"

They gave each other a brief look, then they nodded.

"Good. It's simple, then. We visit Frank the Fence, then we leave. End of job."

"Damn!" Quincy smiled.

"Double damn," Chip echoed. "Let's do it."

Fifteen

Roland returned to the museum Monday morning to study the security videos. He'd seen the crime scene last night, and he had a pretty good idea how the theft was done. Something clever went down when the alarms were set off, but Roland was more clever and soon enough, he'd have this case in the bag. Yale could tease all he wanted . . . Roland would show him how crime solving should be done.

The operator explained the system and brought up both of the feeds from the necklace room. "This is from Saturday, when the alarm first went off. The necklace display is on the left." On the screens, people milled around, entering and exiting the room.

The man pointed to the video on the right. "Here's where the kid loses his ball. See? He goes for his phone, and the ball rolls against the display case. Then, like an idiot, he follows it . . . And there she blows." Lights started to flash, and everyone was suddenly moving much more quickly.

Roland frowned as he watched security guards descend on the culprit. "He never gets anywhere near the necklace."

"I know. That's what's confusing us." He backed up the video and played it again, pointing to the left-hand screen this time. "See? Nothing happens over by the necklace."

Roland focused on the case, but the only people who even got close were running for the doors. "So it wasn't taken while the alarms were ringing. Hmm. This still seems like a distraction to me. Something must be going on over there."

"I'm telling you, I've watched that video a dozen times. Nobody touched the display."

Roland smirked. If this was part of the theft, then it was beautifully executed. "OK. What happened Sunday?"

The security man fiddled some more. "This time, it was some girl who got dumped by her boyfriend. She's by the crowns in the center of the room, so you can see her on both screens." He pointed her out. "Look at her! She's on her phone the whole time, not even looking at the jewels . . . And there she is, suddenly upset and throwing her phone. Lands against the crowns, and bingo!" Lights flashed once again. Roland kept an eye on the necklace display, but—as before—nothing happened there.

"And you say these alarms rarely go off. You'd think with just some rope keeping people away, they'd trip the floor sensors more often."

The security man shrugged. "The floor sensors sit in a narrow band around the display cases, so if someone steps over the line a little, they don't set it off. Almost never happens. Truth is, in all the years I've worked here, I've seen them get tripped only three times. So to have them go off twice in a row makes me wonder."

"Me too." Roland stared at the video. He was convinced that the alarms were related to the theft. Now, all he had to do was figure out how. "Can you freeze the frames so I can get a look at the two kids?"

"Already done." He pulled up still-frames of the boy and the girl. "Both teenagers, from the look of it. The thief must like to hire young helpers."

Roland glanced at their pictures. "I know this is a stretch, but what if the thief is young too?"

The security man furrowed his brow. "Seriously? You think a band of teenagers took the necklace?"

"Well, someone stole it. Why not someone young? Mind if I spend some time looking this over?"

"Knock yourself out." He got up from the chair and walked away.

Now came the magic, where Roland's skills would be put to the test. He was about to get started when a call came from the police officer handling the case. Anxious for every bit of evidence, Roland answered quickly. "What have you got?"

"Well," the officer hesitated. "Nothing. No recent fingerprints on the display case, no damage to the glass, no clues. There was some dust on the floor near the back of the case, but the museum people blame lazy janitors."

"Any damage to the case itself?"

"Nothing visible. The museum people say the cabinet's empty . . . never used."

Roland sighed. "OK, thanks." This convinced him that a professional was at work, but he was a professional too, so he'd need his A-game to catch this one.

Roland sent the pictures of the teenagers to his FBI people to have them do a search. He didn't hold out much hope of finding them that way, because the FBI's criminal databases didn't have many minors in it. Another reason why the thief was clever to use them.

Next, he decided to follow the two trouble-makers through the museum, scanning every camera in the building before and after they set off the alarms. If either one of them interacted with someone else, he'd have new leads. It took a few hours to track them, hopping from camera to camera as they moved through the museum, but he was able to reconstruct their paths.

Both of them had arrived shortly before coming to the jewelry room. This wasn't surprising since the exhibit was the big draw, so most visitors went straight there. Both also left the museum soon after their alarm incident, but given the trouble they'd just made, it's no surprise they left. They barely even glanced at the necklace display and never got close to it while they were in the room. And neither of them interacted with anyone else the entire time they were in the museum.

He had nothing but a wasted morning, which annoyed him. This was supposed to be an easy crime to solve, but so far he was unsuccessful.

Fortunately, Roland was having dinner with his parents that night, and he looked forward to telling them about the case. As a rookie FBI agent, he'd recently moved to a place of his own, but he still visited them for much-appreciated home-cooked meals. And they were great for solving crimes. Roland's mother was a court reporter, and his father was a former detective in the Portland police department, now running his own private agency. They knew all sorts of things about the criminal mind, and Roland grew up listening to many crime-solving dinner conversations.

He knew his parents would ask all sorts of questions about the case, and they'd ask about the parking lot cameras, so Roland expanded his search to follow the teens outside the building. These cameras were very wide views, so each person's face was an indistinct blur. In order to track them, he had to synchronize the interior footage of them leaving, then match their clothing color. One of them surely met with an accomplice outside the museum, and Roland was determined to find out.

But once again, he came up blank. From what he could tell, both of them arrived alone, and both left by themselves without talking to anyone in the parking lot. The boy went straight to his car after triggering the alarm. The girl got lost and circled the museum before finding hers. Perhaps she needed some space after being dumped by her boyfriend and grilled by museum security. He certainly would.

But if they were involved in the theft, which he still suspected, then they were every bit as professional as the thief. This case wasn't nearly as simple as he'd hoped.

Sixteen

The four kids sat in the mall's food court, Neil and Andy practicing trick shuffles with a deck of cards while Penny worked her laptop and sipped from a bottomless cup of juice. Elle's head buzzed with thoughts so she turned to her new colleagues for help.

"Hey, guys, you know this town better than we do. Where should we meet the banker to sell him the necklace?"

"That's easy." Neil turned left and right, gesturing at the space around him. "Do it here at the mall. I'm sure there are a few vacant shops we can use. Security cameras watch the main passageways, but not inside the shops."

Andy smirked. "What rich banker wants to show up at a mall to buy hot goods?"

"No, I like it." Elle nodded to Neil. "The mall provides great cover if things go bad. Lots of people all the time, so nobody's going to start shooting. I get that it's a little low-brow for a millionaire banker, so we'll meet by one of the sit-down restaurants, then do our transaction in an unused store. Let's take a walk around and see what's available."

The four of them toured the mall, noting the unused shops with steel grates over the entrances. Down a quiet side concourse on the upper level, they found two shuttered spaces that were close to each other, separated by an underappreciated perfume store with one lonely clerk. The other shops in this short corridor were a shipping store and an optometrist, specialized businesses that few shoppers visited.

Elle looked through the steel grate of one empty shop, but she couldn't see very far. "I like having two shops near each other. We can arrange to meet at one store, then move the money to the other one after the deal so the mark can't find us if things get dodgy. And mall shops often have a service corridor in back that connects them, which would save us from having to move the money openly."

Penny pulled a set of lock picks from her backpack. "Let's take a look."

"Wait." Elle held up a hand. "We don't want to pick a lock when we meet the mark, it will make him suspicious. Let's contact mall management and pretend we're opening a business. They'll give us a key."

"No way!" Andy shook his head. "If you go to the mall management, they'll ask all sorts of questions about how come a bunch of teenage kids are opening a store. Why expose yourself when you can get the key much more easily?"

Elle curtsied with a smile. "Go right ahead."

Andy leaned against one of the steel grates, pulled out his driver's license, and slipped it through the bars, dropping it into the shop. "Oops!" He winked at them, then ran into the main mall and ducked into a toy store.

"What's he doing?" Penny asked her formerly fake boyfriend.

Neil shrugged. "No idea. But I think we shouldn't be standing here when he gets back." The three of them wandered to the end of the side concourse. From there, they could watch without being too close.

A few minutes later, Andy returned with a mall cop in tow. "I feel so stupid!" he slapped his forehead. "I was just playing. You know, flapping my license against the grate as I walked by. I like to toy with the bars and drum on them. But then it snagged on something and fell behind the grate. I'm really sorry."

"It's OK, kid." The guard stood before the shop and pulled out a big key ring.

Andy's eyes widened. "That's an awful lot of keys. How do you keep them straight?"

"Well, there are ten master keys for different areas of the mall." He fumbled with them a bit more, then held one up. "This is for the shops down here." He unlocked the grate and rolled it open.

Andy bent down to get his license. But instead of grabbing it, he "accidentally" kicked it deeper into the shop, disappearing into the darkness. "Oh jeez! I'm a total klutz today." He chased after it.

"Wait a minute," the cop followed him in. "Let me get that. I know where the lights are." He walked to the back of the dark shop while Andy came out front.

While the cop was in the back, Andy pulled the master key from the grate and pushed it into a lump of modeling clay that he must have bought at the toy store. Then he put the key back into the lock.

When the lights came on, Andy quickly found his driver's license. "Thanks, buddy. You're a life saver." The cop smiled as he locked up, but when he pulled his key from the security grate, a bit of clay that had stuck to it fell out in his hand.

Andy stepped back as the cop studied the detritus. "Something's jamming up the lock." He brought it closer and poked at it. Turning to Andy, he frowned. "Are you messing with me?"

Andy gave him a confused look. "Not me. You think someone's trying to jam the lock?"

"Someone's trying to do something, maybe steal stuff. This doesn't look good to me."

"Hey," Andy pointed to the grating. "Who would want to rob an empty shop? Heck, if I were trying to steal things, I wouldn't bother here."

The mall cop stood tensely for a few seconds, then his shoulders relaxed. "Yeah, you're right about that. And if I report this, I'll be filling out paperwork for the rest of the day. OK, nevermind." He turned and sauntered back into the busier parts of the mall.

Andy held up the clay to show the others as they returned from their hiding place. "See? Easy."

Penny grinned. "Still, you nearly got busted. Want me to make the key?"

"It's OK, I got this." Andy waved her away and wandered off.

Penny sighed. "There's hardly anything for me to do in this caper. I feel useless."

Elle hugged her. "You're anything but useless. And there's plenty to do, especially if your guy, Dearborn, decides to buy the necklace. In the meantime, watch out for Larry Smith, the guy who's been following us from Los Angeles. He'll be here soon."

"Ugh, I know!" Penny groaned. "I tried to find him, but the name's too common. I feel stupid." Her phone buzzed, so she glanced at it, then hugged Neil with a sad smile. "OK, maybe I'm not stupid, but I must have messed up with my hacking because now someone's looking for me."

Elle was happy to see Penny and Neil bonding . . . they really liked each other. She wondered how well Neil would do if he ended up swindling Marshall Crew, the banker he'd investigated. Penny would be nervous if she got to trick her banker, but Elle knew she'd handle it. Neil would probably be able to do it too. Depending on which banker called, any of them could end up as the "inside man."

Elle was also impressed with Andy, and she knew he'd do fine tricking Galt Baxter. He'd handled the key scam beautifully, and he had useful contacts in the Portland area. All in all, she was beginning to like him.

Of course, Andy was a con artist, so perhaps he was tricking everyone including Elle and Penny. She'd keep her eyes on him in case he turned out to be hiding something.

After Andy ran off to make the key, Elle gestured to the lone shipping store, Move It Out. "We'll need this shop too, so I'm going over there. See you back at the food court."

She entered the store and approached the clerk. "I need to send a few hundred packages, all local deliveries weighing a pound or two. I'll package them. How fast can you deliver?"

"Set up an account with us, then you can print your own shipping labels." The clerk handed her some papers. "If you get the packages to us by 4:30, we'll deliver the next day." Elle filled in the papers with one of her fake identities, then she returned to the food court.

Back at their table, Andy was showing off his key. "It opens both shops, and the good news is they *do* connect in back. One of them even has a separate office with a desk and chairs."

Elle fist pumped the air. "Excellent! Let's go there—I want to show you something." They returned to the upstairs corridor and slipped into the shop with the office.

Gathering at the table in the private room, Elle pulled five beautiful wood jewelry boxes from her backpack. "This, folks, is the key to the swindle. Custom jewelry boxes made by my uncle in L.A."

Andy lifted the lid to one of them then let it drop. "What's so special about this?"

"Watch." She reached into her backpack, pulled out one of the fake necklaces, and laid it in one of the jewelry boxes. Then she closed the lid. "OK, here's what happens. We put the necklace in this case, then we bring it to the mark." She pushed the case to Andy.

Andy flipped the lid part way then let it fall closed. "Oh wow," he deadpanned. "Napoleon's necklace. I think I'll buy it."

"Yeah, yeah." Elle pulled the case closer. "Now comes the fun part." She tapped her finger twice in the back corner of the case. A quiet whirring, barely audible, ran for only a second, then stopped. She pushed the case back to Andy. "Now check out the jewels."

Arching an eyebrow, he opened the lid again. "Whoa!" He laughed and turned the box so Neil could see. It now contained a completely different necklace made out of cheap pop beads. "Neat trick."

Neil picked up the case and studied it. "What just happened?"

"What happened is that the fake necklace was sitting on a hidden tray in the lid of the case. When I pushed this secret button two times, the hidden tray dropped down and pushed the real necklace underneath it."

He studied the box more closely. "How do we get the real one out?"

Elle's smile was huge now. She tapped the button again, and a panel opened at the back of the case. With a modest tilt, the hidden copy of Napoleon's necklace slid out into her hand. She tapped the button once more to quietly close the panel.

Neil whistled. "Clever stuff."

Andy twisted his mouth. "Yeah, but won't the mark notice the mechanical sound coming from the box?"

"Not if it's done right. A little distraction goes a long way. Practice with these and you'll be ready." Elle gave each of them one of the trick cases.

Andy drummed on his box. "OK, here's the million-dollar question: how much are we asking for the necklace?"

Elle answered instantly. "Five million. Besides forcing all of the homeowners to refinance, the bank is demanding twenty-five thousand dollars in extra fees, points, and trick clauses. So that's how much I want to give to each homeowner. Quincy has a list with nearly two hundred customers on it, that comes out to five million dollars."

"Then there's nothing left for us."

"There's plenty. Quincy's list actually has 190 names on it, which leaves a quarter of a million dollars left over. I say each of us should get the same as the homeowners: twenty-five thousand dollars. Then, whatever is left after expenses gets saved in case we discover more customers who got cheated. How's that sound? Is twenty-five grand enough for you, Andy?"

Andy's smile ran clear across his face. "It's a good start."

With trick cases and secured mall shops, the four of them returned to the food court to celebrate. Soon they were back to their usual activities, Penny happily sipping juice as she worked her laptop.

Suddenly, she screamed and slammed the computer's lid, pushing away from the table. "Damn! I liked this one." She stroked the machine. "Sorry, baby."

Three sets of concerned eyes waited for Penny to explain. Frowning, she hissed her breath. "Big trouble. Someone just hacked my computer."

"How do you know?"

"Because the little light next to the camera turned on, and I'm not the one who did it. Someone else did, and whoever that hacker is, they now have a picture of me." She turned around to survey the scene behind her, groaning at the sight. "And that means we have an even bigger problem, because behind me, you can see at least six different shops in the food court. Now the hacker will be able to figure out where we are, even what table we're sitting at. We have to get out of here." She got up, roughly shoved the laptop into her backpack, then started to walk away.

Elle got up and followed. "Who did this? Could it be Larry Smith?"

"Could be. We know he spotted my hacking somehow —he's no fool. But this could also be related to the heist. Word's spreading, so the heat's on. We have to play this more carefully, and it starts with me and my computer disappearing."

Neil caught up to take Penny's hand. "Can't you just rebuild the machine?"

Penny shook her head. "It's toast. The built-in addresses have been compromised, so I can't use it anymore. I'll pull the disk to get my data, but I have to destroy the computer."

Andy caught up with them too. "Shouldn't you be smart enough to cover the camera with a band-aid or something?"

Penny grumbled. "Yeah, you're right. And I do have a camera cover, but I forgot to close it after video chatting this morning."

"So . . ." Andy looked around the mall. "We can't hang out here anymore?"

"*I* certainly can't. You three haven't been seen, so you're probably safe. But I can't be here and I don't have a computer. Gah! I feel naked."

They followed Penny as she returned to one of their empty shops. Once inside, she pulled some tools from her backpack and dismantled the computer to get the disk. Then she set the rest of it on the floor of the shop.

"Time for some demolition." She jumped on her computer with both feet, causing it to emit a loud cracking sound. Stepping back, she gestured to the boys to have at it. With unrestrained glee, they took turns stomping the machine, smashing it over and over. Within seconds, pieces were scattered all over the floor.

"Well, that was fun." Andy practically overflowed with excitement as he and Neil gathered up the remains of the computer and threw it in the trash.

Penny regarded her former machine with a sigh. "That was something, all right. But I'm not sure 'fun' is the right word."

Seventeen

Roland felt bleary after staring at security footage all day. His partner wouldn't watch this much video. Yale would bust both those kids and get them in a small room with no cameras. Not that a little questioning would be wrong. But Roland needed to find them first, and he simply couldn't stare at the screen anymore.

Besides, his parents were expecting him for dinner. He stopped for a bottle of their favorite red wine, then went to see them.

Roland's father was home from his detective agency, his short hair more salt than pepper with each passing year. But even when home, he never stopped working on cases, so there he was, comfortable in a bathrobe, tinkering with his latest surveillance camera. Roland's mother couldn't understand how he kept buying these gadgets, especially when money was tight for them. The situation was aggravated by his annoying habit of working for free, either because the clients were poor, or because they cheated him. Her salary as a court reporter wasn't much, but at least it was steady.

At a dinner with three crime fighters, one would expect focused conversations, but the Watsons always insisted on lighter subjects, because tales of grisly murder tended to ruin the flavor of food. Roland waited until the meal was over before presenting his case.

His father jumped right in. "Any ID on the kids?"

Roland shook his head. "Nothing in the FBI database ... we're trying juvenile agencies, but I'm not hopeful. All I have is the security footage, and I can't see anything suspicious even though I watched until my brain started to melt."

His father folded his arms, a gentle smile on his face. "Maybe you should stop looking so hard."

"Excuse me?"

"Well, sometimes when I'm looking at grainy security footage, my head starts to hurt from focusing too much. I did a case once that was so annoying, I couldn't resist having a few extra beers at lunch. When I went back to staring at the screen, I was too bombed to really focus. And that's when I noticed the clues."

Roland smirked. "So that's your secret, Dad. I'll admit that after a few glasses of wine, I'm not feeling as bad about this case. But still, how will getting drunk help?"

"You don't have to get drunk, just step back from the evidence. Watch the footage less closely. Squint, push your chair away, or look to the side and watch with your peripheral vision. You can even play the video backwards. You never know what you'll see."

His mother laughed. "It's like the old saying, 'By letting it go, it all gets done.' Let it go, at least for tonight. Get some rest."

This wasn't the sort of problem-solving Roland expected. His parents typically brought up theories they would argue and rate. Letting go of evidence wasn't much of a theory. It wasn't even much of a problem-solving technique. But it was all he had.

"Here's to letting it go." He raised his glass and finished his wine.

As Roland drove home, the museum's alarm lights kept flashing in his head like a throbbing hangover. He wasn't really drunk, but the case wouldn't let go of his brain, so ignoring his promise to rest, he returned to the museum's control room. Sitting at the console, he queued the videos on the first and second day, started playing them on the largest screen, then pushed his chair back to the opposite wall.

The boy was still a stupid kid, chasing a ball like he was at school recess. The girl was every bit as stupid, overreacting to a breakup by damaging an expensive phone. So instead of looking at the kids, he watched the lonely display case with the necklace, where absolutely nothing was happening. Nothing at all.

And that's when he saw it.

The clue was very subtle, just a slight dimming near the bottom of the case. With all the flashing lights, he hadn't noticed it before, but between flashes, the floor got a bit less bright for a few seconds. He rolled his chair forward and watched it again.

Yes, there it was. A darkness on the side of the cabinet, almost like a shadow. Something was going on near the floor. Not only that, but the light changed on both days, soon after the alarms started, and it lasted much longer on the first day. This couldn't be a dimming of lights in the room from the surge of the alarms, because the lighting in other parts of the room didn't change. The only change was near the necklace's case.

Thank you, Mom and Dad! Hiding in all that nothing was a little something of value. Roland leaped from his chair so fast that the security man on duty spilled his coffee. "I need you to turn off the alarms so I can explore the exhibit."

The man typed a bit into a console, then nodded his head. As soon as he did, Roland ran to the exhibit hall, leading the guard the entire way.

They entered the room with the now-fake necklace and Roland raced to the back of the case. The museum people had assured him that the cabinet was empty, but now he wasn't so sure. Convenient how it faced away from the camera. "Can you open this for me please?"

The guard fumbled with a big ring of keys and found the one for the case. But when he turned the key, it wouldn't open. He played around for a bit, then chuckled. "Get this, it isn't locked. But for some reason it still won't open."

"I don't care if you have to kick it in. Open that door."

The guard tugged harder, and the door finally gave way with a loud ripping sound. "Look at that! There's tape on the inside holding it closed." He reached out to peel some of it off, but Roland stopped him.

"Don't touch anything. Let me see." He put on gloves and squatted down in front of the door.

The first thing Roland noticed was the air hose, shoved into the bottom of the case. That explained the dust outside. He followed it to a pump, taped to the top of the cabinet. He also saw tape covering two of the seams as well as all around the door.

He sniffed the air in the case and was surprised to notice the smell of food, mixed with a light edge of sweat. It reminded him of a former girlfriend, a fitness enthusiast who used to show up at his place when she was done working out. Could a woman have been in here? He wasn't sure, but given the air pump, the food, and the sweat, he was sure of one thing. Someone had spent a lot of time in this cabinet recently. When he looked up and saw the underside of the display surface, he knew exactly how the necklace had been stolen.

To be certain, he walked over to the entrance where the security cameras were mounted, then he asked the guard to squat down behind the case and open the door. As expected, a shadow was cast by the door, exactly as he had seen on the security video.

Everything was clear now. The kids purposely tripped the alarms on the other side of the room so someone could get in and out of the cabinet with the necklace. Then, the jewels were taken in the middle of the night from underneath. This made sense, because the first alarm went off near the end of the day, and the second one that freed the thief had occurred in the morning. He'd bet anything that a search through the video from Saturday night would show the necklace disappearing into the case, then reappearing later.

Take that, Yale. Crime solved.

Eighteen

After Penny's laptop got hacked and her presence in the mall's food court was exposed, she stayed in the motel room. Elle suggested that they go to her parents for dinner, but Penny was busy setting up a new computer. Besides, she felt guilty about being discovered, and that made her too grumpy for polite conversation, so Elle went alone.

It surprised her how readily her parents welcomed her back into their lives. She'd expected a long period of adjustment where her presence would be a challenge for everyone. But instead, her parents happily included her in every possible dinner subject, from cooking and homework issues to favorite movies and sporting teams. The contrast between this home and the one she grew up in was hard to believe.

After the meal, Wendy and June ran to the living room and started trading "Does" and "Does not" declarations, eyeing their new sister with each accusation. Curious, Elle followed them. "Does or doesn't what?"

"OK," Wendy took the lead. "Do you have brothers and sisters?"

"Yeah," June continued the inquiry, "And aunts and uncles!"

Elle smiled. "I have all of those people, but none of them are really related to me. I'm the youngest of three foster kids. The oldest was Jay, who unfortunately died years ago. The middle is my sister, Dee, who lives in New York City."

June's eyes bugged out. "Your brother died! What happened?"

"He, uhh . . . He got really sick." What she couldn't say was that the sickness began when a bullet entered his brain. Even Elle didn't want to think about that.

June nodded. "Gee, that's awful. What about your sister? Has she met her real parents?"

"No, she's still mad at them for abandoning her. And she ran away from our foster mother, so now she doesn't have anyone to call Mom."

"That's too bad. Why did she run away? Is your foster mother mean? Does she hit you?"

Elle blew out a long breath. "She doesn't hit us, but she's very strict and can be pretty mean, like locking us in a closet all day. She can be scary if we mess up, but when we do as we're told, she's very happy, even proud of us. It wasn't easy, but I learned how to make her happy."

"Sounds like she didn't love you very much."

Elle grunted an unamused laugh. "Love? I don't think so. She didn't even feed us all the time. Dee used to go out and scrounge extra food. But I'll tell you this much, my foster mother taught me how to be tough. How to survive in this world."

Wendy frowned. "Your real mom is much nicer."

Elle hugged her sister. "You're so right. But it wasn't all bad when I was growing up. I have an aunt and uncle who were there for me. Of course, they're not really my aunt and uncle—they're not even related to my foster mom. But they'll always be Aunt Franny and Uncle Carl. *They're* my family."

Wendy and June seemed transfixed by Elle's story. She wished she could tell them the truth about all the dishonest things she'd done as a kid, but she wasn't ready to do that yet.

She decided to change the subject and stop talking about herself. Wendy and June were her own blood sisters, and that fascinated her.

"What about you two? Wendy, you're in seventh grade, right?"

Wendy nodded, so June jumped in. "I'm in third grade. We're doing arithmetic." She bounced on her toes. "It's fun."

Elle gave Wendy a half smile. "Do *you* think school's fun?"

Wendy shrugged. "It's OK. This boy is bugging me lately. He keeps following me around."

"He probably likes you."

"Yeah? Maybe. But does he have to be such a dork about it? You know all about boys. What's up with them?"

Elle was so surprised to be thought of as an expert on boys that she laughed. The laughter came from a sad place, where she wished she knew more, where she longed to have a boyfriend. She pulled her sister close.

"Oh, Wendy, I'm afraid I'm going to be a huge disappointment. I understand people and the way they think, but boys are still a mystery. The way they act around girls confuses me—I really don't get them. If you want to know about boys, ask Penny. She knows them best." Elle chuckled. "She already seems to have found a boyfriend up here, and we've only been around for two weeks!"

"So you've never had a boyfriend?"

"I had one. Just one, though, and it ended badly. It happened soon after Dee left town."

"Was he mean to you?"

"No. He was actually very nice. But I did something stupid and made a mess of it. That made him angry, so he broke it off. I didn't blame him."

Wendy narrowed her eyes. "What did you do?"

"I . . . I told him a secret that I knew about his father. I shouldn't have done that, it made everyone mad at me. I thought he'd appreciate knowing, but I was wrong."

Elle remembered how upset she'd been when Bea had announced that they were swindling the boy's dad. She pleaded to leave the man alone, but Bea wouldn't hear of it. After agonizing for days, Elle finally told her boyfriend. It was, after all, the only honorable thing to do. Unfortunately, he didn't see it that way, especially after finding out that his girlfriend was a crook. At least his father was saved, but the boy dumped her instantly, and Elle spent the next day locked in a closet. A total lose-lose, and not something she was ready to share with her new family.

Wendy gave her big sister a hug. "It wasn't your fault, Elle."

"You might think that, but it's important to know when to speak and when to stay quiet. Sometimes, the truth hurts more than lies. I didn't understand boys back then, and after the breakup, I stopped trying. They just aren't worth it." She sighed. "I'm not a normal girl, Wendy, and I don't have a normal life. I'm the last person you want to ask about boys." She clamped her hands into tight fists to keep her sadness at bay.

A phone in Elle's purse started to chime with the ringtone reserved for Frank the Fence. This was such excellent news that it wiped away her disappointment with boys and reminded her that she still had some wicked skills. She jumped to her feet, apologized to her sisters, then wandered down the hall to take the call.

"You believe me now, Frank?"

He grunted. "Maybe. But seeing is believing, if you know what I mean."

"I'd love to bring it by. When's good?"

"Tomorrow afternoon. Four p.m. Tucker Bail, in the northeast."

"I know where you are. See you tomorrow." She disconnected.

As she turned back to her sisters, she saw Wendy staring with a curious look. "What was that about? Sounds like you got a date with a boy named Frank."

"Yeah, a date." Elle didn't bother to point out the absurdity of dating Frank the Fence.

"Yay!" Wendy flapped her hands in the air. "My sister's got a new boyfriend."

Elle gave her sister a thin smile and suppressed the urge to snort.

Nineteen

After seeing the inside of the necklace display cabinet, Roland knew exactly how the theft was done. But he didn't know *who* had done it. The two kids who'd set off the alarms were mere accomplices—they'd done their work then left the museum. The thief was someone else, and Roland was determined to find out who he—or as he suspected—*she* was.

He arrived at the museum Tuesday morning, prepared for another tedious day watching security video. To find the thief, he needed to catalog every person in the room, right before and just after the alarms went off. Anyone still there after the alarms on the first day was not the thief. He needed to find the one person who was there before the alarm and then disappeared.

As he watched the feed from both cameras in the room, he made notes of every visitor. He printed screen shots and wrote numbers next to each person. Then he advanced the video slowly, following each person while looking for new people. The process was slow, and was made much more difficult when the alarms went off, because everyone in the room started to run all over the place. It took over three weary hours to finish this critical task. But even worse than the mind-numbing waste of time, he had to admit that he couldn't find anyone who'd disappeared from the room. The thief must have hidden from the cameras.

After lunch, Roland went to work on the second day's video, once again tracking everyone in the room. This time, he wanted to find a new person, someone who wasn't there before the alarms but who magically appeared after they went off. It took another three hours to finish this task, made worse by post-lunch lethargy and the knowledge that the thief was hiding from the cameras. He'd been hoping for a mistake, a slip-up where the thief appeared on camera, even for a second. But whoever had stolen the necklace was just too good.

Roland went outside to clear his head. While he was there, he called the office to see if they'd been able to identify the two teenagers who had triggered the alarms.

They had bad news and good news. The bad news was that the girl was completely unknown. Probably younger than 18, she didn't have any adult records, locally or at the federal level. And a search of juvenile records also came up blank. She was nobody.

Roland assumed that this would be the case. After all, the thief was very clever, and by choosing innocent young people as accomplices, it would be impossible to find them.

But the good news was that the boy who had tripped the alarm on the first day *did* have a juvenile record. A local kid, Andy Burr, he had been caught picking pockets in the Bridgeport mall and had spent six months in juvenile detention. Roland wondered if the jewel thief used him because he was young and presumably innocent but didn't know about the boy's arrest record. In any case, Roland now had a name and an address. He could follow Andy and hopefully find the thief.

In the meantime, Roland wanted to know more about the other accomplice, the thin young woman with dark hair. He visited the employee break room to interview the guard who'd apprehended her after she tripped the alarm. "Tell me about the young lady who threw her cell phone on Sunday."

"I actually noticed her the minute she came into the room."

Roland arched an eyebrow. "Why?"

"Well, most people show up craning their necks, desperate to see the famous jewels. This girl couldn't care less. She had her face down in her phone the whole time, running a whole conversation—she never stopped."

"Did you get her name? Her phone number? Did you see what she was doing that was so interesting?"

"Yeah, she showed me her phone. Big long conversation between her and some boy. It ended with him dumping her. Kind of sad, so I didn't question her much. I'd have thrown my phone too. I could see from the conversation that her name is Penny, but I didn't get a last name or her phone number."

"Did you get the boy's name?"

"Uhh," the guard thought for a second. "Yeah, right. His name was Neil."

"Was there anything else unusual at the museum that day?" Two other guards were sitting in the break room, so Roland leaned back to include them. "Did either of you see or hear anything unusual over the weekend?"

One of the other guards shrugged. "Define 'unusual.'"

"Anything at all, even if it means nothing to you. Tell me, and I'll decide if it's significant."

"Well," the guard hesitated. "It's no big deal, really. I stopped a girl for having a yellow sticker instead of a purple one."

Roland gasped as a smile crossed his face. "Let me guess, yellow stickers were used on Saturday and purple stickers were used on Sunday, right?"

"Yeah! How'd you know? Anyway, I took her to the lobby to buy a new ticket."

This was his lucky break—she had to be the thief. Someone who'd spent the night in the museum would still have the previous day's sticker. And the thief was a woman, as he'd suspected. Roland found it interesting that she'd executed the crime so carefully but made such a tiny mistake. A number of crimes got solved that way, and this was no different.

He scrambled to his feet with so much energy that his chair fell over. "Come on!" He headed down the hall, waving at the guard to follow. "Let's see if she's on any of the security videos."

Roland couldn't wait to find out more about this fascinating thief who'd pulled off such a clever heist. He was convinced at this point that she'd be older, because the entire job was so professionally done.

After running to the control room, Roland had to wait for the guard, who ambled in at a normal pace and took his time getting comfortable in a chair. Meanwhile, Roland worked the controls like an excited kid on Christmas morning. The prospect of solving this crime made him feel delightfully light-headed.

He pulled up a thumbnail of every camera in the museum. "Which of these cameras covers the area where you stopped that woman?"

"That one." The guard pointed to the screen. "But I definitely wouldn't call her a woman. More like girl. A teenager, I'd say. You'll see."

A *young* woman. Amazing. Roland enlarged the camera feed that the guard had identified, then he set it to the time of Sunday's alarm and let it play.

Very little happened for a while, people walking by, but nothing else. It would probably take a few minutes after the alarms finished ringing before she got to this spot, so he decided to ask some questions and test his theory. "Was she sweaty? Damp hair? Did she smell like she needed a shower?"

The guard cocked his head. "Now that you mention it, yeah. Most kids are slobs these days, but you're right . . . This one was a mess. How'd you know?"

Roland was about to explain when the guard pointed to the screen. "There, that's me." They watched the video for a few seconds. "And there's the girl with the wrong color sticker. See? Now I'm stopping her."

Roland's jaw nearly hit the floor. She was very young, probably a minor. The mastermind thief was no older than her accomplices! That really surprised him. Everything had been executed so cleanly that he didn't expect this job to be the work of a band of kids.

Roland had no doubt that this was the thief. As predicted, her long dark hair was matted down, looking like she'd spent the night underneath a jewelry display. She moved with a sure but relaxed gait as she made her way out of the museum. That smile on her face had to be from the thrill of having a priceless necklace. And even after the guard stopped her, she remained calm. But Roland could see her head turning here and there, eyes darting around to measure her situation. She might be young, but she was every bit a professional.

One thing Roland had to grudgingly admit was that he found this young thief to be pretty. He knew he shouldn't have these feelings, but he was already impressed by her skill, so it didn't help at all to have a physical attraction too. Short yet standing tall, she exuded an aura of confidence, a sophistication totally unexpected in someone so young. He stared with rapt attention at the daring jewel thief, trying to remind himself that he shouldn't be so taken with a crooked underage girl.

Roland grabbed some frames from the video and sent them in for identification. Although he suspected that the search would come up blank, he had to try. Still, even if he couldn't identify her, he had plenty of information now. He had a name and address for Andy Burr, as well as the names of two others, Penny and Neil. From that, he'd definitely be able to track down the clever young ringleader.

In the meantime, there was another angle to follow in this case: the necklace. Those thieves had to sell it to someone. Roland had been in Portland for a few months, but as a new kid at the bureau with a condescending partner, he didn't get out in the field much. Instead, he found himself sidelined at a desk pretty often, so he'd had plenty of time to study the city's players, both legal and illegal.

One thing he knew for sure was that jewels of this rarefied caliber could only be taken to one man. Frank Tucker—Frank the Fence—had his finger in every large theft and hot sale. Even if Tucker wasn't directly involved, he'd know what was going on. Of course, he'd never admit to anything, but Roland still needed to visit him, if for no other reason than to make it known that federal agents were watching this. Roland needed to hurry, too, because those jewels were probably leaving the city soon. Assuming that they hadn't already.

He checked his gun to be sure it was still ready and loaded. Although he fired it weekly at the FBI shooting range, he hadn't ever had to depend on it in the field. Frank the Fence was a known underworld character, so he'd probably have armed men protecting him. To be safe from trouble, Roland logged his planned visit, a step recommended by the bureau when going alone.

As he drove to the northeast side of town, Roland couldn't stop thinking about the thief. A young lady but clearly the leader of the group, a criminal genius. She knew how to hide from the cameras, get at the jewels, and use other minors in the heist to protect everyone from detection and prosecution. Of course, she slipped up on the tiniest of details: the museum's rotating sticker system. But the rest of the plan was brilliant. As much as it bothered him to think this, he wasn't sure if he wanted to arrest her or ask her to dinner.

Twenty

Frank the Fence ran a bail bond service in a seedy part of town, with tattoo parlors, adult toy stores, and by-the-hour hotels as neighbors. Elle stepped carefully over cigarette butts and broken bottles, avoiding the foul-smelling puddles that pooled on the sidewalk.

She came without her crew today, but she brought her parents' neighbors, and they looked fierce. Chip and Quincy wore fitted black suits that wrapped around their bodies like snakes. Chip had a basic black suit, his white shirt open at the collar. Quincy, as usual, was better turned-out, wearing a dark gray three-piece suit with a black-and-white striped tie. Each of them also had dark eyeglasses and ear buds, the threatening bulge of a pocketed gun clearly visible. Nobody needed to know that the guns were toys. Between Quincy's muscles and Chip's sheer bulk, they presented an intimidating show of strength.

Inside the bail shop, two tough-looking men sat in the front office to post bail for the crooks who got caught. For those who got away clean and had loot to sell, Frank waited in back. When the three of them entered, the front office men gave them a silent once-over, sharing a few raised eyebrows. Elle sauntered over and sat on the corner of one of their desks. "Frank asked me to come by and talk about jewelry."

The man picked up his phone and spoke briefly, then he got up and walked to a door at the back of the shop, motioning Elle to follow. She crooked a finger at Quincy, and he stepped away from Chip to accompany her.

The other bail man noticed that Chip was staying. "You sure you don't want to go back there too?"

Chip grunted and folded his arms. "The lady wants me here, so I'm staying."

Elle was impressed with Chip's tough yet professional demeanor, the very image of a bodyguard. He and Quincy were doing exactly the right thing: distracting Frank's men from wondering about the teenage girl in their shop.

Elle and Quincy followed the bail man into Frank's lair. The office was spacious, a big desk, a few chairs, and some side tables along the wall. Seated in his overstuffed throne, with the front-office man now by his side, Frank commanded the room.

Elle approached the desk to get a better look. Frank Tucker was middle-aged, trim, and neatly dressed in a button-down shirt. With his Van Dyke beard, he looked more like a salesman than a purveyor of stolen goods.

Frank was also observing the scene, his eyes darting between Elle and Quincy. After a few seconds, he tightened his mouth. "First of all, I don't know either of you." He squinted at Quincy. "Do much security work around here?"

Quincy delivered a scornful reply as if it was something he'd grown tired of saying. "My clients like discretion, and I like discrete clients. So if you've never seen me before, that's good." Elle wanted to laugh. She couldn't have picked better accomplices if she'd used real con artists. Quincy was also playing his part like a pro.

Now it was her turn. She propped her hands on her hips and faced Frank squarely. "And you've never seen me before because I'm nobody. But my people are serious, and we want to know if you can handle some scalding hot goods. Interested?"

Frank waved his hand over a mostly empty desk. "Show me."

Elle laid her backpack on the desk and pulled out one of the trick jewelry boxes, sliding it across the desk to Frank. Quincy stepped closer, arms folded tight-enough to showcase his muscular build.

As soon as Frank opened the jewelry box, he barked out a laugh. He put on gloves, grabbed a loupe, and studied the stones for a few seconds, then he sat back with a noisy exhale. "You weren't kidding." He eyed her critically. "So you're the one who stole this. Who'd have figured—a girl thief."

Elle propped her hands on her hips. "I never said I stole it. I'm just here to manage the piece."

Frank hummed his doubt and considered her for a few seconds, but Elle remained silent. Finally, he shrugged. "So what's the deal? You want me to take this off your hands?"

"Depends. What's it worth?"

"Well, I can't sell it whole. I'll have to break it up, sell the stones separately, melt down the setting. Too bad, you know, because it really is a beautiful piece." He picked it up and held it respectfully, twisting it to catch the emeralds' gleam. Then he smiled and gently returned it to the box. "OK, I'll give you six hundred grand."

Elle scowled. "The necklace was appraised for over eight million, and that was ten years ago."

"That's if the sale is honest and the necklace stays intact. But I can't offer you either of those things."

Elle leaned forward, fists planted on his desk. "That's a crock, Frank, and you know it. We came to you because you've got connections. You must know people who will pay big bucks for something like this." She slid the jewelry case toward her opened backpack, then she tapped on the case to make her point while her other finger tapped the secret button. To cover the soft whirring sound coming from the trick case, she continued her pitch.

"I heard about a jewelry club where a bunch of Tera bankers show off their latest finds. I bet one of them would buy this necklace as is. Tell you what, connect me with someone who ends up buying this whole . . ." She lifted the case and gave it a little shake to drive home the point. "And I'll give you twenty-five grand. You don't even have to arrange the deal or expose yourself in any way. All you have to do is get them to call me."

What Frank didn't see was that shaking the case let the necklace slide out of the trap door and into Elle's backpack. She closed the trap door, grabbed her backpack, and slid the jewelry box back toward Frank, now with a fake necklace.

Frank considered her offer for a few seconds before making a counter proposal. "Fifty grand."

Elle rolled her eyes. "Fine. But I want guys who appreciate jewelry and will keep it whole. Don't give my number to any chop shops."

"OK, kid. But there's one more thing I need to know. Who did this? I pride myself on knowing everyone in this town: who's playing what, which people don't like each other, who can be trusted. Keeps me and my connections out of trouble. And nobody's gonna believe that a fifteen-year-old girl happened to have . . ."

"Hey!" She cut him off. "I'm *seventeen*." They could fool themselves about who stole what, but they needed to get her age right.

"Well, then." Frank rolled his head like a snooty head-waiter. "Good for you." He stared hard. "It's like this, kid. People ask questions, and they need answers. Who pulled the heist?"

Elle grinned. "The Adjusters."

Frank wrinkled his nose. "Never heard of them."

"They're new."

Frank blew out a breath. "This is getting nowhere. I need to talk to the leader of this gang."

"Easily done. You're talking to her."

"OK, now we're getting somewhere. So you *are* the thief. What's your name?"

"I'm Linda."

Frank groaned. "Here we go again. Linda the Thief ain't gonna fly. You got a last name? These guys I know, they want a name they can respect. Nobody's gonna believe that Little Linda pulled a museum heist."

"How about Linda the Lynx? Exotic enough for you? Tell 'em I'm from out of town."

Frank visibly darkened. "Now you're just making stuff up. I need something real!" He slammed his fist down on the desk, making the jewelry box jump. "All I see is a street rat who thinks she can mess with me, and that won't cut it." He paused, a nasty scowl spreading across his face. "I know. How about I keep this necklace? *It's* real. I'll show it around and let you know if someone wants it." He laid his hand on top of the jewelry case.

Everyone thought they could mess with Elle, the defenseless little girl. People had been underestimating her for years, which usually worked in her favor. But even with big bodyguards, she wasn't fearsome enough to keep Frank Tucker in line. Good thing she'd planned for this.

Elle narrowed her eyes and grumbled. "*I'm* selling the necklace, not you. I need it back *now*."

Frank pushed a button on his desk and gestured to his goon. The man pulled out a gun, pointing it at Elle and Quincy. The other front-office man came in quickly and patted down Quincy. When he pulled out the fake gun, he chuckled and tossed it onto Frank's desk, landing it with the hollow clatter of cheap plastic.

Frank arched an eyebrow. "Seriously? What kind of bodyguard carries a toy?"

Elle spoke up before Quincy could answer. "The kind who doesn't want to shoot anyone. I was rather hoping you'd deal with me honestly, Frank. You could have gotten a nice commission for helping move this piece."

"You got that right, honey. I'll get a whopping commission." He opened his desk drawer and slid the case inside. "Now how about you get out of here before I have my guys show you how real guns work."

Elle's mouth tightened into a flat line. "The Adjusters won't be very happy about this."

"Look, *Linda*, if that's even your name. This whole thing stinks like a horse toilet. A child thief with an unknown crew and a fake bodyguard? You're ringing too many alarm bells here. So until I can figure it out, I'm keeping the necklace. Now go away." He nodded to his muscle men, who raised their guns to drive home the point.

It was time to leave.

Twenty-One

Roland stood outside of Tucker Bail, taking in the sights, sounds, and smells of this seedy neighborhood. One part of him was worried about the notorious underworld figure, but the other part was excited, like being a stage star on opening night. Finally ready, he took a long breath and marched in.

Two desks sat up front, both empty but showing signs of recent activity: coffee cups, an opened notebook, and a half-eaten doughnut. A tough-looking bald man stood by the door, wearing a crisp black suit and glasses as dark as the ones Roland liked to wear. Frank Tucker's muscle, no doubt.

The man held out a hand. "This is a bad time right now. Come back later."

"I don't think so." Roland pulled out his badge and flashed it. "FBI. And who might you be?"

The man instantly lost his swagger and held up his hands as if Roland had pointed a gun. "Sorry. My name's Chip Ungar." He took off his sunglasses and gestured around the office. "I don't work here."

"OK, Chip, and why is this a bad time?"

"Well, it's not really that bad. I'm waiting for someone who doesn't want any trouble." He glanced at the door to the back room, then quickly turned away. Not quickly enough for Roland to miss, however.

"What's going on back there?"

Chip shrugged. "I really don't know."

Roland knew a lie when he heard one, and this man was definitely lying. But that bulge in his jacket looked like a gun, so he needed to be disarmed before Roland could explore further.

"You look like you've got a gun, Chip. I'm going to have to take that from you." Roland laid his hand on his own holstered gun to establish authority. Chip has been cooperative, so it didn't seem necessary to start pointing weapons.

Chip smiled. "It's just a toy."

Roland tapped his gun. "Maybe compared with this, but I don't need any trouble. Put your hands up, please."

Chip raised his hands while Roland reached for the gun. When he touched it, he was surprised to feel a warm rough surface instead of cold smooth metal. He pulled it out and realized he was holding a water pistol.

Roland frowned as he examined the fake weapon. "Who carries a toy gun?"

Chip sighed. "Someone who's only pretending to be a bodyguard."

"And what do you do when you're not pretending to be a bodyguard?"

"I'm the men's department floor-manager at the Herbert Walker department store."

Roland's frown deepened, wondering why a clothing salesman with a toy gun was pretending to be a bodyguard. The man was clearly harmless, but it didn't make sense that he'd be here. The only thing he knew for sure was that he was getting nowhere with this conversation.

"Stick to your day job, Chip, and stand over there where I can see you." Chip obeyed while Roland slipped closer to the back room door. He grabbed the knob and tested it, glad when it turned. With one swift movement, he flung it open and jumped inside. "FBI!" he shouted, flashing his badge. "Nobody move."

The five people in the room turned to stare. He'd seen Frank the Fence's picture, so he spotted the man quickly, sitting behind a large desk. Two other men stood near him, both holding guns. Real ones. On the other side of the room, closer to the door he'd entered, were two more people, the target of those guns. One was a big muscular man, even more crisply dressed than the fake bodyguard out front. And the other person was the most pleasant surprise Roland could have wanted. Fresh off the museum video, but without sweaty matted hair, the young jewel thief stood next to her bodyguard. *How convenient.*

Before trying to learn more about this thief, Roland had to deal with the gunslingers. He didn't want to aggravate the situation by pulling his own gun, so he went for bravado. "You two," he barked at the men whose guns pointed at her. "Put away those guns." He looked Frank Tucker in the eye. "The bureau knows where I am, so don't encourage your men do anything they might regret." Tucker nodded at the men, and they holstered their guns. Roland noticed another toy gun on the desk and guessed that it came from this other bodyguard, who was probably as harmless as the man out front.

"Good. Now what's going on here?"

Tucker volunteered an answer. "Can you believe this stupid girl?" He pointed to the thief. "Little Linda thinks she can come in here and tell me what to do." He shook his head slowly, a disappointed parent coping with his foolish daughter's recklessness. "She was just leaving. I told my boys to make sure she and her bodyguard made it out the door safely. I wouldn't want any trouble." His smile failed to convince Roland that he didn't already *have* trouble.

"I see." He'd arrived as Tucker was throwing the thief out, but why? Roland guessed that she'd tried to fence the necklace, and things had gone badly. It would explain the guns on Tucker's side, and why Linda and her bodyguard were at the door, about to leave. But it wouldn't explain the cool demeanor of this young thief and the look on her face like she was in complete control. She betrayed no concern over being surrounded by four powerful men, three of them her enemy, and two of those with guns aimed at her. Nor did she appear to be concerned that an FBI agent had her cornered. She really was a pro.

Desperate to know more about this woman, he blurted out, "Who are you?" As soon as the words left his mouth, he realized it was a stupid question. She probably wasn't named Linda, but she'd never reveal her real name.

"My name's Lisa Fisher." Her smile was pure innocence. "What's yours?"

Roland chuckled. First Linda, then Lisa. And now that he'd heard her speak, she was probably also Lorie McNee, the fake journalist who'd reported the theft. Not one of those names was hers.

He switched to something more relevant. "Let me ask you folks if you've seen a stolen necklace." He tossed out a photograph of the treasure, one eye on the thief to see how she'd react. She didn't bat an eyelash.

But when Tucker looked at the picture, his cheek twitched slightly. "Never seen it before."

The thief laughed. "You're lying. It's in your desk drawer."

Roland's eyes grew wide, and Tucker looked like he'd stuck his finger in a socket. Why was she revealing this information? Had Tucker's men taken the necklace from her? He approached the desk. "Is that so?"

"Of course not!" Tucker's voice cracked like a pubescent teenager.

Roland leaned over the desk. "Then you won't mind showing me what's in your desk drawer.

"I . . . " Tucker's eyes circled the room, then he sunk down in his chair. "Aw, shit." He got up from the desk and walked to the side.

Roland opened the drawer and saw the jewelry case sitting at the top. "Well, well, well. What's in here? Wait, don't tell me. Let it be a surprise." He flipped open the case, and his face burst with delight. "Yep, this sure looks like the very item that was stolen from the museum. See how much it resembles that picture?" He squinted at Tucker. "And you said you'd never seen it before."

Tucker scowled at the thief. "You set me up."

She slapped a hand to her chest. "I don't know what you're talking about. And I can tell from here that this is no priceless necklace." She pointed her chin toward the case. "That's nothing more than a crappy piece of costume jewelry."

Tucker darkened. "It's not . . ." He choked off the rest of his words and turned to glare at Roland.

Roland watched the two of them, fascinated. Tucker was clearly flustered, but the thief continued to act like she owned the room. He couldn't resist a taunt. "What are you two, a comedy team? This is obviously the necklace that was stolen from the museum."

The teen thief offered a mischievous grin. "Then the joke's on you, Mister FBI, if you can't tell real gems from glass. Look at that thing! Chipped diamonds, scratched emeralds." She smirked. "Go ahead and bring it to the museum. They'll laugh you out the door."

Roland's face fell as he gave the necklace its first serious look. She was right; it *was* fake. He'd studied jewels as part of his FBI training, but it didn't take an expert to see that this necklace was not just a fake, but a truly pathetic one. He'd seen poor forgeries before, but this piece of trash was one of the worst fakes ever, with chips, scratches, and flaws on nearly every stone.

He wondered what was going on. Everything about this job seemed fake. Fake versions of the necklace, here and at the museum. Fake guns on fake bodyguards. Even fake adults; young kids pulling jobs so professionally that he still couldn't believe it. This girl, now that he could see her, seemed like she was only sixteen, and she'd managed to rob a museum, then somehow trick a dangerous underworld figure. As much as he knew it was wrong, he liked her more with every passing minute.

Roland still couldn't figure out this bizarre game she and Frank Tucker were playing. The fact that he had another fake necklace certainly linked him to the heist, so perhaps they were working together. It would explain the show of guns by his men; a way to protect him from the young thief. That would make Tucker the ringleader, the boss who sent her out to do the museum job.

Nah! The more Roland considered the people here, the more he doubted that Tucker was the leader of anything. Given the look of shock on the man's face and the ever-cool look of calm on that girl, Roland much preferred the idea that *she* was the boss, the mastermind of something he still didn't understand. He couldn't wait to bring her in for questioning.

Since Tucker was off his game, for whatever reason, he was the right person to ask. "So where's the real necklace?"

He'd certainly never get a straight answer from the thief. She couldn't even give out her name without lying.

"I have no idea." Tucker seemed more calm now that he'd avoided being caught with the goods. He gestured to the four walls of his office. "Look around if you like. This here's a respectable business. No stolen goods in my place."

"No, of course not." Roland pulled out his card and flipped it onto the desk. "But if you do run across the necklace, be sure to let me know."

He turned to the thief and her bodyguard, desperate to learn about this magical young woman who stole priceless necklaces, then manipulated Frank the Fence with nothing but toy guns. "I understand you were about to leave."

"Yes, we were." She started toward the door then turned back. "Bye, Frank."

Tucker had been staring at the necklace, so he looked up with a blank expression. "Bye," he muttered, then returned his gaze to the jewelry case.

Roland took the young thief's arm. "Good. Come with me." He wanted to arrest her right there, but decided not to do that with Tucker's gunmen around. The interaction between her and them was still confusing, so he needed to get her outside first.

In the front office, her pretend bodyguards made eye contact, then they followed her and Roland out of the shop. When they got to the sidewalk, he reached for his handcuffs. "So, Lisa, you're under arrest for . . ." Before he could even finish the sentence, she twirled around in a convoluted way that freed her from his grip, then she bolted down the street. "Stop!" he cried but to no avail. She moved faster than anyone he'd ever seen, like a jungle cat on the attack, weaving left and right as she sprinted away. He wanted to pull out his gun, but before he could even reach for it she was halfway down the block with people in the way.

The two fake bodyguards stood there, making no attempt to follow her. He could question them, but she was far more important. Besides, he knew where the clothing salesman worked, so he could find them later. He chased the thief down the street, following her into an alley that he'd seen her enter. The space between the two buildings was narrow and dark. It also ended very quickly at a solid wall. He knew she'd run in here, but once he got to the end, he realized that he'd lost her. Looking up, he saw an open window, two stories higher, but he doubted she could climb there so quickly. A garbage bin at the end of the alley had very little in it and definitely no young woman. She was gone.

Roland went back to the street to see if she might be somewhere else, but he knew he wouldn't find her. Even the fake bodyguards had left. The young jewel thief had evaporated without a trace.

The nerve of that girl! She might be clever, capable, and cute, but she was also a liar, a trickster, and a thief. And now she'd managed to escape from him, which was impressive but intensely annoying. She'd made a fool of him, and he got more than enough of that from his partner.

It didn't matter, though, because he'd already solved the case, and eventually he would catch her. Then he'd put her pretty face behind bars.

Twenty-Two

The FBI kept tabs on a wide range of shady characters in Portland, from the petty crooks hiding in alleyways to the power players who ran things behind the safe walls of their big offices. Included among the unscrupulous rich were a few executives at Tera Bank who had a private jewelry club. One of them had spent a million dollars last year on a bracelet that had previously been owned by two mob bosses, a bishop, and a prince. Another banker was rumored to be collecting stolen pieces. Since these men loved jewels, it made sense to warn them that this was one shiny bauble they needed to avoid.

The reputed leader of the club was the CEO of the bank, Damien Artemis, and Roland had an appointment with him this morning. The executive elevator arrived at the top of the bank's downtown office building, where everything was lavishly decorated with dark wood paneling, gold filigree, and antique furniture. Even the carpets were rich, with pile so deep, Roland couldn't hear his own footsteps. At the end of a hallway hung with modern art, he arrived at Artemis's corner office that provided a spectacular view of the city.

The banker stood to shake hands, a small smirk on his face. "You're FBI? You look younger than I expected." He chuckled as he settled back in his chair.

Roland chose to get down to business so he wouldn't have to defend his youthful appearance. He sat down and tossed a picture of the necklace on the desk. "Ever seen this piece?"

Artemis glanced at it and nodded. "It's been in the news . . . Got stolen from the museum. Why are you asking me about it?"

"I know you and your colleagues at the bank like to collect jewelry. President Baxter is even rumored to have some 'missing' pieces. So I want to warn you about this one —the French government wants it back." He handed Artemis a picture of the young thief. "Another thing we know is that the theft was done by this person."

Artemis glanced at the picture. "You're telling me that a teenager stole the necklace?" He grinned widely. "Guess that explains why the FBI sent another teenager to find her. What is this, a Hardy Boys mystery?"

"This is serious, Mr. Artemis."

"Good for you, son. But I haven't seen this necklace or this girl, so I can't help you." He picked up the thief's picture. "I'll keep this photo, if you don't mind, and give it to my security people. They'll want to know if she's armed and dangerous."

Roland wanted to laugh. The thief hadn't even let her bodyguards use guns. "No, sir. We do not believe she is armed."

Artemis set the picture aside. "Good to know. Now, are we done?" He stood from his desk, clearly indicating that the answer was "Yes."

Roland stood too, an amused smile on his face. "Thanks for your help."

He never expected to have an honest conversation with Artemis. If the banker had heard from the jewel thief or from Frank the Fence, he wouldn't admit it. But he'd been warned and would think twice before buying the necklace. Roland turned and left the office.

As he exited the bank building, he got a call from his partner. Yale was on a different case now, so it was annoying to have him call like a hovering parent. "What?"

"Boss wants me to check in with you, see if you need anything. How's it going, *kid*?"

Roland ignored the dig. "It's going well. I've figured out how they stole the necklace, and I have a lead on the thief. Yesterday I talked to Frank the Fence, who seems to be involved."

"Yeah," Yale rumbled. "Frank's involved in everything. I've got enough on that guy to bust him six ways to Sunday."

"Oh, so why don't you?"

"Are you kidding? Frank's immune. Sure, he fences goods from all over the state, but I let that go because he helps me when I need it. Informants are good to have, so we don't bust them on the little stuff."

"The French necklace isn't 'little stuff,' but he still didn't offer any help."

"Sorry. Frank gets to move as many hot goods as he wants. I don't bother him on theft, and you would be smart to do the same."

"Wow, Yale. Do you two take baths together?"

"Very funny, wise guy. That would probably be the way you'd get to know someone. But me and Frank, we like to have burgers and beer together. He was at my place last weekend for a barbecue."

"Seriously!" Roland couldn't believe this. "You're friends with Frank the Fence?"

"I'm telling you, he's a good guy. Sometimes you got to work with the criminal element if you want to get things done. God, kid! Do I have to teach you everything? You clearly need my help with this case." Like a petty child who needed to have the last word, he hung up before Roland could respond.

Roland was stunned. Nobody told him that Frank the Fence could be cooperative. That they could share beers instead of trading threats. Life would be easier if he could question criminals at barbecues instead of in holding cells. If he worked the way Yale did, he *would* take that young thief to dinner. But for now, he would start by arresting her, and he needed to do that soon.

Perhaps it was time to visit her accomplice, Andy Burr. Andy would know all about Lisa the thief. Or was she Linda the thief? Maybe Lorie the thief? Definitely none of the above.

Elle returned to the mall's food court that afternoon, without Penny who was hiding at the motel, setting up her new laptop. Neil was by himself at their favorite table, eager to catch up with everything, so Elle told him about her visit to Frank.

By the time she finished the story, Neil's face had drained of all color. "You've got a lot of nerve, running away from an FBI agent. Weren't you worried about being caught?"

She shrugged. "I had the necklace in my backpack, so I figured it wasn't the best time to chat with a fed. And I'm good at disappearing. I went down an alley and climbed a drainpipe to an open window on the third floor. Folks in there were surprised to see me, but I told them I was hiding from an angry boyfriend, so they let me stay for a while." She grinned. "Easy."

Neil grunted. "So we have the FBI chasing us now? That can't be good."

"Don't worry."

"Oh, come on! This seems like a very good time to worry. Don't you ever do that?"

Elle laughed. "I always worry, but I love it. I've lived my whole life with the thrill of swindles that have dozens of ways to go wrong. And they *do* go wrong, nearly all the time. Sometimes you have to walk away. But before that happens, you do your best to salvage it, and pretty often you can. So don't give up, we'll figure something out."

Neil's eyes grew bigger than an anime cartoon princess. "Being hunted by the FBI isn't something you simply 'figure out.' It's trouble. I mean, it's really . . ." He stopped and looked past Elle, one eyebrow arched. "Andy's coming, and he's acting weird."

Elle turned to watch Andy approach. He was weaving through the mall, looking left and right as he went, ducking into shops then coming back out. He finally made it to their table, flopping onto a chair with a sheen of sweat on his brow.

Neil scooted closer to his friend. "What's going on, Andy?"

"We've got big trouble, folks. I just had an FBI agent visit me at home. A guy named Roland Watson."

Elle sat up straight. "Young guy?"

"Yeah, looks like a kid, but he's pure cop."

Elle huffed out a breath. "He was the one at the fence's place yesterday. Persistent fellow, that's for sure. What did he say?"

"For starters, he found me from when I set off the alarms on Saturday. He also had your picture, and he knew Penny and Neil's names. I didn't admit anything, I swear, but he already seems to have all the answers. Knows you hid under the display all night. Knows how Penny and I were the diversions. I'm telling you, this guy's trouble."

Neil dropped his head into his hands. "We're screwed."

"We're *not*," Elle snapped. "Get it together. All this does is complicate things, but we're not through yet. What did you tell him?"

"I tried to keep my cool when he told me all this stuff, but it kind of shook me up, and he probably noticed." He cleared his throat. "The FBI, Elle! This isn't a cheap trick at the mall anymore."

"This was never a cheap trick at the mall, Andy. I told you that from the start. But I'm still not worried. I've faced worse in L.A. At least FBI agents observe established rules. Vigilantes and criminals aren't as nice. One of them even killed my brother. So if all I have to worry about is some young FBI agent, I'm good with that." She grabbed Andy's backpack and started looking through it.

"Hey!" He tried to snatch it back from her, but she held it tight and kept searching. "What are you doing?"

Elle ignored his irritation. "Did Watson follow you?"

"I don't think so. I was careful when I came here. What should we do?"

"Well, first of all, come closer." She abandoned his backpack and moved to sit next to him. Her hands roamed across his back and down his sleeves, giving him a quick pat down. It was a little strange to be doing this, especially considering that the two of them didn't get along that well. But she had to know if he was being followed.

Andy squirmed when she reached into his pockets. "Stop that!"

"Sit still. I'm looking for tracking devices." Her search ended at his belt. Stuck on the inside, at the back of his pants, was a slim disk. She pulled it off and tossed it on the table.

Neil picked up the disk, turning it slowly. "Is this a tracking device?"

"Afraid so. Now the FBI knows Andy's here. Hang on." Elle took the disk and approached another table where two young men were having a snack. They looked to be about the same age and build as Andy, so she dropped the disk into one of their shopping bags.

When she returned to the table, Neil scowled. "You really think that will fool the FBI? The guy already knows where Andy lives."

"Yeah, but they don't know we meet at the mall. Andy's visit could simply be some retail therapy."

Andy groaned. "I don't know. We probably shouldn't meet here anymore. The place is already too hot for Penny. Now none of us can be here."

Elle sighed. "I suppose you're right. Guess we'll have to go into hiding for a few days. But that's OK—it'll give us time to make arrangements with one of the bankers. You and Neil should stay away from the mall and from each other. Penny and I will stay at the motel."

Neil got up from the table. "OK, this sucks. What do I do when the FBI guy knocks on my door?"

"Tell him you don't know anything about the theft. You had no idea Penny was doing anything shady, and anyway, you two broke up. You're not involved, so you get a free pass." She stood up. "If either of you hears from Agent Watson, let me know. OK?"

Neil laughed sadly. "I knew it would be trouble to fall for a girl like Penny." With a shake of his head, he wandered out of the food court.

Elle bought a cup of juice for Penny, then she drove back to the motel. When she got to the room, her friend was pacing back and forth, muttering and cursing, her black hair unkempt. "What's the matter? You're always glued to your laptop. Is something wrong?"

"This is what's wrong." Penny lifted her phone and pointed to it. "That guy is at it again."

Elle frowned. "Who?"

"You know who. Larry Smith, or whatever his name is. The guy who followed us from L.A. The guy who hacked my laptop. The guy who's now sending me messages." She looked down at her phone and read the screen. "'Sorry about taking your picture the other day, Penny. We need to talk.'" She glowered. "This isn't good. He even knows my name."

"Well, of course he knows your name. He visited your mom, and she probably blabbed everything about you. It was easy to get your phone number."

"Yeah, OK. But finding my laptop and hacking into it was impressive. The guy's no fool. He knows all sorts of things about me, but I can't find a single thing about him. Do you know how many people are named Larry Smith? Too many."

"So, you gonna answer him?"

"Yeah. Here's my answer." She spelled out a reply with dramatic stabs of her finger. "N-O." Then she powered down her phone.

"He's still after you, Penny, and apparently the FBI is after me. The agent who found me at Frank's visited Andy this morning, and he knows how we stole the necklace. Pretty good for a rookie. I'm sorry you couldn't find out anything about Smith, but can you locate an FBI agent named Roland Watson? In his early twenties, I'd guess."

"OK. But I can't use this new machine, because if I login to any of my accounts, Smith might find me. And I can't use my phone anymore either, so if you want me to investigate your FBI agent, we'll have to visit a computer store. Their demo machines are anonymous."

Elle nodded. "Let's do it tomorrow. I'm having dinner with my folks tonight. Want to come along?"

Penny shook her head. "They're your family. I'll stay here. Besides, they'll be upset if I sip juice and ignore their food. Go have fun."

"Oh, stop it! You obviously need to get out of here, so come on! Spend some time with normal people and relax for a while."

"How can I relax when things have gotten so gnarly?" Penny grimaced. "You've got the FBI on your tail, and I've got a hacker on mine. Maybe we should give up and go back to L.A."

Twenty-Three

Elle returned to her parents house for dinner, with Penny grudgingly in tow. To avoid the many people looking for them and possibly following them, they parked up the street at a random neighbor's house, then they sneaked into the back yard and climbed a few fences until they were behind Harry and Trish's home and could enter through the kitchen door. She needed to keep her parents safe from her shady activities.

Wendy and June were home from school, baking cookies with Trish. Elle knew that cookies weren't typical at the Burnside home, but her mother was rolling out her best hospitality now that she'd found her oldest daughter. Today's chocolate chip cookies had everyone in the family excited. Even Penny joined the enthusiastic baking party, though she had no intention of eating all that sugar.

At one point, Elle noticed her Father sitting in the living room, so she joined him, hopeful to learn more about her own history. "I have a question," she began tentatively. "When did you two get married?" What she really wanted to know was whether they were married when she was born, but that might be a touchy issue.

Harry gave a knowing smile as he answered the question. "As I mentioned, Trish's parents weren't my biggest fans, so we eloped. Went down to city hall and got married one day. Then we got in our car and headed south. We didn't have much money, but we were determined to have a honeymoon, one way or another. We drove around, trying to enjoy the journey, and it only took a few weeks before Trish was pregnant with you."

Rather than showing any pleasure over Elle's conception, Harry seemed downcast as he flopped back in the sofa. "I thought her parents would be happy that they were going to have a grandchild. But a few bad things happened while we were on our honeymoon trip. First, I lost my job, only one week in. They told me I could take the time off, then they changed their mind. Next, we got evicted from our apartment, since we couldn't afford the rent. So when Trish showed up at her parents door, homeless, pregnant, and married to a guy with no job, they hated me even more. They told her to choose between them and me. When she chose me, they cut her off."

Trish came into the living room and sat by her husband. "Talking about the good old days, when we had no home, no money, and no food?"

Wendy and June were in the doorway with Penny behind them, so they heard their mother's question. Wendy's eyes widened. "You didn't have food? How did you live?"

Her mother pulled her into a hug. "It wasn't easy. We ate at soup kitchens. When I got visibly pregnant with Elle, they usually gave me extra food. Somehow, we made it work."

Now it was June's turn to be surprised. "You ate soup all the time?"

"No, dear." Her mother pulled her close. "They just call it a soup kitchen. But we ate regular meals." June seemed relieved at that.

Wendy furrowed her brow. "So where was Elle born if you had no home? Was she born in a soup kitchen?"

Harry laughed. "No, Elle was born in a hospital, like you two. Mom and I were living in our car back then, and we had to move it every day to avoid getting a ticket. One morning, as we were driving away, her water broke."

Wendy's mouth fell open, but June didn't seem to understand, so Harry explained. "That means she was about to have a baby. We went to the hospital, and that's where Elle was born."

Wendy propped her fists on her hips. "Then how did you lose her?"

Trish sighed. "We couldn't afford the hospital costs, so someone came to discuss our money situation while I was still in labor. They pointed out that we were too poor to raise our child properly. She'd be cold and hungry, which is never a good thing. They suggested that we consider putting her up for adoption. We weren't happy about it, but we knew they were right, so we agreed to let Elle be adopted by a different family." She paused for a few seconds, then wiped a tear from her eye. "It was the hardest thing I ever did."

Silence descended on the room for a few seconds. Finally, Trish waved her hands to dispel the sour mood. "No more sadness. Elle is back with us, and I think the cookies are ready!" She got up and went to the kitchen, followed by Wendy and June.

While they were in there, the burner phone with Frank's name started to ring. Elle tried her best to cover the excitement of the call, but nothing could hide the importance of this next conversation. It could be Frank, calling to arrange a deal. Or it could be someone Frank contacted, assuming he spread the word. She and Penny shared a secret smile.

Elle apologized to her father and quickly stepped outside. After a moment to calm herself, she answered. "Yes?" She needed to keep it short and businesslike.

An unfamiliar voice spoke, oozing authority. "A client of mine is interested in some jewelry you claim to have."

Elle gave a silent fist pump and danced in place. Frank had done exactly what she'd wanted: he'd told others about the necklace. Now they were calling. With any luck, this would be one of the Tera bankers. "And who might your client be?"

"My client's identity is irrelevant. You'll be dealing with me."

Not good. She was afraid people would use intermediaries. This man needed to be corrected. "Let me make one thing clear. Your client's identity is not irrelevant. It's essential. I don't deal anonymously, because I care about this piece. Whoever buys it has to be someone who appreciates it as a work of art and will keep it whole. I don't mind dealing with you to set things up, but come the day of the sale, I insist on meeting with the person who's buying it."

"I'm not sure my client will agree."

"In that case, let me put it in terms your client can understand. If this sale is done anonymously through you, then the price is *fifty* million dollars. If your client shows up, however, and can convince me that it will be kept whole, the price is only five million. See? It's simple. If your client is willing to pay forty-five million dollars to avoid meeting me, then I can live with that."

"Hmm." The man paused for a few seconds. "I'll have to get back to you about this." He ended the call.

Elle was pleased to have her first nibble, and hoped it was someone from the bank. If not, she would ignore the request and keep waiting. Sooner or later, someone from Tera would call, especially now that Frank seemed to be getting the word out.

Unfortunately, the Tera bankers were having their jewelry club meeting in only two days. They might not be ready to buy the necklace before this month's meeting, but they had to know that stolen property wouldn't stick around for long. If they wanted Napoleon's necklace, they couldn't dawdle.

Elle returned to the living room as her mother arrived with a plate of cookies. Penny was sipping juice, off in the corner, so Elle went over there to give her the "Frank" phone. "We're getting calls, but it's awkward with my folks around. You better hang onto this for now."

Turning to her family, Elle picked up a cookie and took a bite, happier with a home-cooked treat than she might have imagined. Her sisters were already on their second cookie, no longer able to savor each bite as they stuffed their mouths. "Sorry about that call. Stuff from back home."

"Of course." Her mother took another bite of cookie and regarded her family with a proud look. But her father frowned, not making eye contact even once. She could sense the tension in his body but decided not to say anything.

When Elle got up to leave the room, Harry cornered her in the hallway. "I hate to be a snoop, but I overheard some of your phone conversation, and I'm confused. Are you really dealing in jewels worth millions of dollars?"

Elle blushed, hoping that her father hadn't heard too much. But she couldn't completely lie to him. "I am, Dad. I feel really bad mixing that up with my visit here. Can you forgive me?" Penny was heading their way, but Elle shook her head, sending her friend back to the living room. Elle and her father needed to discuss this privately.

Harry shrugged. "I don't care about your personal business. I'm just surprised with how well you seem to be doing. God!" His eyes lit up. "You show up in a brand new car, think nothing of staying at a motel, and you're moving millions of dollars for your work." His mouth fell open. "You're clearly better off than I ever was. Are you a millionaire? A one percenter?"

"Neither. Penny and I work together, sometimes with large amounts of money. But we don't keep much of it."

Harry blinked a few times, seemingly unsatisfied with that answer but unsure how to proceed. "I guess I'm not used to this whole thing yet, where a complete stranger, with a life of her own, is suddenly part of my family. It's got me kind of confused."

Elle threw her arms around her father and gave him a hug. "I know I'm still a stranger. And there's so much I want to tell you and Mom. Can it wait a few more days, though? I promise I'll tell you everything. But until then, it's best if you don't ask too many questions about my work."

"Don't ask too many questions? What does that mean?"

"Well, unfortunately, that's one of the questions you can't ask. When this business is done in a few days, I'll explain it all."

Her father paused for a few seconds. "Can I ask you one thing? Is it legal? You were talking about million-dollar jewelry. Is this related to the theft at the museum?"

Elle stared at her father with tight lips. He *had* heard the conversation, and that raised all sorts of questions. This probably wasn't the best time to tell him that she'd robbed the museum. Of course, he might have heard enough to figure it out for himself, so it wouldn't be that much of a surprise. More like a disappointment. Still, she had to tell him something.

"It *may* be." She blushed, unsure how this answer would be received.

Harry's mouth dropped open. "Oh damn! Are you in trouble? Are the police after you? This sounds dangerous."

"I've been doing dangerous things my whole life, Dad. Foster homes aren't the most normal places to grow up, and I've survived by going undercover to arrange deals. This deal's important because it will save your home and make sure the museum gets the necklace back. I promise I won't involve you in anything illegal, but you have to keep it secret and let me and Penny do our job."

Harry looked hard, clearly trying to understand his daughter. "Aren't you a little young to be doing undercover work?" They faced each other for a few seconds, but Elle had no answers, so she kept quiet as a chill air enveloped them.

Harry suddenly snapped to attention, his head held high. "OK then, is there anything I can do to help?"

Wendy picked this time to make an appearance. "Me too! I want to help you."

Elle stepped back to regard her new family. They sincerely wanted to help her, even though they had no idea what they were asking. "Listen, you two. Neither of you wants to help me. It's too much trouble, and I don't want to expose anyone else in this."

Wendy pouted. "You're no fun. First I get a new sister who's cool. Then, I find out she's dealing with a museum robbery, which is *way* cool. But she won't even let me help her or anything, which sucks."

"Wendy! You can't tell anyone about this."

"Duh! I'm not stupid. And I know how to trick people. I've been stealing extra milk for June all year."

Harry's eyes shot wide open. "You've been *what*?"

"Oh, come on, Dad, I'm twelve years old and I know stuff, like the fact that you guys don't have a lot of money. But June misses the chocolate milk she used to drink last year, so when I buy lunch, I slip one into my backpack. Nobody sees me, and I pay for the rest of my lunch, so I've been able to get away with it."

Harry groaned. "We are going to have a little discussion about this, young lady." He turned to Elle. "At least I can't blame you for being a bad influence. I see it runs in the family." He wrapped his arm around Wendy, and together, they faced Elle. "Are you sure we can't help?"

Elle thought for a few seconds. She did have a task that needed to be done by innocent people who nobody else knew about. Chip and Quincy were no good for that since they'd been seen with her at Frank's place. But Harry and Wendy were unknowns, willing to help, and had a necessary skill. Maybe it was time to let them in on the caper.

Elle blew out a long breath. "There *is* something you can do . . . I see you have a drone." She turned to her sister. "And I hear you're a good pilot. I could use some drone flying."

Harry grunted. "The last time we flew it, a propeller broke. I need to go to the hobby shop and get some parts."

"Well, I have a better idea. Buy a new drone. A really good one that's reliable." Elle reached into her backpack and grabbed her wallet. Then she pulled out a fistful of cash and pushed it into her father's hand.

"Wow," He sputtered, then stared with large eyes at the five hundred-dollar bills he was holding.

Elle leaned closer to her sister. "Make sure he buys the very best—don't cheap out. If you need more money, let me know."

Wendy's jaw dropped as she examined the big bills, but she recovered quickly. "If you want best, it's going to cost more. That much will get you a four-propeller drone, but I always wanted one with six propellers. They're faster, and I've heard they can handle minor collisions better."

Elle peeled off a few more bills. "Will that do?" Wendy nodded with a little smile.

Harry was still having trouble forming words. "I . . . I mean . . ." It took him a few seconds before he could go on. "Why do you have so much cash? You're not dealing drugs, are you?"

"No, Dad. Definitely not." Elle didn't know what else to say. She couldn't explain that con artists prefer cash, because she couldn't admit to being a con artist. At a loss, she stood there, rocking back and forth.

Harry finally showed mercy and broke the ice. "OK, why do you need a drone?"

She was much more comfortable discussing this question. "It's going to make a very important delivery in a few days, so make sure it can carry a few pounds. Don't get too attached, though, because it'll be making a one-way trip. You won't be able to keep it. Also, I want both of you to wear gloves when you touch the drone. The work I'm doing to return the necklace is secret, so you have to stay hidden too. No fingerprints on it *anywhere*. Got it?"

Harry darkened. "Fingerprints? You said this was legal."

Elle sighed. "It is, but the drone will raise questions, and I'd rather you not be forced to answer them. Just play it safe, please." Her father nodded, then he stuffed the money in his pocket.

Elle turned to her sister. "And you . . ." She handed Wendy a twenty-dollar bill. "Stop stealing milk for a while. The last thing I need is for you to get nicked on petty stuff when you're needed for something important. OK?"

"Definitely!" Wendy gave Elle a kiss on the cheek then scampered off, practically dancing with delight.

Harry went back to the kitchen, but Elle followed Wendy to her room. She crooked a finger at her sister. "I need a special favor from you. Is there somewhere around the house where I can hide something small? I don't want June or Mom and Dad to find it."

Wendy thought for a second. "I keep my diary in the bottom of a shoe box in the corner of the closet. Nobody messes with that."

"Good." Elle pulled out a brown leather pouch from her backpack. "Put this in there. It's incredibly important, so don't lose it. And don't play with it."

"What is it?"

Elle grinned. "What do you think this is?"

"Uh, something to do with the necklace that was stolen from the museum?"

Elle was pleased with her sister's savvy. But she knew she had to reveal the necklace, because if she didn't, Wendy would look at it anyway. By showing her now, it would keep Wendy satisfied.

Elle tilted her head toward the bathroom, and the two of them ducked inside. With the door closed and locked, she held a finger to her lips to make sure Wendy stayed quiet.

Her sister was about to hold a priceless necklace in her hands, probably more valuable than anything she'd ever touch again. Why shouldn't she get the full experience? For the rest of her life, she'd remember the time she held

Napoleon's dazzling jewels. Elle pulled out two sets of cloth gloves and tossed one to her sister. Putting them on, she pulled the necklace from the pouch and held it out.

Wendy's mouth fell open, but she managed to control her excited response. "Oh my God!" she whispered loudly. "You found it!"

Elle spoke quietly in an attempt to keep her sister calm. "Yes, I found it, but I can't return it for another two days, so I need to hide it until then. Do *not* mention this to anyone, even Dad. And do *not* take it out of the pouch, even to look. This is your only chance to see it, then we have to hide it. Here . . ." She thrust the necklace into Wendy's hands.

Wendy held the necklace close to her chest and looked in the mirror. "It's really pretty." With an excited little hop, she turned and held it out to her new sister. "Put it on. I want to see how it looks on you."

Wendy's gesture came as a delightful surprise, a truly sisterly offer that Elle hadn't felt in a long time, since her foster sister Dee left town. And Wendy was a real sister, a concept that was still somewhat alien.

Was this the sort of thing that family members did, proudly sharing in their relatives' achievements? If so, she certainly wanted these people to be her family from now on. They even offered to help her, without fully understanding what they were doing. She wiped a tear from her eye before it could run down her cheek.

The necklace's clasp was difficult to work, especially when wearing gloves, but she got it open and put it on. When she turned to look at herself, she couldn't believe the image in the mirror. There she was, in torn jeans and a ratty T-shirt, perhaps the worst ensemble ever worn with Napoleon's emerald necklace. It looked like someone had made a joke and drawn the necklace over a picture of her.

Elle never expected to wear Napoleon's necklace. Of course, she never expected to find such a wonderful family, either. But there she was, the girl who could do any number of tricky things, staring at herself with total disbelief. How could her life get any more amazing?

Twenty-Four

After hiding the necklace in Wendy's closet, Elle went down to the living room. Now that she wasn't carrying the jewels, she felt lighter and freer, convinced that she could pull this swindle even with an FBI agent breathing down her neck.

Penny was alone in the living room, so Elle pointed to the back door, and the two of them slipped out to the small fenced-in backyard. At the far end, they perched on a pile of rocks.

Penny pulled out the "Frank" phone and waved it in the air. "You're not going to believe this, but we got another call while you were talking to your dad. There are six bankers in the Tera jewelry club, but we only checked-out four of them. The call I got was from someone we missed, Ivan Jackson. Probably for the best though, because he was just fishing. He asked if we really had it, but he didn't bother to ask the price. Just said 'OK' then he was gone."

"You never know. He could still be our mark. The call that came before was from someone who wouldn't tell me the buyer's name. It might be a Tera banker, too."

The suddenly-popular "Frank" phone rang once again, eliciting big eyes and shared smiles. Frank had done well, and the jewelry club whales were sniffing the bait.

Penny answered quickly and held the phone away from her ear to let Elle listen. "Yes?"

The voice was coarse and full of bluster. "I'm callin' about the French goods. Let me talk to the boss."

Penny gave Elle a thumbs-up. "Your name, please?"

"I'm Crew, Marshall Crew." Neil's guy, the banker who disliked his fiancée but still hired a thief to get her something to wear at their wedding. Penny and Elle nodded to each other.

"I can help you, Mr. Crew."

"Screw that! Put the boss on the phone. I ain't got time to waste."

Penny scowled, but continued to speak calmly. "I'll handle the arrangements for now, then the man with the goods will call you back to finalize things."

"What kind of an operation are you running here? I'm not talking to some chick about this. Get him on the line now, or the deal's off."

Penny's grip on the phone tightened and she gave it a quivering shake. "In that case, the deal *is* off. Thanks for calling, Mr. Crew." She disconnected the call, then picked up a rock and pretended to smash the phone with it. "That miserable little dirtbag."

Elle took the phone away. "Easy, girl. We'll let Neil deal with this—he's the one who investigated the guy. Imagine stealing five million dollars from the jerk. Wouldn't that be nice?"

"I suppose . . ." The phone rang again, startling them once more. Frank must have just notified the bankers, because they were falling over themselves for the jewels.

Elle answered this time, holding the phone so Penny could hear. "Yes?"

"I understand that you have something rare for sale. Frank Tucker said I should call you."

Aha, another potential lead. "Who are you?"

"I . . ." The man hesitated, clearly uncomfortable giving out his name. Finally, he acquiesced. "The name is Dearborn."

Elle and Penny beamed with excitement. Orson Dearborn was the one Penny had investigated, the man in charge of the bank branches.

Penny crooked her finger at Elle, demanding the phone. Dearborn was her banker, and this conversation belonged to her.

Elle completed her conversation. "One moment, please." She gave the phone to Penny, but they both continued to listen.

"Hello, Mr. Dearborn." Penny was smooth and professional. "I understand you're a fan of emeralds and diamonds."

"I'll take anything that sparkles, my dear. You really have Napoleon's necklace?"

"It could be yours." She knew better than to state openly that she had stolen goods.

"How much?"

"Five million dollars."

"Oh." They could hear him deflate. "Too much. I'll give you *one* million."

Penny grunted. "You can give me one million, Mr. Dearborn, but that won't get you what you want. The price is five."

Dearborn grumbled. "You call that negotiating? We're supposed to bargain here. I'll go up to two million."

"OK, I'll counter with, hmm, let's see . . . five million." This was the amount they needed to help the bank's victims. She wouldn't take less.

"That's not how the game is played."

"That's how I do it. But since you want to play, fine. The price is twenty million dollars. Your turn."

"Yeah, yeah. I get it. The price is five." Dearborn grumbled. "Too rich for me. Never mind." He ended the call.

Penny sighed. "Count him out." She turned to Elle. "Did I do something wrong?"

"No, that was exactly right. Firm and friendly. Now he'll think about it, and he may decide to come around. We've got lots of leads lining up already. It's still a horse race to know who will be the one."

As if by magic, the phone rang again. With the jewelry club meeting in two days, the bankers were falling all over themselves.

Elle took the call. "Yes?"

"We spoke earlier about buying that item you have." The mystery buyer was back, and Elle could hear his hunger. They may not have Dearborn, Crew, or Jackson but someone else was definitely interested. With any luck, it would be another banker.

"So has your client decided to reveal his name?"

"His name is Artemis."

Bingo! Not only did Elle have a banker, she had Damien Artemis, the man *she'd* investigated. If she could get him to commit, she'd be the one doing the swindle. This was super-good news.

Elle cleared her throat so she wouldn't come across as an overexcited teenager. Which she was. "Good." She grumbled the word, adding weight. "Mr. Artemis is a sensible man. Can he get the money by Friday?"

"Yes, he'd like to do this Friday, in the morning or early afternoon."

"That's fine. Tell him to bring the cash to the Bridgeport Mall, Friday at one. You'll see a young woman with a white carnation in her lapel outside the Chinese restaurant. Got it?"

"You need to know that he's coming with two other people. One will be a jeweler who can authenticate the goods. The other will be a bodyguard. Is this acceptable?"

"Yes, that's fine. Thank you for setting this up." She put her phone away.

"We did it, Penny!" Elle jumped from the rocks and did a little dance to celebrate, hugely relieved with the progress. "Artemis is the mark."

Penny laid back on the stones, smiling at her friend. "OK, you win. And you're right about the hunger. Artemis called back quickly. None of the others showed that much enthusiasm. Interestingly, the only one who didn't call was Andy's mark, Baxter."

"Yeah, he really had his hopes on that guy. But face it, Artemis is the CEO, the top dog. It makes sense that he'd reach for the prize first. I've got to tell the others about this."

While Elle sent messages to Andy and Neil, Penny stared into the dark, her mouth tight. "I'm worried about doing this at the mall. Smith keeps getting closer to me and that FBI guy knows too much. He even knows Andy hangs at the food court. I think we need to move the necklace around on the day of the deal."

Elle nodded. "A shell game?"

"Yeah. Shuffle it from one of us to the other, passing it off discretely. We can even get Chip and Quincy to be part of it. The FBI guy knows them, so if we get them moving around without the necklace, it will add to the confusion. If we work it right, you won't have it on you until it's time to sell it."

"Good idea. Let's go visit them and ask for their help."

They climbed through a few more back yards on their way to Chip and Quincy's house, then they knocked on the kitchen door.

Chip answered and invited them in, pulling Elle aside. "Quincy's a little mad about how things went at the fence's place. I'm just sorry we abandoned you there. Everything was going so wrong, we didn't know what else to do."

"It's OK," Elle patted his arm. "You did the right thing by leaving when you could. Let me talk to him."

"Quincy," Chip called out as they headed to the living room. "The international jewel thieves are here."

Quincy raised his head, a guarded look on his face. "You back for more?"

Chip sat down next to Quincy, then Elle and Penny took seats facing them. "We do want more. Much easier this time, I promise, and it will be the last thing we ask of you." Elle paused to take an excited breath, then went on. "The deal is happening on Friday, and we need you then."

Quincy groaned. "You know we'll help—we agreed to that. But this time, can we avoid having people point guns at us? You took us to the seediest part of the city, had thugs threaten to shoot us, then left us standing on the street with an FBI agent who wanted to arrest you. I'm sorry things messed up so badly, but you really should have planned this better."

Elle reached across the table and patted his knee. "Actually, the visit to Frank went perfectly. You two did a great job."

"You call that perfect?" Quincy frowned. "You angered the fence *and* the FBI. What's perfect about everyone being mad at you?"

"At least they know we have the necklace. Look, guys. I'm sorry it got weird, but we're running a scam here, so things aren't always as they seem. The good news is that it ends Friday at the Bridgeport mall. Can you spare a few hours? I promise there'll be no guns, and it's a nice neighborhood."

Chip smirked. "What's the plan?"

"Since that FBI guy knows you, you're going to be decoys, walking around to distract him."

"And what do we tell him when he stops us?"

"He can't arrest you for being at a mall . . . Nothing wrong with that. And you can tell him anything because you won't know what's going on. See? No guns and a safe place to take a stroll."

Chip relaxed his shoulders. "OK, we can do that."

"You might also stand guard at one point when I do the deal, a simple matter of looking tough, as you've done before. Then, when you're done walking the mall, we'll need you to move cash."

Chip's shoulders tensed back up. "Move cash? That doesn't sound too innocent. The FBI will certainly stop us if we do that."

Elle shook her head. "You're just moving it from one back room to another, so you'll be hidden from any mall activity. The FBI won't see you. But I'm warning you, it'll be heavy."

The men looked at each other and exchanged little nods. Then Quincy grinned and flexed his arms. "You think we can't pick up some cash? Please!"

Elle smiled. "Do you know how much five million dollars weighs, assuming it's all in hundred-dollar bills?"

Quincy blinked a few times. "You're going to get five million dollars? Damn, you ladies are intense. But don't worry, we can lift it."

"Yes, I suppose you can. But for your information, it weighs about a hundred pounds. It'll be even heavier if they use fifties."

Chip straightened up. "Really? Why don't you ask them for thousand-dollar bills?"

"Because," Penny interjected. "There aren't any. The government stopped printing large bills years ago. There used to be $1,000 bills, $5,000 bills, even a $100,000 bill at one point. But when they realized those big bills were being used to fund illegal activities, they pulled them. Now folks like us have to use hundred-dollar bills or risk exposure with electronic fund transfers."

"I see. So you need us to be at the mall and move your money."

"Yes, please. And one more request." Elle clasped her hands in a gesture of supplication. "After you move the money, we're going to need help packaging it and taking it for delivery. This will be in a back room again, so no FBI oversight. You'll get your share of the money then, and we'll be done."

Chip shrugged. "Sure, why not? But I have a question. What if we see the FBI agent before Friday? As you said, he knows who we are, and he might find us sooner."

Elle shrugged. "You can tell him anything, but please try to keep Harry and Trish out of it. They still don't know what we're doing, and I don't want any trouble for them. Other than that, you can tell Agent Watson anything, because he seems to know it already. You can even tell him that it's happening at the mall on Friday. I've a feeling he knows that, too."

"Aren't you worried? What if you get caught?"

"Not a problem. Agent Watson already caught me, but I'm still here. Don't worry about him."

"How ballsy is that?" Quincy chuckled. "You aren't even afraid of the FBI."

"Hey, it's part of the job. Besides, I've dealt with much sketchier people. Three years ago, I had to sneak onto a smuggler's yacht and steal some papers. He had a dozen armed guards, itching to try out their weapons. Compared with them, the FBI is downright friendly." Elle stood up. "Anyway, meet us at the Bridgeport Mall at ten on Friday, outside of the Move It Out shipping store. Be prepared to be around until mid-afternoon. I know that's a lot of time, but I need to make sure everything's safe before I act, which could take a while."

There was going to be a big sale at the mall Friday.

Twenty-Five

Roland had dinner with his parents again, excited to tell them how he'd figured out the case. After hearing everything, his mother gave him a hug.

"This is wonderful, Roland. You've solved your first case. The bureau will be impressed."

"Yeah," his father agreed a little less enthusiastically. "But she got away from you. When are you going to bust her?"

"I know she hangs out at the mall. I'm going there tomorrow to arrest her."

His father stared hard. "Think so, huh? She could be on an airplane by now, heading somewhere with no extradition laws. She knows you're on to her, she's gonna run."

"I've been watching the phone number they gave Frank Tucker. It's still in town and has been getting calls from bankers at Tera. These kids aren't running . . . They'll be at the mall."

His father's frown softened just slightly. "Well, I still think it's reckless. You claim she's a con artist, so maybe she's tricking you."

Roland stifled a laugh. "She probably is—everything she does is slightly off from what I'd expect. There's got to be a plan here. She's not stupid." He shook his head. "And she's completely fearless. She didn't even flinch when Tucker's thugs had guns drawn on her, and she's certainly not afraid of me."

Roland's mother patted his hand. "You're too nice. Maybe you should take a few tips from your partner. He's got a tough hide."

"Or . . ." His father grinned. "Since she likes to play tricks, maybe you should too. For example, you could offer to help her out, which gives you an excuse to keep a closer eye on her. Sometimes you have to work the criminal element."

The idea of working with a criminal made Roland smirk. "Speaking of that, did you know that Yale invites Frank Tucker to his barbecues?"

Roland's dad flinched. "Your partner is friends with Frank the Fence? Huh. I would never do that."

"Really?" Roland tapped the dinner table. "Never had a crook sit here for drinks or a meal?"

His father shrugged. "I knew some guys who did some things, if you know what I mean. But none of them were international jewel thieves."

"Oh? So they can do other crimes, but they can't steal jewels? Where do you draw the line, Dad?" Roland took a deep breath as he prepared to admit his own conflicting issues with the case. "And speaking of fuzzy lines, you're going to hate this. That young thief . . . I like her."

"So?"

"No, Dad. I *like* her. She's clever, and I'm fascinated by everything she does. But worse than that, I think she's cute." Roland gritted his teeth to prepare for his parents' response.

His mother smiled at this but his father scowled. "You're falling for a thief? A *teenage* thief? That's bad news."

"I'm not in love, and I'm sure she's underage. But for some miserable reason, I can't stop thinking about her, and not because she stole a necklace. I'm totally attracted to her both because she's pretty, and also because she's clever. I . . .

I'm supposed to arrest her, but I'd really rather take her to lunch." He blew out a loud sigh.

Roland's mother gave his hand a light pat. "It's too bad she's a thief, but it's nice to finally hear you talking about a woman this way. I hope it doesn't stop you from doing your job."

"Don't worry. I'm definitely bringing her in tomorrow."

Roland's father gave a nod of finality, then he changed the subject. "Hey, you know what I'm doing tomorrow? I'm gonna use this new toy I got, the tiniest bug you've ever seen."

Roland's mother sighed, but said no more. Father and son went to a partitioned section of the garage that doubled as an office. They looked at the new micro bug, then they sat down with a few beers.

"Still having money troubles, Dad?"

His father waved it away. "The usual. Creeps hire me, then they don't pay."

"You have to handle these cases better."

The older man took a swig of beer. "Don't worry, Roland. This is a temporary setback. I'll be fine, but will you? Getting a crush on the thief you're chasing isn't good for your career."

"I know I'm being stupid, but I can't stop thinking about her. I wish I knew more."

"Maybe you should talk to the guys who played her bodyguards. They'd know more."

Roland nodded. "I was planning to see them *after* I arrested her. Didn't want to tip her off." Roland squinted, then got to his feet. "But maybe you're right. I should visit them now."

His father gave him a thumbs-up. "Go have fun."

Roland was grateful for parents who understood the thrill of detective work. He drove to visit Chip and Quincy. Even though it was dark out, he put on shades when he arrived. He liked the effect it gave.

Chip opened the door and froze as he realized who it was. "Uh, damn," he hesitated. "How did you find us?"

"Oh, come on, Chip! How many men's department floor managers do you think the Herbert Walker department store has?" Roland pushed his way into the house. "Quincy around? The three of us need to talk." He air-quoted the word, "talk" so Chip would know that it could go way beyond that.

Soon they were gathered in the living room, where Quincy grumbled at the young FBI man. "If you're looking for Elle, she's not here."

"Her name is, 'L'? A letter of the alphabet? I know she likes to use fake names that start with that letter, but I never imagined she used the letter as her name."

"Uh, no. I believe her name is Elle, as in E-L-L-E."

"Of course!" Roland slapped his knee. "She's a slippery one, but right now I want to talk about you two." He leaned closer. "Why'd she pick you guys to be her fake bodyguards?"

Chip smiled uneasily, so Quincy took up the question. "Because we're big, strong men, and she's a small woman. She heard that the fence guy has serious muscle, and that he's connected to lots of security people in town, so she couldn't trust real bodyguards."

"What?" Roland frowned. "Let me get this straight. She doesn't trust professional bodyguards, so she picks two random men to fake it, gives them toy guns, and brings them to a heavily armed underworld figure. How did she convince you to do that?"

"Hey! She was right about one thing. If we'd had real guns, it could have gotten messier than it already was. This way, the only thing that got damaged was our pride, and I honestly don't care what Frank the Fence thinks of me."

Roland stared for a second, amazed at Elle's ability to trick people. With a quiet chuckle, he continued his questioning. "How did she swap the necklace? Frank obviously thought he had the real one. I saw his face when he looked at it in his drawer—the guy was practically in shock. She must have shown him the real one, then switched it."

Quincy grunted. "I don't know what went on, and I was in the room when it happened. We're minor characters in her little game. We don't even know how to find her."

"Oh, don't worry. I'll find her. But I still don't see the connection. Is she related to you two?"

"Related?" Chip rolled his eyes as if it was the stupidest question he'd heard all day. "Hardly. We only met her last week for the first time."

"How did that happen?"

"She knocked on our door and offered to help us with our mortgage."

Roland narrowed his eyes. "What does your mortgage have to do with stolen jewels?"

Chip looked to Quincy for an explanation, but neither had one. "We've been trying to figure that out ourselves. But if the little lady wants to help us with our money problems, then we're more than willing to pretend to be bodyguards. It's the least we can do. She's trying to help all the people who got bad mortgages."

"All? How many people are you talking about?"

Quincy was the one who had made the list, so he explained. "Nearly two hundred, as far as we can tell. It seems like they're tricking homeowners to get them out so they can redevelop these poorer neighborhoods. A few dozen on the list have already gotten eviction notices."

"Can I see that list?"

"Sure." He wandered off and returned with his laptop, pointing out the names.

Roland studied it for a minute, impressed with the large number of names. Then he handed the laptop back. "She wants to help all these people?"

Quincy nodded. "She says she does. Want me to send this list to you?"

"No, that's fine. I just needed to understand why you're helping her. What else has she asked you to do?"

Both men fidgeted for a few seconds, so Roland pushed a little harder. "Don't lie to me, fellas. I know she has something planned, and you *do not* want to be accessories to this crime. When and where?"

"OK," Quincy paused. "The Bridgeport mall on Friday."

"And?"

"Hey, that's all we know. She doesn't tell us much. She asked us to be there at ten in the morning. Beyond that, we're clueless."

Roland eyed them carefully, fairly certain they weren't lying. "OK, thanks. I think I've got everything I need."

He got up to leave, unable to shake a feeling of surprise. Once again, the young thief was acting in a most unexpected manner. At least he had her name. Elle. As he considered all her fake names and now her real one, Roland began to form a curious theory about the thief named Elle.

Twenty-Six

Elle awoke Thursday morning to Penny's pacing around the motel room. She sat up and smiled at her frustrated friend. "You really are helpless without a computer."

Penny flopped down in a chair. "I'm bored. Can't use my computer and can't use my phone. Gaa! I don't even know if I'm safe here." Her eyes darted around the room. "I feel like Larry Smith is watching me."

Elle gave her friend a hug. "Let's get you out of here. Besides, we need to find out more about Roland Watson, and you said you could do it on a tech store's demo computer. There's one at the mall, and I wouldn't mind going there to check the shops where the deal's happening tomorrow. If we steer clear of the food court, we'll be OK."

"I might not be able to go to the food court, but *you* can, and maybe you can get some juice for me." Penny blew out a burst of air. "I know I shouldn't whine, but you get to have fun tomorrow swindling Artemis."

Elle rested her hands on her hips. "Look, Penny. Just because you didn't steal the necklace doesn't mean you aren't essential here. We'd never be able to pull this off without you."

"I suppose," Penny sighed.

Elle understood that her friend hungered to do more and learn as much as possible. A similar situation existed between Andy and Neil, with Neil being the one who strived to be as good as his teacher. In both cases, the student seemed to feel inadequate but was actually very important. Penny had her hacking skills, and Neil was an accomplished forger. The four of them were a good team.

Elle and Penny drove to the mall. The first stop was the computer store, where Penny wandered over to one of the display machines and started working.

At one point, a salesman approached her. "Can I help you?"

"Oh, don't mind me." Penny batted her eyelashes, then pointed to the machine. "This model has a hyper-threaded processor, but only one floating point unit. Do you know who makes the mother board?"

"Uh," the salesman sputtered for a few seconds, then attempted a reply. "It's definitely one of our better machines." Elle silently laughed at her friend's ability to bamboozle even a tech nerd.

Penny tapped the machine. "Do you mind if I run some tests? It'll only take a few minutes."

"Sure." The salesman fidgeted nervously while slowly backing away.

Elle wrapped an arm around her friend. "I think you scared him."

"That was the idea." Penny worked the machine for a while. "Aha, here he is. Roland Watson, FBI. Local kid—parents still live around here. Looks like he moved into his own place recently. Hmm . . ." She clicked some more and stared for a few seconds, then she slapped the table. "Well, look at this!" She pointed to the screen.

Elle studied it for a few seconds, then she gasped, a huge smile on her face. "My oh my, agent Watson." She and Penny gave each other a high-five. "See, Penny? You're an essential member of this team . . . You just solved our FBI problem. Come on, let's get you some juice, then we can celebrate. And if this Smith guy is looking for you, I want to know more. Let's both go to the food court, but I'll go first and scout it out."

Penny held back when they got close, and Elle went in. Most of the tables were full today, everyone busy eating. There was even someone in the corner where Neil and Andy liked to sit, but he had a drink and a sandwich in front of him, so he didn't seem like trouble. Still, she kept a careful eye on him as she waited by the Juice Moose shop.

Soon, Penny entered the food court, came to the shop, and ordered. The man in the corner got to his feet.

"Um . . ." Elle faced away from Penny as she spoke so the two of them wouldn't appear to be together. "I hate to say this, but I think we've found Larry Smith. He's heading your way now."

"Think he's dangerous?" Penny managed not to turn her head.

"Hard to say. He's been sitting where we usually do, and he got up as soon as you arrived."

Penny started to walk away while the man followed discretely. He kept his pace calm, but Penny had a head start, and she walked more briskly.

Elle let Penny head off on her own, then she started to run. She quickly passed her friend, muttering, "Follow me," as she went by.

Elle turned down a corridor that led to the bathrooms. She had intended to hide Penny in the ladies room, but the first door in the hallway said, "Maintenance," and someone had just wheeled a service cart in. She grabbed the door before it closed, then with a single smooth motion, she shoved Penny inside and closed it behind her. The workers might object to someone in their space, but Elle felt certain her friend could manage.

With Penny safely tucked away, Elle needed to hide too. If Smith had noticed the two of them together, he'd use Elle's presence as an indicator of where to look. She continued down the hallway to the women's room, slowing her pace so he would see her go in. She didn't turn to look as she strolled through the door.

After an appropriate amount of time, Elle came out, intending to return to the food court. Smith was waiting in the corridor, and he didn't react when she walked by, which meant that he probably hadn't connected the two of them.

Since Elle was free to roam the mall, she went back to the juice shop to grab Penny's order. Then she wandered the mall for a while, waiting for Smith to leave. On her third trip around, he was gone, so she returned to the maintenance room. As she suspected, Penny had made herself at home. She was chatting with the workers, showing them interesting things they could do with their phones.

They took the long route out of the mall to avoid the food court. As they walked, Penny finished her juice. "Would you do me a favor and get me a few more juices? You're still able to go there. I know you want to check out our shop for tomorrow . . . I'll wait for you there." Elle nodded, and Penny walked to the escalators.

Back at the food court, Elle ordered three more juices for Penny as well as one for herself. Then she sat down to enjoy a moment of calm. Penny was safe, and tomorrow would be a big day. Elle looked forward to swindling Damien Artemis.

As soon as she'd finished her first gulp of juice, her "Frank" phone rang again. A very popular phone. Did someone else want the necklace? Was Frank calling to confirm things?

Elle leaned back and took the call. "Yes?"

"Let me start by saying that I'm very impressed. You're a tricky young lady."

The man sounded like Frank Tucker, but she couldn't be sure. "Is that you, Frank?"

The man laughed. "You must be confusing me with Frank the Fence."

"OK then, who are *you*?"

"I'll give you a clue. I'm not Frank, but you and I first met at his place."

Damn! It was that FBI agent. Of course, he went back to Frank and got this phone number. Now he could trace it and locate her. This was bad. If he arrested her now, it would ruin everything. Elle disconnected the call instantly and powered down the phone, shoving it into her backpack.

"That won't help, you know." The same voice was speaking, only now it didn't come from her phone. Standing at the table was Roland Watson, his dark glasses reflecting ominously.

She got up to get away from him as quickly as she could, but Roland was a little quicker. He grabbed her wrist and snapped a handcuff onto it. She tugged on her arm but this was one hold she couldn't break easily. "Let me go."

"Why? So you can run away again? You're quick and you're good, but I'm not letting you go this time." He snapped the other cuff to the table leg, and since the table was bolted to the floor, Elle was caught.

Twenty-Seven

Handcuffed to a food court table by the young FBI agent, Elle took a moment to regroup. She couldn't run away, but she was not without options. Penny's investigation provided some confidence that he'd be reasonable, but there were no guarantees. Good thing the necklace was hidden at her parents' house. Otherwise, she wouldn't feel as safe.

The dark glasses made it hard for Elle to assess Roland and determine what was going on behind that annoyingly smug grin, so she tilted her head and offered a light smile. "You're kind of cute for an FBI agent. I don't suppose you'd take off those ridiculous shades and let me see your eyes."

Much to her relief, Roland removed the sunglasses and slipped them in his pocket. "Better?" He gave her a smile that sparkled from now-revealed eyes.

This encouraged Elle to continue the easy conversation. "Say there, Mr. FBI. I don't believe we've been properly introduced."

"How rude of me." He held a hand to his chest. "I am Special Agent Roland Watson, and *you* have been caught."

Ignoring Roland's threat of imprisonment, Elle's hopes were buoyed by the easy way he gave his name. He was certainly aware that she knew this already because he'd visited Andy, and in so doing, introduced himself to the entire team. Still, it was nice of him to pretend that he was telling her something new.

"What makes you special, Special Agent Roland Watson?"

Roland seemed willing to play along. "First of all, I work for the FBI, and all their agents get that title. But second, I think I deserve that honor for having found the young lady who robbed the museum last weekend. I'd say that's pretty special, don't you think?"

Elle cocked her head. "So what if you saw me talking to a fence about fake jewelry. It doesn't mean I robbed anyone."

"I know all about your little heist, but I don't know anything about you. Let's talk."

"Oh my!" Elle gushed, eyeing him coyly. "Are we on a date?" She rattled the handcuff beneath the table. "I don't do that much, but I doubt you're supposed to handcuff me. You must be a very naughty boy."

"Me? *You're* the naughty one. I'm the sort of person your parents would be happy to meet, assuming they'd raised you right." He squinted at her. "You were raised right, weren't you?"

"Well," Elle chuckled, relieved by this irrelevant conversation. "I'll tell you this much. My foster mother told me not to go out on dates with FBI agents, and you can be sure she *never* did."

Roland let out a quiet laugh. "I can imagine. So, no foster father to teach you how to behave properly?"

"Never had a foster father. Are you volunteering for the job?" She leaned closer and examined his face. "You barely seem old enough. Doesn't the FBI have a minimum age requirement?"

He raised his chin in a show of pride. "I'm twenty-three, which I bet is a lot older than you."

"Twenty-three? So they *do* let children join the FBI." Roland was quickly becoming her favorite FBI agent, which really wasn't saying much because she hadn't met very many, and they were all annoying jerks. But in this case, it felt like the two of them *were* on a date, although she had very limited experience with that. "Is this your first case, Roland?"

Roland waved his hand briefly. "Doesn't matter. I solved the case and I caught the thief. Things are going well."

"Oh, I don't know. I think this date is going pretty badly. You sneaked up on me and handcuffed me to a table. Not very romantic at all."

Roland exhaled loudly. "Look, all I want to do is talk."

"Just talk? No visit to 'Fedquarters'? Aren't you going to read me my rights?"

"I never said you were under arrest. Let's start with some questions."

Elle rolled her eyes. It always started with questions, but how would it end? What if she couldn't answer him satisfactorily? She scanned the food booths, especially the ones with low counters she could leap over if she needed to run.

Roland began his inquiry. "Let's talk about Frank Tucker. You seem to have him twisted around your scheming little finger. I don't think you intended to fence the necklace, or else you wouldn't have tricked him like that. But you obviously didn't expect trouble, because your bodyguards were packing toy guns. So enlighten me, what's with you and Frank?"

"Frank's scum."

Roland bolted a laugh. "He certainly is. And what were you doing at his scummy underworld shop?"

"I must have taken a wrong turn somewhere."

Roland closed his eyes and pinched the bridge of his nose. "Stop. Lying."

"I can't help it. You're so much fun to tease."

"It won't be fun when I take you downtown for some serious interrogation. My partner, Yale, doesn't do witty banter, and if you tease him, he'll get all kinds of angry. Want to avoid that? Get serious and answer my questions. Who are you?"

"Well, let's see. Our crew has decided to call itself, 'The Adjusters.' Catchy name, don't you think?"

Roland scrunched his mouth. "Adjusters? What does that mean?"

"It means we find people with too much money and power, then we adjust their point of view so they're happy to do the right thing."

Now it was Roland turn for an eye-roll. "Look, when I asked who you are, I didn't want a sales pitch for your heist team. I expected you to tell me your name. You've been handing out fake names all week, telling me you're Lisa and telling Frank you're Linda. And if I'm not mistaken, you phoned the museum to tell them the necklace was gone, telling them you're Lorrie. That's a lot of names that start with 'L.' Oh wait!" He pounded the table. "That's your name. Hello, Elle. Pleased to meet you." He held out a hand to shake hers.

Elle's breath caught in her throat as she reached out to shake his hand. Roland was no fool, which was both intriguing and concerning.

Her unease was fueled by another small problem. Some creepy older man kept staring at her from across the food court. This sort of thing happened to Penny all the time, but it was unusual for Elle to get such attention. Good thing she had an FBI agent nearby. Perhaps Roland Watson wasn't the scariest person here.

The feeling of discomfort drove out any attempt to be civil. "You're not pleased to meet me. Just pleased to have me handcuffed to a table."

"Good point. Yesterday I was certain that I'd arrest you, but I've changed my mind. Instead, I have an unusual offer to make. Answer my questions, and if I like the answers, I'll let you go. I'm not reading you your rights, and none of this is admissible in court. Just talk to me."

Roland's offer was promising but offered no guarantees. "Seriously? What if something I say makes you think I need to be arrested?"

"Elle, everything you say and do convinces me, beyond any doubt, that you *do* need to be arrested."

"Then why are you letting me go?"

"Because I think there's something bigger going on here, and I want to understand it better. I've already got a pushy partner who won't stop telling me how to do my job. If it were up to him, he'd have you behind bars by now. But I'm not doing things his way, so stop complaining. If I decide to let you go, I expect you to leave without giving me any flak."

Elle held up her free hand in a sign of surrender. "You've got a deal. But how did you find out my name?"

"Quincy told me. But I'm asking the questions, remember? Let's try a simple one. How old are you? I've never met a band of children who could pull off a heist like that."

"I'll be turning 18 in three days. And flattery will get you nowhere."

"No, I'm being honest with you. I'm quite impressed. Of course, that necklace has to be returned to the museum, so

I'm going to search your belongings." He grabbed Elle's backpack.

"Sorry, Roland, but there's nothing of value here." She leaned back in her chair.

Roland sorted through the contents. The first thing he found were her lock picks. "You know, Elle, these are illegal. I'm going to have to take them."

"Come on, Roland. Give a girl a break. How else can I get out of these handcuffs?"

"Exactly." Roland continued his search, this time pulling out two phones. "How many do you need?"

"I'm very popular. Lots of people want to reach me."

"Like Frank the Fence." He held up the one that had 'Frank' written on the back.

"I know lots of guys named Frank. Besides, you called me on this phone . . . Is *your* name Frank?"

"Ha, ha," he deadpanned. "I don't expect Frank's phone to keep working for long, so give me your other number."

"Sorry, that number's a trade secret."

"Not today. We have a deal here. If you expect to walk, you're going to have to talk."

Elle nodded and gave him her other phone number. It had Penny's location-scrambling hack that made it untraceable. The "Frank" phone didn't have that extra layer of protection since they didn't want the bankers to get suspicious. It would be a much better way for Roland to find her, but she didn't bother mentioning that.

Next, Roland pulled out her wallet and found her driver's license. After examining it, he arched an eyebrow. "This is a pretty good forgery, but look at this! It also says you're about to turn eighteen. Maybe you are." He studied her for a few seconds. "I think we're having a breakthrough, Elle. You told the truth."

"Ha, ha, very funny," her mouth curled to the side.

He leaned closer. "I need that necklace back."

"That will be happening tomorrow. Hey! Maybe we can go to the movies afterwards and celebrate."

"Then you *do* have it?"

"Did I say that? No. I simply happen to know people who are committed to getting it back to the museum. And they plan to do it tomorrow. So if you want to solve this case, give it one more day. I recommend some personal time. Take a walk, get a massage, visit some friends." She shook her head slowly. "Look at you, all tense about your assignment. I hate to see you this way, Roland, and I want you to do well at the Bureau, especially with your difficult partner. Take my advice and chill a bit."

"I see. And I can trust you because you've been so forthcoming with me. The only true thing you've said is your age. Everything else is lies. Not only that, but you won't sit still to talk to me. The first time we met, you ran away. Then today, I had to handcuff you to the table to get you to stay put."

"No, you didn't have to handcuff me to the table. I decided on my own to stay and talk to you." She pulled both hands out from under the table and set the now-opened handcuffs down with a flourish. One of the cuffs had picks sticking out of the lock which she quickly grabbed and slid into her sleeve.

Roland's jaw dropped. "You *are* good." He put the handcuffs in his pocket.

"Seriously, Roland, I'm telling you the truth. And look at me." She waved both hands in the air. "I'm free but I'm not running away. The museum's missing jewelry *will* be returned. All you have to do is pretend it took you a little longer to solve the case. Then we can all pretend that nothing was stolen."

He smirked as he folded his arms. "God! When I started this job, I had the impression that criminals were afraid of law enforcement, especially the FBI. But you act like you don't even care."

"I'm not that blasé. And I certainly don't want to spend the rest of my life running from the FBI, especially an agent as clever as you. But I have a vision of a perfect future, where the missing jewelry gets returned to the museum. Let me make this vision come true, and all will be well."

"Except for one thing. You stole the necklace, and letting thieves walk is not in my job description. I could bring you in right now, but as I've already said, I'm doing things my way. So I'm going to ask you one more question. Then I'll decide what to do with you. And don't think you can hide from me. I *will* find you, and I'll send you away for a long time. Our light repartee and your cute little innocent act are not going to save you."

Roland pulled a small pad of paper from his jacket and wrote on it briefly. Then he folded the page in half and set it on the table. "I've written down what I think is your plan. Now you get to tell me your version. If it's the same as mine, I'll let you go. But if you make up more lies, we're going downtown. Does that seem fair?"

Elle groaned, then she tucked her chair closer to his. This was the moment when some carefully edited truth was needed. "OK, here's my plan. I'm selling something rare to Damien Artemis, CEO of Tera Bank."

"I know who Damien Artemis is. I've already talked to him."

"Good. But what he doesn't know—and what I'm hoping you won't tell him—is that after I get his money, I'm going to swap this rare item for a fake, something you may think I pulled on Frank the other day, although I can't confirm anything. In the end, I'll get Artemis's money, and the rare item will be returned to its proper place."

"Artemis will want his money back."

"No, he won't. If you visit him next week and offer to return the money, I predict that he'll refuse." She folded her arms and leveled her gaze. "What do you think of my plan?"

Roland nodded slowly, then slid the folded piece of paper across the table. Elle read it with increasingly wide eyes. "Say, you *are* special, aren't you? How did you figure out I was targeting Artemis?"

Roland winked. "Trade secret. I get to have them, too, you know."

"Fine. How would you like the jewelry to be returned? Would you like it delivered to your desk at the FBI building? I'm sure you'll get a commendation for that."

"More like a demotion. My supervisor would *not* be happy for me to receive a stolen necklace. He'd only send me out to bust you even harder for playing games."

"Then there *is* such a thing as too much game playing." Her smile twisted with churlish pride. "OK, since you're being nice, let me fill in the details. First of all, the necklace will be delivered to the museum at around two o'clock tomorrow afternoon. Secondly, Artemis won't want his money back, as I've already said. Nobody will press charges against me or anyone else, so I'm hoping you won't want to arrest me. And thirdly, if you do decide to arrest me, or if you want to talk some more—maybe go to a movie—I promise to stick around."

Roland laughed and got to his feet. "OK, you can go. The Bureau will certainly think I'm crazy, but I'm cutting you a huge break. Just don't confuse that with any sort of immunity—I'm watching you and your Adjusters. And I don't know about a movie, but I'm definitely coming for you when this is over."

The creepster across the food court was on his feet now, and he had his eyes fixed on Elle with unnerving attention. She'd never encountered someone who stared that brazenly.

"Say, Roland. As long as you're watching me, perhaps you should check out this gnarly dude across the food court. He can't seem to take his eyes off of me. Blond guy with a determined look on his face."

Roland turned and looked for a few seconds, then he walked over to the man. "Yale, what the hell are you doing here?"

Yale? Elle swallowed hard. Roland had mentioned that his partner was Yale. Could that creepy guy be another FBI agent? This would be a good time to leave, to get away while she could, but she somehow felt safe around Roland, even if his partner seemed dangerous.

Yale stood tall and proud, one hand clamped tight on Roland's shoulder. "I'm checking up on you, dummy. Frank Tucker told me you've been snooping around. Claims to have met the thief, but he couldn't be sure because she gave him a fake necklace. You wouldn't happen to know anything about that, would you?" He pointed his chin at Elle. "Is she the thief?"

Before Elle could defend herself, Roland jumped to the task. "She's an informant who was at the museum when the necklace was stolen."

Yale darkened. "Is that so? Because she was with another young lady a few minutes ago, who I followed to a closed mall shop on the second floor." He propped his hands on his hips and gave Elle a withering look. "You wouldn't happen to know about that, would you?"

"Know about what?" Elle refused to flinch. She once faced three squad cars of police breathing down her neck, and compared to them, these two FBI agents were easy. Especially since they didn't seem to like each other very much.

Yale grinned. "Well then, let's go up to that shop and see." He took a few steps toward the escalators, then stopped. "Are you and your young informant coming, or do I have to do all the work myself? Jeez, kid. You really are helpless." He gave Roland a nasty leer.

Elle and Roland followed Yale as he ascended to the secret mall shops. On the way, she pulled out her phone to warn Penny, but Yale grabbed it from her. "Your accomplice waiting for you there? Good." He slipped her phone in his pocket and kept walking.

They got to the shop, and Yale pointed to the metal grate which was unlocked and slightly open. "See, Roland? You're such a stupid kid. If you weren't wasting all your time chatting up teenage informants, you might actually solve this crime. Watch and learn."

He pushed open the metal grate and stepped inside. The shop was dark, but a light glowed from the back office. Badge in hand, Yale stormed the room. "FBI! Nobody move." Roland and Elle followed him.

Penny yelped when Yale barged in. Sitting on the table by her chair were the four remaining trick boxes. Next to them, three brown leather pouches held the remaining fake necklaces. Elle watched grimly as the FBI agents began to examine it.

Roland opened one of the boxes and found it empty. He looked through the others as well, but none of them had a necklace. Yale kept tapping the gun on his hip to make sure everyone stayed still. Penny sat with an impassive look, clearly trying to be brave. But Elle could see a light sprinkle of sweat on her friend's forehead.

When Roland finished with the boxes, he opened one of the pouches. As the fake necklace spilled out on the table, Yale started to laugh. "Too bad, kid. Looks like I cracked this case for you. Maybe someday, you'll get to be a real FBI agent. But not today."

Roland examined the necklace, then frowned at his partner. "This is a fake, Yale. The necklace isn't here."

Yale pointed to the other pouches. "Check them all."

Roland turned to face his partner. "I'll bet you anything they're fake too." After all the fakes he'd seen, at Frank's, at the museum, and now in this first pouch, he probably understood that the real necklace wasn't going to be found easily.

Yale sneered. "If you believe that, then you're dumber than a box of rocks. Check them!"

"Fine!" Roland quickly examined the necklaces in the other two pouches, then he sneered back. "All fake."

Yale grumbled. "Well still, let's bring it to H.Q. These girls are coming too."

Roland shook his head. "Listen, Yale. This one is an informant too, and I'm not busting either of them. They're part of my investigation, so leave them alone. We can take this stuff, but I need them here to keep their eyes on the mall." He pointed to Elle. "And give this one back her phone. She needs it to contact me."

Yale glowered at his partner for a few seconds, then shifted his disdain to Elle and Penny. Finally he blew out a puff of air. "Stupid kid. You want to screw up your first case, I won't stop you. I'll take this stuff down to headquarters and you can have fun with your mall chicks."

"No." Roland stood his ground. "We'll both take it in. I'm done here." He grabbed the trick boxes and the pouches with the necklaces, then he walked off with Yale.

As they stepped out of the back room, Roland gave Elle an apologetic shrug. She pointed to the cases under his arm and silently mouthed, "I need that." He gave a barely perceptible shake of his head, then he was gone, along with everything they needed to do the swindle tomorrow.

Twenty-Eight

Andy was startled by the sound of furious knocking on his door, and even more surprised when he opened it to find Elle. He leaned across the door jam, blocking her. "How do you know where I live? I never gave you my address."

"Come on, Andy. The FBI found you . . . I can too." She pushed past him into his apartment.

It still irked Andy to have her run this swindle. With fists clamped tight, he followed her inside. "What's going on?"

"What's going on is the FBI. I just finished chatting with our friend, Roland Watson, and another FBI agent who's certainly not our friend, his bulldog partner at the Bureau. They're making all sorts of trouble."

"You ran away from them?"

"No, they let me go."

Andy squinted hard. "Watson knows you stole the necklace. How come he didn't arrest you?"

"Because I told him we're returning it tomorrow."

"And he believes you? Wow, you must be really good if you can convince the FBI of that."

"Well, there may be other factors in play here. But he wants the necklace returned before he makes his move."

"Well then, you better get it right when you see Artemis tomorrow."

"Yeah, that's the problem. The FBI let me go, but they took all our stuff, so I have no idea if the deal will even

happen. In the meantime, I'm tired of carrying this phone."
She pulled out the "Frank" phone and handed it to him.

Andy shuffled the phone from hand to hand, frowning.
"Why do I need this? You're the one doing Artemis
tomorrow. You know I wanted to play Baxter—he loves
stolen goods and buys it by the bucket. But it's your deal,
and you might need the phone. Keep it."

Elle refused to take it. "I can't have this on me anymore.
It doesn't have Penny's location hack, because we didn't
want the bankers to get suspicious. That means Watson can
track it, and I don't want him knowing about my parents.
But since he knows about you, he won't be surprised to see
it here. Hang on to it, and tell any last-minute callers that
they're too late." She turned and left his apartment.

Andy closed the door and stood for a few minutes,
white-knuckling the phone hard enough to crush it. He
wanted to scream at her for following him home, for getting
him in trouble with the FBI, for ordering him around like he
had barely half a brain. *Who does she think she is?*

The more he thought about it, however, the less any of
it mattered. After all, the deal was going down tomorrow,
and he might make some money. Then, when it was done,
he could reevaluate his relationship with Elle and Penny. He
simply didn't like being told what to do all the time.

As if the phone was aware of his anger and wanted to
make things worse, it began to ring. It annoyed him to be
her secretary, arranging things like some devoted gofer. He
stared at the phone for a few seconds then finally took the
call. "What?" Not the friendliest greeting, but too bad.

"My name is Galt Baxter, and I understand . . ."

Wahoo! The banker he'd investigated was on the line.
Andy was so excited that he cut the man off mid-sentence.
"I know who you are, Mr. Baxter."

He began to consider his options. Would it be possible to nail the banker who deserved it the most? He could arrange to meet Baxter first. It might alter Elle's plans, but at this point, he didn't care. Baxter was within reach, which was all that mattered.

Andy switched to his smoothest voice. "I understand you have an appreciation for the finer things in life, including jewelry so dazzling as to leave you breathless."

"Very poetic. Am I to believe that you actually have such a breathtaking object?"

"Yes, I have a very fine piece. Belongs in a museum, if you know what I mean. And I'm willing to sell it for five million dollars. But there are a few catches."

Baxter chuckled. "Always are."

"First, we're doing this tomorrow. Can you get that much cash in time?"

"Easy. What else?"

"Your CEO, Artemis, thinks he's buying the jewels, but he's getting a fake."

"Aha. I wondered why he was going on about that theft. So you're cheating him. Why shouldn't I worry that you'll cheat me too?"

"Bring a jeweler along, and verify it for yourself. I have the real thing. I'm tricking Artemis because he's a cheap son-of-a-bitch who refuses to pay the full price. But if you have the right money, I have the right jewels."

"I understand. And by the way, we need to finish this deal by mid afternoon. I have . . ."

"Yes, yes, Artemis already explained it . . . your jewelry club meets at four. You'll make a big splash when you show up with this, won't you?"

"That's what I'm hoping. Let me warn you that I'm also bringing a bodyguard."

"Of course. Meet me tomorrow at eleven, in front of the Chinese restaurant at the Bridgeport Mall. I'll be wearing a white carnation." He disconnected before Baxter could say anything more.

Excited, Andy called Neil. "Guess what! Baxter just contacted me. I'm selling him the necklace tomorrow, two hours before Elle meets with Artemis. I told Baxter that he's getting the real one, and his buddy, Artemis is getting a fake. That ought to amuse Elle."

"Amuse? I don't know. She'll probably be pretty annoyed. This could sour her deal with Artemis."

"Let's not worry about Elle, OK? She can take care of herself."

"Not when you're plotting behind her back."

"Trust me, Neil, I'm doing the right thing. Now are you going to help me, or are you going to mess me up when we're about to score our biggest haul ever?"

Neil paused for a few seconds, then blew out a groan. "You know you can count on me, Andy. And this works because we're playing a shell game at the mall tomorrow, confusing the FBI by moving the necklace from person to person. I get it at ten, and I'll give it to you at eleven."

"We make a good team, don't we, Neil? By this time tomorrow, we'll be rolling in money."

Elle sat in her parents' living room, trying to relax. They were neck-deep in trouble from a mysterious hacker and *two* FBI agents. And now that they'd lost their fake necklaces and trick boxes, she wasn't sure how she could pull this scam.

But Elle had seen con games change in the strangest of ways. Usually the changes made things worse, but sometimes they saved the day. Rather than give up, she decided to move forward with the plan, prepared for the worst but hoping for the best.

She was taking a huge leap thinking Roland would help her, but it wasn't completely out of the question. After all, he did let her go after catching her today. And he'd defended her and Penny from his overzealous partner, calling them informants instead of thieves. He even seemed sorry to take their equipment.

Too bad the game would finish tomorrow. That didn't leave much time to recover her props from FBI lockup. She'd give Roland and Yale a while to study their haul, then she'd call him and see if she had a chance.

While these thoughts echoed in her head, Harry came home, bringing Wendy and June from school. June bounced on the sofa a few times. "I'm going to a friend's house now. See you later!"

Elle caught her sister mid-bounce, gave her a squeeze, then let her continue to jump. "Have fun with your friend." After a few more bounces, June ran out the door with her father.

That left Wendy, fidgeting quietly on the sofa. "Dad says I can take the day off from school tomorrow." She tightened her mouth. "I'm a little worried. Never piloted a drone in city streets. We're not supposed to do that, you know. But honestly . . ." She let her excitement finally show. "I can't wait!"

Delighted with Wendy's enthusiasm, Elle gave her sister a high-five. Then a thought bubbled to the surface, a risky possibility, but something that could be very helpful.

Someone needed to bring the necklace to the mall tomorrow, and it couldn't be anyone on her team, because Roland was watching. Wendy would be perfect because she was unknown, and also because she had the necklace in her closet. But could Elle trust her sister with something this important? Stealing chocolate milk for June was a far cry from handing off million-dollar jewelry. But nobody else was available.

Elle cleared her throat. "Listen, Wendy. Can you help me with something else too?"

The young girl's eyes widened. "Sure. What's up?"

"I need you to bring the necklace to the mall and give it to my friend, Neil. He and I are being watched, and people might try to take it from us. But nobody knows you, so if you're sly, you can slip it into his backpack. Can you do that? I know it's a big ask."

Wendy grinned broadly. "Does this mean I get to join your team?"

"Well, yes, but you have to act like you don't know us. Let's go upstairs and I'll show you."

They went to Wendy's bedroom and retrieved the pouch with the necklace. Elle gave her sister instructions. "OK, have this in your backpack when you come to the mall tomorrow. Sit on a bench near the food court and wait for me. Get a snack first, then act normal, play with your phone, stuff like that. Let's see you do this now."

Wendy pulled out her phone and looked down at it. When Elle sat next to her, she smiled. "How am I doing?"

Elle wagged a finger. "You're not supposed to know me, so ignore me when I sit next to you."

Wendy nodded and looked back at her phone. Elle continued the lesson. "When I sit down, I'll pretend to talk on my phone, but I'll really be talking to you and telling you how to spot my friend, Neil. Then he'll come sit by you and you slip it into his backpack. Do it carefully so nobody notices. Just act casual and it will go fine."

"OK, I get it. Sound's easy."

Elle marveled at her sister's enthusiasm. She remembered being young and learning her first tricks. Bea would be proud. Harry and Trish certainly wouldn't.

She couldn't worry about that right now, so she put it out of her mind and hugged her sister. "You're going to be great."

"Thanks. When do I fly the drone?"

"That comes later. After you hand-off the necklace, go shopping." She gave her sister some cash. "Get a new outfit and put it on. Get a ball cap, too, and tuck your hair into it. I want you to look completely different when you fly the drone so nobody recognizes you from before. You and Dad will have almost four hours, so take your time, have lunch, do what you like. But be changed and back at the mall by 2pm when I call."

"Do I take the necklace from someone's backpack?"

"No. This time, I'll show up and give it to you. But remember, you still don't know me. I'm simply a stranger giving you a gift. Thank me, then go with Dad to the car. Strap the pouch to the drone, then fly it back to the museum. And remember that you and Dad have to wear gloves so you don't leave any fingerprints on the drone. Got it?"

Wendy nodded. "Definitely!" She collapsed in her desk chair. "Sorry, but I've got homework. Big report coming up next week." Elle left her alone and went back downstairs.

As she sat in the living room, trying to calm her breathing, her phone rang. Her personal phone. The caller ID said, "Hidden." Could it be Roland? She took the call.

"Yes?"

"I have a theory about you . . ." Roland had dived in as if they were in the middle of a conversation. Elle was happy to hear his voice, and not just because he might be returning her confiscated items. For some bizarre reason, she actually enjoyed talking to this particular FBI agent, so she leaned back to hear his theory.

"I was wondering about all the fake names you use. Lisa, Linda, Lorrie. A definite pattern here. When Quincy told me that your name is Elle, it seemed to fit with the fake names. Then I got this wild idea. It may be completely off-base but hear me out."

"Go on . . ."

"What if a con artist changed her name to Elle, a name that sounds like a single letter, then used fake names which always begin with that letter? It would be perfect, because if she ran into someone who knew her while she was working a job, they'd call her 'Elle,' but the marks wouldn't suspect a thing. They'd assume it was a nickname for Lisa or Linda or Lorrie. Perfect cover, right?"

Elle swallowed. "Jeez, Roland. You nailed it on your first guess. I was named Elle for that very reason. You know, maybe you're in the wrong line of work. Ever think about becoming a con artist?"

"Ha! So your foster mother's a con artist too."

Elle exhaled loudly. "Yeah, we're not from around here."

"You live in Los Angeles, right? I can hear Valley-Girl in the way you speak."

Elle took a second to calm herself as another layer of secrets got peeled away by this man. She decided to ignore his statement, to neither confirm nor deny it.

"My foster mother thought up the idea of having single-letter names and used it on herself, changing her name from Beatrix."

"Of course. She's Bea now. Got any sisters or brothers?"

"I've got one of each. What's my sister's name?"

"Let's see, Kay?"

"Buzz. Guess again."

Roland took a few seconds, probably running the alphabet in his head. "Dee?"

"Yep. Now tell me my older brother's name."

"Well . . . Jay?"

"See? You're pretty smart for an FBI agent."

"All I need to know is your last name."

"Not today, Roland. Too much to think about and a big day tomorrow. Are you going to help me with that?"

"Well, I know you need one of those fake necklaces back."

"I need a jewelry case too."

"Why?"

"They're unique. Tell you what. Meet me with a necklace and one of the cases, and I'll show you."

"I can't do that. Our tech guy is examining them now, and we'll know why they're unique soon enough. After that, they may not be in good enough condition for you to use. Also, my overbearing partner already thinks I'm incompetent. If I steal evidence, he'll have my head."

"Come on, Roland. You're going to solve this case soon and impress everyone at the Bureau, even your angry partner. But you have to help me work the deal."

"I don't *have* to do anything. And there are some things I simply can't do."

Elle scaled back her request. "OK, how about this? Go visit Frank the Fence and get his fake necklace and the case it's in. He's not going to sell that junk, so he'll be willing to part with it."

"Hey! I'm not your errand boy. Why don't *you* visit Frank?"

"Frank and I didn't get off on the best foot, as you know. But you're FBI, so you can go in there and demand it as evidence. I'll even pay you for your effort. Just get me a necklace and a jewelry box."

Roland snorted. "Oh, come on now! You're trying to bribe an FBI agent? Not a chance."

Elle sighed. "Fine, I won't pay you for it. But I'll buy your ticket when we go to the movies. See? Not a bribe, just a date."

Roland's laugh was loud and hearty. "If we end up going to the movies, you're definitely buying the tickets. Let's talk again at the mall tomorrow morning. I assume you'll be there."

He paused for the briefest moment, then changed the subject. "And by the way, why can't I trace this phone? I can track any cell phone within seconds. How come the system thinks you're in Dallas?"

"Jeez, Roland. I can't reveal *all* my secrets."

"Look, I don't care about the other stuff you've done. And I'm sure you've done plenty. I'll grant you immunity on all your former crimes if you tell me how you're able to mask your location. I asked Yale if he'd ever seen someone who could do that, and apparently he hadn't, because now he's even more desperate to drag you in for questioning. You don't want Yale questioning you, so give it up. How do you do that?"

"I've got a hacker girl on my team who *might* be willing to explain it if you offer her complete immunity."

"You mean Penny? She's an accomplice in the museum theft, so I can't guarantee her immunity. But I might be able to keep some secrets. I simply want to know how she hacks the cell phone system."

"Look here, Roland, if you want to know how she does it, you're going to have to keep the museum work a secret, too. You can try to pin things on me, but you have to promise to leave my friend alone."

"Hmm." He paused for a few seconds. "OK. Penny is safe. But *you* are not, so beware . . . I'm watching you tomorrow."

"Ooh! Are you some kind of creepy stalker?"

"Compared with the other people watching you tomorrow, I'm your best friend. Don't spoil it by making me mad." He ended the call.

Elle couldn't say for sure why she liked Roland so much, why she enjoyed talking to him, teasing him, even simply being with him. She had to remind herself that he was an FBI agent, that he was the enemy here and a truly dangerous friend.

Twenty-Nine

Elle awoke Friday morning in a haze of uncertainty. The heat had become oppressive, with two FBI agents and a mysterious hacker lurking at every turn. Too bad they'd arranged to do the swindle at the mall, because it wasn't safe there anymore. She wondered if they'd even be able to do it.

The only hope was Roland, who might return some of their confiscated equipment. Before leaving the motel room, Elle called him, fingers crossed. "Morning, Elle. I see you're in Winnipeg today. You've got to let Penny tell me how she does this—I'm amazed."

"Well, Roland, you've got to do something for me first."

"Already done. I'm in your empty mall shop right now."

Elle released a long-held sigh. Thanks to Penny's hacking, they knew Roland wouldn't prosecute them for this caper, but they weren't as certain that he'd actually help them. "You're a life saver, Roland. But how did you get in there?"

"Give me some credit. I used the lock picks I took from you—very nice tools. And you were right: Frank was more than happy to get rid of the fake necklace and jewelry case. As for understanding how your cases work, our tech tore one of them apart and showed me. Very clever."

"Thought you'd like that. Custom made for this job." Now that the scam was back in force, one little point needed clarification. "I hate to be a bother after you've been so nice, but what about your aggressive partner?"

"No problem. He's back on some other case, after having solved this one. You should have heard the dressing-down I got. He thinks I'm a total fool. You better come through for me today, or I'm going to need another job."

"You can always join our crew."

Roland groaned. "You keep thinking I'm a crook, but that's not how I roll. I'm just giving you enough rope. It's up to you to do the right thing or to hang yourself." In the background, she could hear a metal grate sliding closed. "Anyway, I'm done here. See you later."

"You're a good man, Roland. And that's a huge compliment, considering you're FBI." She disconnected, then she and Penny danced around the room to celebrate the good news.

Since she was meeting with the CEO of a bank today, Elle wore slightly fancier clothes than her usual T-shirt. The light-blue button-down blouse gave her a modicum of class, and would look good with a white carnation in the lapel. Of course, her black skinny jeans had tears in both knees, which gave her a casual-kid look. Part of her simply refused to pander to this man.

They drove to the mall for what promised to be an interesting day. As she and Penny got close to the food court, Elle looked around carefully, wondering about each person she saw. Mall crowds usually provided safety, but today she doubted nearly everyone. Roland was out there, and Larry Smith probably was too. But what about Damien Artemis's people? Were they watching? At least Wendy was there, sitting on a bench. It was nice to be able to trust someone.

They needed to keep the necklace in motion today so anyone watching wouldn't know who had it. That's why they planned to send it on a complicated journey. Neil would take the necklace from Wendy now, then it would go to Andy at 11am, to Penny at noon, and finally to Elle for her 1pm meeting with Damien Artemis. After that, Wendy would fly it home. And through it all, Chip and Quincy would wander the mall, talking to the kids and even exchanging packages with them in an attempt to divert attention from the real action.

Penny went ahead and entered the food court carefully, joining Neil and Andy who were already there. Elle stopped near her sister and sat down on the bench, pulling out her phone to fake a call. Wendy munched on a cookie, never even flinching when her big sister sat down.

With her back to Wendy, Elle spoke into her phone. "Watch me now. I'm going to give my friend a pat on the back. He gets the pouch." Elle put her phone away, then got up to walk to their table in the food court. She patted Neil on the back, glancing briefly to make sure Wendy noticed the signal. Then she sat down next to him and finished the connection. "The girl with the yellow T-shirt, eating a cookie."

He turned discretely. "Got her."

Before Neil could get up, Elle noticed Roland. "Head's up! Fed on the way." She wanted to laugh when he walked past Wendy, never suspecting that this preteen girl had the necklace.

Roland arrived, sporting his signature shades, a cocky grin clear across his face. "Well, well, well. It's the entire heist team, all in one place. Hello, Elle." He turned to the next person. "Nice to see you again, Andy." He pointed at Penny next. "You and I need to talk." Finally, he completed his circuit of the table. "And you must be the horrible boyfriend who just broke Penny's heart. Neil, right?"

Neil might have been nervous with the upcoming swindle, but he kept cool and offered a completely blank look. "Do I know you?"

Roland squinted at Neil and Penny for a few seconds, slowly shaking his head. "You two look like you might make a good couple, after all. Who knows?" He pulled up a chair and sat down.

Andy and Neil leaned away, but Elle gave him a level stare. "Hey, Roland, go away. You're scaring my friends."

He leaned back and considered the four of them. "They should be scared. They helped you steal millions of dollars worth of jewelry. Jewelry you think will be magically returned today. So . . ." He leaned closer. "Who's got the necklace?"

Elle smiled and tossed her backpack on the table. "Not me."

Roland looked at the backpack, then he turned to the other three. As his eyes circled the table, each of them tossed out their backpacks. He gave them a cursory examination, pawing the contents and shaking solid objects that might have jewels in them. Then he pushed them away, probably convinced that the kids wouldn't have allowed a search if the necklace was there.

"All right, never mind. I can wait. Don't mind me." He leaned back with his hands behind his head like a family patriarch presiding over an unruly clan.

Elle slapped a hand on the table. "We're busy, Roland. We can't keep meeting like this."

"Come on, Elle. I'm starting to enjoy our little chats."

"Fine, then. Let's chat. But leave my friends out of this. Let them go."

Roland shrugged. "The boys can go. I don't care about them. It's you and Penny I came to see." He looked at Neil and Andy and jerked his head, motioning them to leave.

They quickly got to their feet. Andy headed in one direction, and Neil went a different way, toward Wendy. Roland was about to say something when a confused look clouded his face. It gave Elle a moment to glance around, and to her great relief, she watched her sister deftly slip the pouch into Neil's backpack.

Roland's attention stayed glued elsewhere, his head now tilted to the side. Elle and Penny turned to follow his gaze as the mysterious Larry Smith arrived at the table, sat down in Neil's seat, and grabbed Penny's wrist.

"Hey!" She protested, using a twist Elle had taught her to escape his grip. "Back off."

Smith leaned away in his chair, making no attempt to grab her again. "I've been telling you for days, Ms. Herman, we need to talk." He looked over at Elle, sitting next to Roland. "I'm guessing this is your friend, Elle Kirkland."

Elle blew out an exasperated groan and dropped her head into her hands. "Jeez, buddy. Too much information."

Roland just laughed.

"Oh, sorry." Smith glanced at him. "Your boyfriend doesn't know your name?"

Roland flashed his FBI badge. "I do now. And I'm very interested in hearing what else you know about her and Penny. Penny *Herman*, is it?" He tapped a note into his phone. "And who might you be?"

The man glanced at the badge and sat up straight. "The name's Larry Smith. I'm a private investigator, and I've been looking for Ms. Herman for a few weeks now."

"Tell you what, Mr. Smith. How about you and I both talk to her. I've got some questions for Ms. Herman too.

And I'd love to hear what you want." He glanced at Elle. "I believe I've wasted enough of Ms. *Kirkland's* time right now." He bobbed his eyebrows as he spoke her last name.

Penny was already aware that Roland wanted to talk, and that Smith would eventually find her. She couldn't run from either of these men, but the information Roland wanted might protect her. She got to her feet as Roland and Smith stood on either side, boxing her in and leading her away.

"Wait, you guys." Elle jumped to her feet. The three of them stopped and turned back toward the table. "Two things, Roland. First, you promised to keep Penny out of this. I'm holding you to that. And second, I need her back by noon, so you only get her for two hours."

Smith frowned at Roland. "Who's in charge here, you or these girls?"

Roland glanced skyward. "Despite appearances, I am. But this is a complex case."

"Or," Smith grinned as he considered Roland and Elle. "Maybe I was right when I thought you two were a couple. Anyway, I don't need much from Ms. Herman, as long as she's cooperative."

Roland nodded. "I probably don't need her for long, either." As they led Penny away, he tossed a hand in the air to wave behind him. "See you later, *sweetheart*." The word was soaked with sarcasm.

Once they were gone, Andy came out of hiding and returned to the table. Neil was elsewhere, wandering the mall with the necklace. "That was close. I still can't believe he let us go."

Elle looked around. "Well, as he said, he's watching us. And he and that detective are interrogating Penny, which I'm not happy about."

Andy chuckled. "I bet she's even less happy about it. You really do live in a world of trouble."

Thirty

"Hey, Andy." Neil waved as his buddy entered the storage room of the mall's game store, a shop where the boys spent enough time that the owner let them hangout in back. Neil had gotten the necklace from Elle's younger sister an hour ago, and now it was time to pass it to his friend.

Andy winked. "How's it going?"

"Awesome!" Neil shouted it out, then glanced around with a sheepish look and continued more quietly. "I just had the most amazing time with this thing. It made me feel like a total pro, a real trickster." He pulled a brown leather pouch from his backpack and handed it off.

Andy smiled. "I'm proud of you, Neil. You're becoming a real con artist." He opened the pouch and gazed at the jewels for a few seconds. "This necklace really is something, isn't it? Hard to believe it's worth five million dollars."

Neil laughed. "It's just a pile of rocks right now. You still have some work to do if you want to turn it into money."

"No problem." Andy gave a single crisp nod. "I'll see you later." He slipped the pouch into his pocket and left.

Minutes later, he stood in front of the mall's Chinese restaurant, a white carnation dangling from the drawstring of his red hoodie. Some people stared as they walked by, but nobody stopped to comment. The carnation was the only thing out of place about him—the rest of his outfit was pure mall, with a backpack, blue jeans, and a sweatshirt, the hood pulled tight on his head.

In the distance, three well-dressed people approached, looking even more out of place than Andy's carnation. Galt Baxter, the bank president, wore a surprisingly loud three-piece suit, sapphire blue with a crisp white dress shirt. His black patterned bow tie matched a handkerchief in the jacket pocket. Clean-shaven except for a tiny soul-patch of a beard, he was every bit the eccentric banker that his administrator had claimed.

Standing next to Baxter was a big man wearing a black suit and tie. His hair was short on top and shaved to the scalp on the sides. With dark glasses and dark clothes, he seemed like Baxter's shadow, and even though he wore a white shirt, the small amount of it that showed did little to lighten his appearance. He dragged a large roller bag that was probably full of cash, and he moved it slowly with constant glances back. Andy didn't want to mess with this guy.

The third member of Baxter's team was a slight woman with long straight blonde hair. In keeping with the rest of Baxter's people, she wore a black tailored suit over a light green blouse. If the big man was the bodyguard, then the woman was the jeweler who would validate the necklace. The three of them stopped in front of Andy, the muscle man carefully straddling the mountain of cash.

"You?" Baxter squinted as he considered Andy's slouching form. "I expected someone more . . . Oh, I don't know. More mature."

"Nice, Pops. Way to get things off on the right foot. Did you bring someone who can verify the goods?"

"That's her job." His head angled toward the woman. "But even I can tell a fake from the real thing."

"Good for you. Let's go." Andy turned and started to walk through the mall.

Baxter frowned. "Go where? I thought we were doing this here."

"We are, just someplace a bit more private upstairs." Andy marched on, but Baxter waited for his bodyguard to start rolling the bag before the three of them followed.

At the base of the escalator, Andy looked around to see if anyone else was following the banker. He had stationed Neil nearby as a lookout and made brief eye contact with his buddy to be sure. Neil gave a raised thumb of assurance.

They rode to the second floor then marched down the side concourse. Andy unlocked the grate to the empty shop, but before going in, he pulled out his phone and waved it at them. "Hope you don't mind if my people listen in. I'm outnumbered three-to-one here, so I could use some protection." Baxter nodded, and Andy let the three of them slip inside before sliding the grate closed.

Once in the small back office, Baxter stood to the side while the strongman hefted the luggage onto the table. Andy pulled out a jewelry box, which he handed to Baxter. When the bank president flipped open the lid, he froze for a few seconds, clearly dazzled by the necklace's brilliance. Slowly, he reached out and lifted it from the case, bringing it close. "Beautiful!"

He handed it to the woman who examined it carefully. She rolled the stones back and forth, staring at every part of the necklace including the intricate setting. After a bit, she pulled out a loupe and focused intensely on the main emerald. Finally, she laid the necklace back in the box. "It's the real thing."

Baxter smiled. "I'm impressed. You really stole Napoleon's necklace." He closed the lid, then he kissed his fingers before touching the box. "This is going to be my good luck charm."

Andy watched Baxter's superstitious gesture, and it gave him an idea. "This will be mine." He kissed his own fingers and touched the huge bag of money.

When he unzipped it, he needed a few seconds to take in the enormous quantity of cash laying there. Bundle after bundle of hundred-dollar bills filled every corner of the bag. It was stuffed so full that the zipper practically burst apart when it first slid open. He started to pull out random bundles and check them.

As he examined the money, Baxter slid the jewelry box closer to himself. Andy quickly reached out and pulled it back, jamming it next to his backpack. "Let's wait until I'm satisfied here, OK? It's a good luck thing with me, too."

Baxter folded his arms and started to tap his foot as Andy continued to check the money, pulling out piles and setting them on the table. The jewelry case got shoved to the side by all this activity, nearly falling off the table at one point. Andy had to reach out quickly to bring it closer again. Finally, after satisfying himself that the money was good, he stuffed it all back and zipped up the luggage.

"All good, Mr. Baxter." Andy pushed the jewelry case back across the table. "I'll let you leave first. I recommend a quick exit because I heard there might be law enforcement at the mall today. You can use the service corridors in the back of the shop."

Baxter scowled as he regarded the back door. "I never hide from anyone. Bad luck, you know."

"Then perhaps you should send the necklace out back with someone else."

Baxter grinned. "You seem eager to have me use the back door, so I'm leaving through the front. But he's carrying it." Baxter handed the jewelry case to his bodyguard, and the man cradled it in his arms. In the quiet of the unused mall shop's back room, they could hear the stones rattling as the man handled the case.

"Let's go." Baxter slid open the shop's grate and walked out, stepping with a pronounced bounce to his step. His two people followed.

Andy waited a few minutes to be sure he was alone with the money. Then he got up and rolled the suitcase away. Good thing it was on wheels, because it was heavy with cash. He couldn't wait to see the look on Elle's face.

An hour later, Elle stood in a women's lingerie shop and waited for Penny to arrive. When she did, Elle waited a bit longer until she was convinced that her friend wasn't being followed. Finally, she went to the changing rooms and entered the one with a black stocking hanging over the knob. Penny sat inside.

Elle gave her friend a hug, happy to see her still on schedule. She had a million questions she wanted to ask, most of them about what Roland and Larry Smith had to say. How much trouble was Penny facing? And more important, did she have the necklace? She was supposed to have had it for the past hour, after Andy ran it around, and now Elle would take it to sell to Damien Artemis.

Unfortunately, she couldn't ask any of these questions, because her deal was happening soon. Also, the changing room might be a safe place to make an exchange, but it wasn't a good place to talk, with other customers nearby. Glancing around the tiny space, Elle went for the most basic question, which would cover all of the others. "Are you OK?"

Penny smiled. "Oh my God, yes." She hissed the last word to emphasize it without being loud. "Your buddy,

Roland, was very nice. And Smith, well, not too bad. I'll tell you about it later. But oh!" She was having trouble controlling her enthusiasm, and covered her mouth to keep quiet. "I've never had this much fun. I . . . I mean . . . Well, whoa!" She paused and took a calming breath. Then she pulled out a pouch and handed it over.

"Good work." Elle was thrilled to see that Penny had gotten away from Roland and Larry Smith with time to spare. She was even happier to know that her three crew members had kept the necklace in play, from Neil to Andy to Penny, and finally to her. Things were going well.

Penny left first, then Elle followed a minute later. She did her best to blend in with other shoppers, her heart beating faster now that she had the necklace. Up on the second floor, Elle went to the alternate unused shop, next to the one where the deal with Artemis would take place. With gloves on, she pulled the necklace from the pouch and quickly set it in the trick case. Then she moved the case to the other shop's back room to await sale. Threading a white carnation through a buttonhole on her blouse, she wandered to the Chinese restaurant.

The deal was still ten minutes away, but she wanted to get there early. This was the big one, for her parents, for Chip and Quincy, and for many others. She could feel the thrill pulsing through her body.

As she approached the meeting place, she saw Artemis standing with two other men. All of them looked quite proper, with black suits and white dress shirts, although Artemis's suit was perfectly tailored, making the other two seem rumpled in comparison. The muscular bald man was probably the bodyguard, standing with one hand on a large camping backpack that was likely filled with cash. It certainly seemed heavy enough—he'd taken it off and set it by his feet. The third man was most likely the jeweler, so hunched over that he looked like the smallest of the three, although he'd be as tall as Artemis if he stood up straight. Elle could sense the jeweler's nervousness from a distance.

Artemis was early for the meeting, and he paced back and forth, talking on the phone and pausing occasionally to make brief comments to the jeweler. By contrast, the jeweler stood silently, rocking from foot to foot. The bodyguard watched the other two with a minimal smile.

Elle let them fidget—she liked her marks to be off-balance. She ducked into a store to keep watching, gauging their level of impatience. She also looked for any gestures or head motions they might make to others in the vicinity. As near as she could tell, these three were the entire team meeting her.

At the appointed time, Elle stepped out of the store and walked up to them. "Mr. Artemis."

When he looked at her, his mouth fell open. "You really *are* a kid! How old are you?"

"We're not here to talk about me. Let's go. We can indulge in small talk along the way." The big man hefted the backpack into place, then he followed Artemis, who was already following Elle. The jeweler scampered to bring up the rear.

"Well?" Artemis still wanted an answer to his question.

"I'm seventeen. Getting ready for a big eighteenth party Sunday, which I know you'll want to be at."

"Yeah," he drawled. "It's at the top of my list." He followed her up the escalator. "Did you really steal the necklace?"

Elle turned to stare at him. "Can we not talk about that here?" She turned and led him down the side concourse, where Quincy stood guard in front of the empty shop.

Smooth and powerful looking, he slid open the grate to let Artemis and his team enter with Elle. Then he closed the grate behind them.

In the back room, the jewelry case waited on the table. The bodyguard's backpack fell next to it with a loud thud. "Check it out, gentlemen." Elle opened the case and stepped away.

The jeweler reached to take the necklace, but Artemis grabbed it first. He studied it for a few seconds. "This really is gorgeous."

"Yes," the jeweler agreed. "Let me check it more closely."

Artemis held up his hand. "No point in doing that yet." He set the necklace back in the case and closed the lid. "We have a problem here, and unless I get some straight answers, I'm not buying anything."

Elle shrugged. "The necklace is real—isn't that the only truth you need?"

"Yeah, but an FBI agent talked to me the other day, and according to him, you stole the necklace."

"Maybe I did. Why does that matter? You already know it's stolen."

"Yeah, but this guy claims to be following you. Warned me that he intended to recover the necklace and that I was about to commit a federal crime. Then there was your insistence that I be here today instead of letting my lawyer handle this." He grumbled. "Makes me wonder if this is some kind of trap. You obviously wanted me here at the moment of the sale. Why else would you give up forty-five million dollars?"

"First of all, if we were being followed my people would notice. Don't trust me? Have your man go look around. Second of all, buying stolen jewels from foreign countries was *always* a federal crime. Don't go soft on me now, dude.

And thirdly," She leaned on the table to get closer. "I demanded fifty million if your lawyer did the deal but only five million if you showed up, but that's because I like this necklace, and I wanted to look the new owner in the eye to be sure it would be kept whole. Your lawyer couldn't guarantee that—he wouldn't even tell me your name. That's why I added the extra forty-five million to the price, but it was never really part of the deal."

"And you're not worried about that FBI agent?"

"I believe you're referring to Special Agent Roland Watson." Artemis widened his eyes. "Yeah, I thought so. I've met him—nice guy. He doesn't worry me at all. Now, do you want the necklace or not?"

"Sorry, too much heat. If you want to sell it, I can only pay half price."

Elle propped her fists on her hips. "That doesn't make any sense. If you're worried about being busted for buying this, then you're in the same amount of danger regardless of what you pay."

Artemis grinned. "I've done plenty of shady deals, and I know my lawyers can get me off if I'm caught. But the money will be gone along with the necklace. I'm not risking a full five million on a gamble like that."

"You're not risking *any* money by cutting the price, because I won't sell it to you. This isn't a used car dealership, Mr. Artemis. Your man lugged that cash all this way. Do you really intend to make him haul it back out of here?" The bodyguard merely rolled his eyes.

Artemis smirked. "Why don't I call up Agent Watson and tell him where he can find you and the necklace?"

"If you bring Agent Watson into this, he'll take the necklace, and you'll be missing out on some fabulous emeralds." She shook her head, disappointed with the man.

Elle had seen this sort of thing before. When marks got nervous, they needed a stark dose of reality. Her next move would be to walk away, hoping he'd change his mind.

"It's too bad you don't want this. Maybe some of the others in your jewelry club will be interested."

Artemis chuckled. "You're a big talker, young lady, but your jewelry's too hot. Sell it for half price or I'll call in the feds."

Elle was about to walk out, but she turned and got into his personal space for one last attempt. "Let's get one thing straight. If you're not buying it from me, it's going right back to the museum. Buy it for the agreed-on price, or *I'll* be the one who calls Agent Watson."

She paused for a second or two, staring at Artemis in a waiting game. When he didn't flinch, she flipped the lid closed on the jewelry case. "Time's up." She snatched it off the table, shoved it in her backpack, and walked to the door of the shop's office. "Goodbye, Mr. Artemis. Too bad you're such a scared little child. And you think *I'm* a kid!" She turned and walked toward the shop's gated entrance.

Thirty-One

Some plans don't work out, and this was looking like one of them. Sure, she'd stolen a stunning bauble that many would like to buy. And she'd even gotten the attention of the CEO of the bank, exactly the man she wanted to swindle. It could have been perfect.

Except for Special Agent Roland Watson. He'd been more helpful than any FBI agent ought to be, yet his involvement had scared Artemis, making the cheating CEO afraid to buy the necklace. Now she was going to have to return it, unsold, to the museum.

Elle considered keeping the necklace, holding on until she could find another banker to buy it. But Roland was no fool, and he had an uncanny ability to track her down. Also, he'd trusted her and probably took a big risk at the bureau, so she couldn't leave him hanging.

Elle made it to the front of the empty shop and prepared to disappear into the mall. Given the likelihood of FBI agents, detectives, and other difficult people who might be milling about, she needed to do a quick disappearing act. Good thing she was in a mall, an ideal place to get lost, even when it was crawling with adversaries. She'd weave back and forth, duck into a few shops, then call Wendy to meet her at the drop-off point and get that necklace back where it belonged.

Stepping outside their shop, she pulled off the carnation, and gave Quincy a weak smile. He pointed back into the shop. "They still back there?"

Elle sighed. "Yeah, but we're done. You can go."

Quincy shook his head. "I'll wait till they leave."

Elle nodded, then she slouched a bit and started to move toward the main promenade. She quickly joined four young women who were heading toward the big department store, discussing dresses they wanted to get for an upcoming party.

As they were about to enter, Elle felt a hand on her shoulder. Her first thought was that Roland had caught up with her again, but when she turned to look, she was surprised to see Artemis's jeweler. She stopped and gave the man a lidded look.

"What?" Did he want to buy the necklace for himself? She had no intention of selling to this man, but she stopped to hear him out.

"Mr. Artemis has had a change of heart."

This was a good sign, but Elle kept herself from showing it. "Mr. Artemis has no heart."

The jeweler laughed. "Yeah, you're probably right. But he's been kicking himself since you left and finally decided to do the deal. Come on."

Elle followed the man back to the empty shop. Quincy gave her a raised eyebrow but said no more as they went inside. Artemis and the bodyguard were still in back, arms folded like nightclub bouncers. She stopped at the office door and waited for Artemis to make a gesture of concession. After his initial manipulation, she wasn't crawling back to this banker until he lost the tough-guy attitude.

Artemis dropped his arms and took a step toward her. "Sorry for the confusion. I'll buy it."

Elle stared hard, unwilling to declare victory yet. Although usually deferential to her marks, she decided to set some rules and make it clear who was in charge. It wasn't him.

She pounded a fist into her other palm. "We have to move quickly now. You've wasted valuable time, and the Feds may be coming." She pointed to the overstuffed backpack. "Open that. Let's see your money."

Appropriately chastened, Artemis gestured to the bodyguard who quickly unzipped the big backpack he'd hauled to the mall. Elle set the jewelry case on the table, then she started to examine the cash. While she sorted through the banker's money, Artemis lifted the lid of the jewelry case and peeked inside. Then he slammed the lid and hugged the case to his chest. "I love it."

The jeweler cleared his throat. "May I see it?"

Artemis squeezed the case tighter. "Didn't you look at it before?"

"Sure, it looked real when I saw it, but I never got to study it closely. I need more time to be sure."

"You heard the lady, no time. We need to get moving. Besides, I know gems—this is the real thing. And she's the thief, so I know she's got the goods." Artemis squeezed the box.

Elle was pleased to see that he'd accepted her deadline. She moved more quickly to check the cash, which on first glance looked like a full five million dollars. Unfortunately, she hadn't had a chance to swap out the necklace, and now Artemis was cradling it like a newborn baby. She had to get it back for a few seconds.

"You really love that necklace, don't you?" She continued to sift through bundles of hundred-dollar bills.

"It's a true beauty." His arms relaxed slightly.

"Don't you want to take a better look at it? Go ahead, let it sparkle. I need a little more time to check the money, then it's yours."

Artemis peered down at the box, his mouth scrunched. He needed to put the box down on his own now, so she went back to checking the cash. Each bundle she examined was a solid stack of hundred-dollar bills, and there were hundreds of bundles. She dove her hand deep into the mass of cash to test the bottom of the pile.

Slowly, Artemis lightened his grip on the jewelry case and set it down on the table. He opened the lid, and his breath caught when he saw the gems. Even the jeweler smiled. Then he dropped the lid with a nod. He was about to grab it again when Elle pulled out two fists full of cash and dumped them all over the table, including a few bundles on top of the jewelry box. "Oops, sorry." She swept the cash from the jewelry box while discretely tapping the secret button to switch necklaces. "Incredible color on those stones." An even larger armful of cash got pulled out and dumped everywhere. After she'd checked the bundles, she tilted the case to slide everything back into the big backpack, including the real necklace waiting below the jewel tray. Then she dove both hands into the mountain of cash, ostensibly stuffing it in but actually packaging the necklace into a leather pouch, separate from the money. Finally, she zipped the big bag of cash.

"Your money's good." She pushed the jewelry case across the table. "Let's get out of here before anyone shows up." Artemis got up and handed the case to his bodyguard. The three men looked carefully as they exited the shop, then they raced into the mall, no doubt trying to avoid being caught red-handed.

Once they'd left, Elle pulled the pouch from the luggage with the cash and put it in her smaller backpack. Seconds later, Quincy came in and hefted the money off the table. He made it look like it was filled with feathers as he carried it through the back door, into service corridor, and to the other shop.

Roland watched Damien Artemis leave with his men, minus the huge backpack that the bigger man originally had. He knew what had been in that backpack, and he wondered if Elle would be carrying it next. He'd seen Quincy go in to the shop, so perhaps he would lugging it. He marveled at her ability to swindle so much money that it literally weighed a person down.

Soon she stepped out and turned toward the main promenade of the mall. But she didn't have the money. Instead, she wandered the mall with only a smaller backpack, scanning carefully and talking on her phone while she headed toward the entrance.

Roland couldn't wait for Quincy to emerge, so he followed Elle and the necklace. She had promised to return it now, and he needed to make sure that happened. He watched as she stepped outside the mall, pulled a small pouch from her backpack, and handed it to an older woman with some big shopping bags. The two of them exchanged a few words, then the woman thanked her and walked away. Roland knew that this woman now had the necklace.

Before he could start to follow the unknown accomplice, Elle pulled another pouch from her backpack and handed it to a different woman. A third pouch given to a man who was leaving the mall, and a fourth pouch was given to a young girl who was leaving with her father. After five bags had been given out, all to people heading in different directions, Roland realized he was being played. None of them had the necklace—Elle still had it in her backpack as she strolled into the parking lot. She'd handed out those packages to confuse him. After all the trust he'd given her, and all the help he'd provided, her insistence on tricking him further made him angry. He ran ahead, intent on stopping her before she could get away.

Suddenly, from the back of the parking lot, a small drone lifted into the air. Nobody flew drones at busy shopping centers—it wasn't allowed in densely populated areas. He watched the drone for a few seconds, expecting it to fly up into the air then come down again. Perhaps it was being used to make a promotional video of the mall. But when the drone flew away from the mall, across the parking lot, and down the street, he had a pretty good idea what was going on. The necklace was in the air, hopefully on its way to the museum.

Roland turned to watch Elle, but she wasn't controlling the drone. Instead, she kept walking away, never turning back, as if she knew he was watching. Someone else was piloting that drone, probably one of the people who'd received leather pouches from her. She was clever, every step of the way, but if that necklace didn't arrive at the museum soon, he'd make sure she paid for it.

He ran to his car and followed the drone. It was traveling along the roads, which meant that whoever was piloting it was also driving. He looked at every car he could see, but none of the drivers or passengers seemed to be involved. Still, the drone was definitely on a path to the museum, so he raced ahead, hoping to get there first. He called the museum's director, telling him to wait outside.

Roland arrived as the drone made a gentle landing on the museum's steps, directly in front of the museum director who was waiting with a guard. The guard kept curious visitors away while the director unstrapped the pouch and looked inside. With a joyful shout, he patted Roland on the back.

"You did it! The necklace is back, like you said. I can't thank you enough."

Roland took charge. "Come on, let's get this inside quickly." He turned to the guard. "Don't let anyone touch the drone, it needs to be checked for fingerprints." Deep down, though, Roland knew the drone would be clean. Elle didn't leave fingerprints.

When the necklace was safely in the museum, Roland went back to his car. As he was about to drive away, he got a call from his unlikely informant. "Thank you, Elle."

"Thank *you*, Roland. I've never actually worked with law enforcement before."

Roland grunted. "You may think we were working together, but all you do is trick me."

"Apologies for that last bit. But thank you for trusting me."

"Who said I trusted you? I simply saw no reason to stop you from returning the necklace. You still have to deal with the fact that you stole it and tricked Damien Artemis. We're not done yet."

"As I've told you before, Artemis won't mind. And I'm hoping I can convince you to let this incident pass."

"That's not the way law enforcement works, you know. And I guarantee that Mr. Artemis will not be happy to find out that he's purchased a fake necklace. He's going to come after you, either with unfriendly thugs or by calling me for help. You better hope he calls me."

"Roland, listen to me. Artemis will never make that call. In fact, I'd be willing to wager that when this is over, he'll want to thank me."

"I can't imagine how that could possibly be true, but I know better than to make a wager with you."

"Look at it this way. You've trusted me up to this point, and I've been true to my word—the necklace is back at the museum. Now I'm asking you to trust me with these final details, which you'll understand soon enough."

"Come on, Elle. Even if Artemis is not a problem, even if the French government is happy, and even if the FBI is more-or-less satisfied, you still have piles of money that you obtained illegally. I can't let you keep it."

"What money, Roland?"

"Come on! I saw Artemis's bodyguard hefting a huge backpack. My guess is you got four million, maybe more."

"There's no money, Roland. We can talk about that too next week."

"What about now? Meet me for some juice?"

"Can't right now ... Work to do. Don't worry, I promised to stick around, and I will. Besides," She chuckled. "It's my birthday Sunday, and I'm looking forward to our movie date." The line went dead, and as he drove back to the bureau, Roland kept bursting into laughter.

Thirty-Two

After Elle finished talking to Roland, she returned to the mall and used the service corridors to slip into the other empty shop, the one Artemis hadn't seen. In back, Quincy looked up from a table full of cash. "Glad you could make it. The party's in full swing."

Chip was also there, as well as Penny, Neil, and Andy. Over on the side, a table was piling with fat envelopes, and everyone was busily stuffing more of them with cash.

Chip waved at her with a thick stack of hundred-dollar bills. "Looks like you kids pulled it off."

Elle smiled broadly as she surveyed the room. "Wow, everything really clicked." She ran over to Penny and they hugged. "Tell me about Larry Smith."

"He wasn't too bad." Penny stuffed another envelope with cash. "Remember when we scammed that truckload of cars? Well, someone at the Tijuana plant noticed the shipment and got curious. Then they saw the slush fund we used and realized that they were being robbed. So they hired Smith, who found the crook at the plant and busted him."

Elle sighed. "I guess we have to give back the money and the cars."

"What he really wants is to find out how I hacked the plant. They don't want that happening again. Larry's pretty good with computers." She hitched a lopsided grin. "Almost as good as me. We do have to return the seventy grand we got from the dealer in Glendale, but we can keep our two cars. They're not new anymore, and the plant's willing to let us have them in exchange for my help."

"Good news." Elle gave her a fist-bump. "What about Roland? He promised to protect you if you explained your secure phone hack."

Penny nodded. "Yep. We worked that out. He's a nice guy for a fed." She poked her friend with an elbow.

"Yeah, yeah." Elle waved that away and pointed to the cash on the table. "But let's have the real news. How did it go with Dearborn?"

"Oh! It was amazing!" Penny's eyes grew bigger than dinner plates. "When Andy called last night to tell me that Dearborn had changed his mind, I was really nervous. But it went beautifully. I actually got to swindle him. The guy was in heaven, overjoyed to give me five million dollars." She shook bundles of cash in the air. "God, Elle! I feel like a real con artist now."

"You rule, girl!"

Andy cleared his throat. "What about me? I scored five million, too. Stupid Baxter thought I was going to give him the real necklace and cheat Artemis. He loved the idea of tricking his boss."

Elle patted him on the back. "A clever angle. You're a pro, Andy." She paused, then relented and gave him a hug. Andy seemed equally surprised, but after a second, he hugged her back happily.

Finally, Elle turned to Neil. "What about you. Did you have fun?"

Neil blushed. "Yeah, it was pretty awesome. I've never scammed so much money before. After Marshall Crew called two days ago and was so obnoxious to Penny, I called him back, hoping to revive the deal. The guy's such an ass, and he refused to pay five million. I tried using his fiancée as leverage, reminding him that she wanted a necklace for their wedding. Of course, he couldn't care less. I feel sorry for her."

"So how did you change his mind?"

"I called him again last night and took a tip from Andy. Told him he'd be cheating Baxter, and everyone would be impressed with him for duping the bank president. He still balked, and I figured I wasn't going to scam the guy. But he must have thought about it all night, because he called first thing this morning, desperate to give me his money, laughing over how he was going to show up his buddies in the jewelry club. Really caught me by surprise. And I was the first with the necklace today after your sister handed it to me, so I got to be the first one to score." He shuffled around in a victory dance. "What a rush to swindle that jerk! I feel like a total con artist for the first time in my life. I don't think I've *ever* had so much fun."

Elle looked around the room, admiring all the over-sized luggage. Each of them had sold a fake necklace to a different bank officer, scamming the man, then passing the real necklace on to the next member of the crew. In total, they got twenty million dollars.

Good thing Roland had retrieved most of the cases and fake necklaces that Yale had confiscated, as well as the bad fake that had been given to Frank the Fence. They'd needed four cases and four fake necklaces today, and they had exactly that. Unfortunately, the necklace they'd left with Frank was truly bad, making it harder to use it in a swindle. But since they were tricking four bankers in a row, the early ones needed the best fakes so they wouldn't run back to the mall and spoil the later deals. Elle, who sold last, had to use the pathetic fake in her deal with Artemis.

She stepped over to the table and joined the money-stuffing party. When they thought they'd be able to trick one banker, they planned to give each homeowner $25,000. But now that they'd swindled all four, the homeowners were getting a full $100,000. They continued to package the money, wrapping the cash securely and including a cover letter that Penny was printing over on the side. She'd also printed prepaid mailing labels, one for everyone on Quincy's list of mortgage-stressed bank customers. After they filled an envelope, they peeled off a label and stuck it on, ready for overnight delivery. When enough batches of envelopes were filled, Chip and Quincy loaded them into the big backpacks and took them to the nearby shipping store. Soon, all of the envelopes were on their way. Except for two that would be hand-delivered.

Elle gave one envelope to Quincy. "This is for you. I can't thank you enough."

Quincy and Chip traded looks of delight. "No, thank *you*." Quincy gave her a hug. "You're the best!"

Elle nodded, a little embarrassed with the praise. "Do me a favor. Give me some time before you go talk to Harry and Trish. I know you're itching to tell my folks about this, but I need a few minutes first." They agreed, then everyone left the mall.

With Penny by her side, Elle took the last package of money to her parents. Harry opened the door. "Is everything good?"

Wendy stood by his side, bouncing on her toes. "Oh my God! I want to do that again!"

June was still at school, but Trish was home early, so they settled in the living room. "What's all this about? Your father and sister have been very mysterious for the past few days."

"It's about this." Elle handed her mother the envelope. "Your home is safe."

Trish looked at the envelope, then turned to her husband. "What's in here?"

Harry shrugged. "Not sure. Let's take a look."

Trish opened the envelope and ripped apart the heavier black plastic bag. When bundles of cash spilled onto the table, she screamed. "Oh my God! Where did this come from?"

Wendy stared with huge eyes. "Is this real money?" She reached for a pile of hundred-dollar bills, pulling one of them out and examining it closely.

Elle pointed to the letter that was also in the envelope. "Read that."

Trish picked up the letter and read it out loud.

> Dear Homeowner. The directors at Tera Bank have discovered a serious flaw in the mortgage papers that were recently drawn up to refinance your home. This flaw has affected nearly two hundred customers and has cost each of you many thousands of dollars in unexpected fees. In some cases this has endangered the security of your home. We at Tera Bank are deeply sorry for this error and have decided to pool our personal money to help you with your mortgage. Enclosed, you will find $100,000 to cover the excessive fees and to help with the balloon payment that is now due. Be advised that you should deposit no more than $10,000 at a time to avoid federal scrutiny, and we recommend opening a few new bank accounts to discretely distribute

this cash. We hope this helps you and your family, and we thank you for being a Tera Bank customer. Yours truly, Damien Artemis, Galt Baxter, Orson Dearborn, and Marshall Crew.

She turned to Elle, her jaw wide open. "They gave us a hundred thousand dollars. That's incredible!"

Elle smirked. "Actually, I'm the one who arranged this. I wrote that letter, too. The bank officers don't know about this yet, but they will soon when people call to thank them."

Trish's eyes hardened as she glared at her daughter. "You *arranged* this? What exactly does that mean?" She turned to her husband. "Did you know about this, Harry?"

"I don't know all the details, but I do know that she was involved in something sketchy."

"So you robbed the bank?" Trish propped a hand on her hip.

"No, of course not. The bank officers gave it to us willingly."

"That doesn't sound right." Trish tossed her hands in the air. "Oh Lord! What has my daughter done?" She looked up to beseech the heavens.

Before this question could be answered, Quincy knocked at the door. Harry let him in, then waved a pile of hundred-dollar bills in the air. "Look what we got from Elle. I think she robbed the bank."

Quincy laughed. "She did better than that. She tricked four bank officers out of five million dollars each. Gave you, us, and nearly two hundred of our fellow homeowners enough to survive the bank's bad mortgages."

Trish gave her daughter a look of confusion. "You tricked someone? Are you some kind of trickster, like a con artist?"

Silence filled the room as Elle lowered her gaze, unable to face her mother. This was the moment of truth that she could not avoid, and though it would certainly cause pain, it had to be done. She looked up and offered a weak, "Yes."

Trish's head snapped. "Since when? Didn't your foster mother give you enough? Does she even know about these things you do?"

Elle faced them squarely, letting her story unfold. "Mom, Dad, you don't understand. My foster mother *is* a con artist. She taught me everything. Because of her, I've been swindling my entire life."

Trish gasped. "You've been raised to be a criminal? That's terrible! How can you do these things?"

"Excuse me, mom, but crooked things were done to you, and it's costing you your home. Do you want to be on the street again, or do you want help from someone with the skills to fight back?"

Trish paused, biting her lip. "I . . . I guess. But still . . ." She turned to Penny. "Are you part of this too?"

Penny blushed. "Yeah, we work together. My parents raised me to be a good girl, but your daughter totally rocks a scam, so I can't resist. I do the tech stuff and help when I can. But Elle, wow! She's got a really sharp mind. Thinks up some truly clever schemes. And beyond her con artist skills, she's one of the best cat burglars in Los Angeles. This girl can sneak in or out of anywhere."

Trish turned back to her daughter with somewhat less of a frown. "Aren't you worried that they're going to catch you and put you in jail?"

Quincy shook his head. "This one's slippery. She even made friends with an FBI agent who was trying to find her."

Harry blanched. "The FBI? What have you done to get them involved?"

"Well . . ." Elle gave them a nervous smile, praying that the rest of the story wouldn't upset them too much more. "Dad and Wendy already know that I was involved in returning the stolen French necklace to the museum. Wendy got to hold it the other day." She winked at her sister. "It's gorgeous, isn't it? Thanks for helping me return it."

She wondered briefly how much of her scheme she should reveal. Returning stolen property was far less upsetting than having stolen it in the first place. But if she danced around the truth too far, it would come back to bite her later. Her parents needed to know everything.

She cleared her throat, then went on. "This is a secret, folks, so please keep it on the down-low. You see, I also stole the necklace from the museum. A complex game that involved stealing it, using it to trick the bankers, then returning it. Chip and Quincy suspected I did the theft, and they helped me trick the bankers. But Wendy and Dad had no idea. They only helped to return it."

Wendy's face went from excited to explosive. "You stole it, too! Super awesome!"

"Remember, Wendy," Elle admonished. "You can't tell *anyone*." Her sister calmed down, but she continued to gaze intensely.

Trish still had a stunned look on her face, but her frown was nearly gone, replaced with a look of pure surprise. "But even if you returned it, you still committed a crime when you stole it. Can't they arrest you for that?"

"They can. But I've got arrangements that will hopefully protect me and everyone else involved. The FBI agent seems to be on our side, and he even helped me this morning, so I'm hopeful. We'll see over the next few days."

Trish hummed unsteadily. "So let me see if I've got this right. My daughter is a thief and a con artist who robbed a museum, tricked four bankers out of twenty million dollars, then returned the necklace and gave away all the money. She also made friends with the FBI agent trying to track her down."

Elle gave her mother a proud smile. "That about sums it up. But there is some leftover money, since there were fewer than two hundred bank customers. The four of us who did the work each got some, and of course, we had expenses. The rest is being put aside in case we find other homeowners who need help."

Quincy chuckled. "I love your daughter."

Elle turned away, trying to hide a blush she could feel rising. Quincy's pride felt good. Her parents' pride would feel better, but she doubted she'd get unanimous approval. This was the moment she'd dreaded ever since finding her birth parents, when they finally learned the truth about her. She held her breath and waited.

The silence was broken by her father, who started to laugh. That was enough of a relief, but when her mother joined in, Elle's jaw fell open. They *did* accept her, and they appreciated what she had done. Soon, her parents were laughing so hard, they had to hold onto each other for support.

Her father faced her with teary eyes. "We're proud of you, Elle. You've saved hundreds of people's homes."

She couldn't stop grinning.

Thirty-Three

On Saturday morning, Elle wandered into the Tucker Bail shop to visit Frank the Fence. She felt she owed him for helping her find the bankers, and she wanted to apologize for the trouble she'd caused with the FBI. If she expected to have any future in Portland, she needed to make peace with this man.

Frank's shop reminded her of all the seedy places in L.A. where she'd spent her childhood, so she practically danced in the door, bouncing enthusiastically as she made her way to the desks of two familiar muscle men. They sat up straight when they saw her, and one of them quickly made a call. "It's her!" He hissed. "Linda the Lynx." He winced at the reply and hung up.

In seconds, the back door opened with a crash, and Frank stood there scowling. "You owe me, little girl. Fifty grand." He marched up to her with clenched fists. "No tricks this time."

"No tricks." Elle held up her hands in a sign of surrender. "I'm here to pay, to apologize . . . and to explain."

Frank leaned toward her. "OK, start explaining."

Elle relaxed against the desk, relieved that Frank was willing to listen. "I was running a con on some of the bank executives at Tera. I knew they liked jewelry, so I grabbed Napoleon's necklace to use as bait."

"You *grabbed* it?" He arched an eyebrow.

"One of my skills." She wiggled her fingers. "Let's leave the details for another day. Today, I just want to settle up.

You helped me with those bankers, and I'm here with your cut."

"You also made me look like a fool in front of the FBI, and the bankers will hate me for luring them into your trap."

Elle casually flipped a hand out to the side. "I can't fix your FBI relations, but my swindle will cool-out the bankers and keep you safe. Still, if you want to blame me, go ahead. Put it on my tab and let's even the score." She took off her backpack.

When the backpack landed on the table, one of his men grabbed it. Frank sneered. "What ya got in there? More fake jewelry?"

Elle shook her head. "No, much better, Frank. Cash. Go ahead and check it out."

Frank's man emptied the backpack onto the table, ten bundles of hundred-dollar bills. He pulled out a bill and examined it closely, then handed it to Frank.

Elle picked up her empty backpack. "See? I pay my debts. This is for helping me out. You wanted fifty grand, but I decided to stick with my original offer and give you twenty five, *per banker*. Turns out I sold the necklace four times, which means you get a hundred. Are we square now?"

Frank picked up a bundle of cash and thumbed through it. Then another and another. He squinted at her. "What's the catch? You could have given me fifty. Why give me more?"

"The catch is that next time I'm running a game and need your help, I'm coming straight to you. I don't want to have to trick you again or worry about your tough guys. From now on, we're on the same side."

Frank tilted his head. "For a kid, you're pretty smart. Who taught you this shit?"

"My foster mother's a con artist in L.A. She and her friends taught me plenty."

"Hmm. OK, kid, you've bought yourself a friend. And as your friend, I got to ask if this has anything to do with some unusual gifts I've been hearing about where folks get a hundred grand in the mail. Two guys I know told me the same story this morning."

"Were they close to losing their homes because of a deceptive mortgage?"

He tapped his chin. "I believe they were. So you *are* involved in that."

"Yeah, that's me. The goal was to help the victims of the bank's bad loans. We took in twenty million and gave away over nineteen million to these homeowners. Then everyone in the gang, from myself on down, got a hundred grand. Even you."

"Nice." Frank stacked up the pile of cash. "You gonna pay off that FBI kid? He's still after you."

"I don't think a direct payoff's going to work with Agent Watson. He's a little too honest for that. I've got something else, though, that I think will do the trick."

Frank chuckled. "I'll bet you do. You're full of secrets."

Elle turned to leave. "Bye, Frank."

"Wait! I don't even know your name. The boys are calling you Linda the Lynx, but I heard you tell the Fed you were Lisa. That's a lot of L's."

"And that's my name: *Elle*." She stretched it into two lazy syllables. "All those names that start with 'L' are my con names."

Frank scratched his chin for a few seconds then pointed to her. "I know about you. You're from that family of L.A.

kids that all have single-letter names. I remember a girl named Dee who could paint amazing forgeries."

"Yep, she's my older sister."

Frank's face exploded with delight. "So you're Elle Kirkland. Of course. I know about your mom, what's her name?" He snapped his fingers a few times then nodded. "Bea! Yeah, Bea Kirkland. And there was a boy named Jay, I'm pretty sure."

Elle sighed. "Jay died. Shot in the head by some vigilante while playing Three Card Monte."

"Right, I heard about that. The guy was a nasty piece of work—killed a number of card players, then he mysteriously stopped. No one knows why."

"Boy, you really are connected, Frank. Is there anyone you don't know?"

"This is my business, kid. I gotta stay connected. Truth is, if you'd been honest with me when you first came here and told me you were Elle Kirkland, daughter of Bea Kirkland, we could have worked together. But that Linda the Lynx line smelled like rancid garbage on a hot day."

"Sorry about that. Anyway, I have to run now. Just wanted to make sure there are no hard feelings."

"None at all. Drop by any time." He handed her a card. "That's my private line."

On Sunday, Elle was back at the mall with Penny, Neil, and Andy, excited to explain the final details of the swindle. "I've been telling you that the bankers wouldn't be angry with us. That we would *adjust* them and make them realize it was good to give away their money. Well, I contacted a few news agencies and gave them this story." She set her phone down on the table to let the others watch.

A reporter beamed at the camera. "Good news for some homeowners in Portland. The Tera Bank has been refinancing homes with very confusing mortgage papers that have pushed people to the point of homelessness. But thanks to four very generous bank officers, a fund was created to help these people. All over the city, homeowners have been receiving money, and they're incredibly happy. We interviewed the CEO of the bank, Damien Artemis."

The video switched to Artemis, smiling into the camera. "We at Tera Bank were shocked to find out that some of our customers were about to lose their homes. So we banded together and pooled our personal money to help them out."

The off-screen reporter continued the interview. "Wow! How much did you contribute?"

Artemis broadened his smile. "I put up five million dollars. It was really a no-brainer, because I got a huge bonus last year. When I found out that the money came from our own struggling homeowners, I and three of my colleagues decided to do the right thing."

"That's incredibly generous of you. Your bank really cares."

"Yes, we do. Lots of banks are impersonal machines, dedicated to making money at any cost. But at Tera, we go that extra mile for our customers."

The video cut back to the news anchor, her mouth hung open. "Isn't that something? I think I'm going to move my bank accounts to Tera!" Her fellow anchors made similar comments in support of the bank, then the reporter signed-off with one last line. "What a story. Only in Portland, folks."

Neil couldn't take his eyes off of Elle. "You did it! You actually adjusted the bankers' attitudes, or at least tricked them into adjusting. Not only won't they come after us, they'll never even mention the jewelry swindle because that would expose their boast about being nice to the customers."

Andy nodded as he considered this, then he tightened his mouth. "You also said that the FBI wouldn't want to bust you, but I don't see that happening. You think you're such a clever little con artist, but how are you going to avoid Agent Watson?"

"We'll see." Penny and Elle glanced at each other, sharing a private moment. They'd known something about Roland since that day in the computer store, something they hoped would save them. Her next meeting with him would say for sure.

"In the meantime, did you boys have fun with this game?"

Andy laughed. "It *was* fun, except for all the people chasing us. You going to do any more games here in Portland?"

"I'd love to. I've been thinking that The Adjusters could offer their services to others in the city, shifting people's point-of-view and getting them to do the right thing. We've got some connections and a real nice mall. This city could probably keep us busy for a while."

Neil cocked his head. "I thought you two were going back to L.A."

"I've got friends there, but I have to admit, it was fun doing a swindle without my overbearing foster mother getting involved. Plus, if I stay here, I'll have a real family, and I can play games only when I want to help someone." She turned to Penny. "What do you think?"

"Oh, girl. You know I'd love to move here with you. But I've got to finish high school. Maybe in the fall I'll come up for college. In the meantime, I can always help you from

L.A., and if you really need me, I can come visit. So sure, I'm in."

Andy propped his hands on his hips. "One little detail . . . how do people find us? Nobody knows what we did, except four bankers, and they're not talking. Even the news reports don't mention us. We have no website, no phone number, nothing."

Elle raised a finger. "Frank the Fence knows about us, and I've made peace with him. Word will spread, and people will find us."

A voice interrupted the celebration. "I found you." Roland had once again sneaked up to their table.

"Damn!" Andy's eyes darted like a caged animal. "I told you that guy would come looking."

Like a well-rehearsed act, Elle and Roland spoke at the same time. "Relax, Andy." Surprised at their synchronization, they grinned at each other.

"Hey, Roland." Elle pulled out a chair. "Take off those ridiculous shades and have a seat. We're celebrating the fact that we helped a lot of people. I hope you're happy."

"I *am* happy, and by the way, happy birthday." He whipped off the glasses as he took his seat. "Told my supervisor that I'd single-handedly arranged the recovery of the necklace. He was very impressed. Unfortunately, he still wants me to bring in the people who stole it."

"And who would that be?"

He shrugged, looking mildly amused. "I haven't a clue. At one point, I thought a band of teenagers stole the necklace. But seriously . . ." He bolted a single chuckle. "That's just ridiculous. *Teenagers*?"

Andy frowned. "What are you talking about? You knew every detail of the theft when you visited me." He turned to

Elle, who was trying to suppress a laugh. "Don't tell me you tricked this guy too."

"Roland's an honest man—I could never trick him. But I did discover a little secret that I knew would protect us."

"Last minute evidence." Roland's mouth curled on one side. "It really changes things." He pulled out a letter and let it drop to the table. A familiar letter, the one that they'd included in each of the cash envelopes.

Andy picked up the page briefly, then tossed it back on the table. "So what? We sent out hundreds of those."

"Sure, but this one was inside of an envelope full of cash that my parents received yesterday. A dozen of their neighbors got similar packages." He relaxed with a warm smile. "I came to thank you kids for a job well done."

Andy's eyes widened as he turned to face Elle. "You knew his parents were on the list, didn't you?"

"Penny investigated him and found the connection. After that, I didn't think we'd get in too much trouble, as long as we pulled it off." She turned to Roland. "But you've been awfully nice to us for the last few days. I have to wonder whether you also knew your parents were on that list."

"I did. When I visited Quincy, I saw his list. Given how tricky you are, though, I couldn't be sure you'd come through. But you did, and I thank you for that."

"Aha! No wonder you were committed to helping us succeed. You not only got our stuff out of FBI lockup, but you visited Frank to get that last necklace and jewelry box. I'm impressed."

"Yeah, Frank was more than happy to give me what he had, but I had to work harder to get the rest of your stuff from the FBI evidence room."

Elle arched an eyebrow. "How did you know that we needed all four fake necklaces and trick boxes? When we talked a few days ago, you were convinced I was only going to swindle Artemis."

"Hah! You really think I'm stupid, don't you? I put a tap on the phone you were using to talk to Frank, and I heard all your conversations. That's how I knew each of you was selling a necklace. It made sense—if you could swindle one of the bankers, why not all four? Yale and I confiscated four boxes, but we destroyed one to figure it out. I knew you needed Frank's box to finish the job."

Roland managed to surprise her all the time. "And how did you sneak our stuff out of the FBI building?"

"Yale unwittingly helped with that. He makes friends with criminals like Frank, but he treats the support people like crap. In his mind, the field agents are gods who can boss everyone else around."

Roland puffed out his chest. "I, on the other hand, like the support folks. After our tech guy figured out how your boxes work, he and I went out for drinks. Turns out, he hates Yale as much as I do, and he was more than willing to pretend that he had to destroy all four boxes in order to figure them out. Right now, there's a carton full of shattered wood in the evidence room, along with a report about how Special Agent Yale Fulton brought it in. The report goes on to say that the evidence is unrelated to any active case and is of no interest to the FBI."

"Aww, poor Yale." Elle giggled. "He doesn't even get credit for tracking down our stuff. You're a devious man, Roland. Does this mean we have a friend at the FBI?"

"Well, maybe. But I'm tired of getting tricked by you. That has to stop."

"I'm sorry. I couldn't be certain what you'd do, so I had to keep you out of the loop. But you're right, it would be much easier if I could discuss my plans openly without having to worry about FBI rules and procedures."

"You know, I'd like that too. You and your team could be useful in all sorts of ways. Hell, Yale is friends with Frank the Fence; why shouldn't we cooperate?" Roland leaned closer with both elbows on the table. "But in order to make that work, we have to trust each other. Can I trust you?"

"Yes, definitely." Elle slapped the table. "Let's declare a truce. No more lies and no more tricks. I'm thinking of settling here in Portland to help people who need adjustment from an unfair world. It would be great to have you available for advice and help. And by the way, I'm now better friends with Frank the Fence than your stupid partner ever will be, which gives you a direct line to the man." She held out her hand. "Deal?"

"Yes, deal." They shook hands.

Elle slid her chair closer. "Say, weren't we going to the movies? It's my treat."

He smiled and took her hand again. "I'll buy the popcorn."

About the Author

I seem to be all over the map with my writing. My first three books (the Westerley series) were romance novels. My next two books (the Fame series) were also romance novels, although less erotic. And now I find myself writing stories about young con artists, in which there's no erotic content at all.

After a lifetime of reading general fiction, I discovered writing at age 59 and fell in love with it. Now I fill my time reading and writing novels.

Life is full of surprises, including my books and a recent journey from Silicon Valley to South Carolina. I have been happily married for over forty years, and we have raised two wonderful children. I honestly wouldn't trade places with anyone else, living or dead, real or imagined.

www.ingramcontent.com/pod-product-compliance
Lightning Source LLC
Chambersburg PA
CBHW030031180626
46810CB00001B/319